Every Witch Way but Demon

Magical Misfits Mysteries - book 6

K.E. O'Connor

K.E. O'Connor Books

Chapter 1

Vole problem

"Anyone would think it was angel plucking season." I leaped and landed nimbly next to Sage, one large white feather in my mouth and another clasped between my murder mittens.

"They get like this when they're stressed. It's a scientific fact stress makes your fur fall out. I guess that goes for angel feathers, too." Sage blasted off the ground and caught an impressive number of white wing feathers. She landed on her stubby black paws, her wheeled harness clunking behind her.

We sat in companionable silence for a moment, chewing on feathers as the angels darted back and forth like giant sparkly balls of tense righteousness.

Angel feathers had a curious taste. They were a little like sugary, warm cinnamon buns, but there was a sharp aftertaste, suggesting you tread carefully when messing with these almost immortal creatures.

"Look out! More non-magicals arriving." Sage wheeled herself back until she was nestled by the door of Vorana Stowell's bookstore.

I joined her and spat out the last of the feather. The tiny feathers at the base of the spine always got stuck in my throat and made me gag. "It's no wonder the angels are in full-on panic mode with so many non-magicals dropping by. These days, they almost outnumber us." That wasn't strictly true. Crimson Cove was your average-sized cute up-and-coming town. But this little town hadn't had a moment of non-magical peace in ages. And there was no end in sight to their growing obsession with visiting and poking into every corner. And when you poked at magic too hard, it had a nasty habit of turning on you.

"Uh-huh." Sage had pulled herself up using the window ledge behind us and was peering into the bookstore. Just like me, she always kept an eye on her witch.

I didn't mind Sage giving me only half her attention. Our bonded witches were prone to mishaps, so we needed to ensure they behaved.

"The angels will need to be doubly careful when the scarabs' performance begins. The non-magicals will fall under any enchantment those scarabs sneak out while they dance." I glanced over my shoulder. "What's keeping our witches? We should head over there soon, so we get decent seats."

"You'll have the best seat in the house, perched on Zandra's shoulder."

I cat-smiled to myself. Zandra Crypt had shoulders made for my murder mittens to rest on.

Not too broad or too bony, usually covered in some soft or practical material, and always available when I needed to settle in my most favorite of places.

"They shouldn't let it go ahead," Sage grumbled. "Nothing good will come out of this scarab matinee show. Why let those creatures visit when the angels know they'll stir up trouble?"

"It's hard to say no to a scarab performance. They're beautiful. And we all missed out the last time because of that unfortunate angel killing incident," I said. "Their performances are always enchanting. Well worth the risk."

"Sometimes, they're literally enchanting. I don't trust those giant glittering bugs as far as I can kick them with one of my back legs." Sage was still looking through the window, her gaze intent and her paws pressed against the glass.

Personally, I looked forward to the performance. It had been many years since I'd seen a scarab dance. Once experienced, never forgotten. And this scarab lineage, the Scarabetic-Green, was worthy of all commendations for their shows.

I studied my furry friend. "You seem stressed. Vorana is fine, isn't she?"

Sage huffed out a breath, misting the glass. "She's not. She's putting on a brave face in front of everybody, but there's something wrong. I know my witch better than I know myself."

I turned, tucking my wonderfully white tail around me, so no clumsy non-magical stood on it, and peered through the window into the cozy, mildly cluttered bookstore with mismatched bookshelves, comfy reading chairs, and cute knick-knacks on the shelves.

The place was Vorana's pride and joy. She was a wonderfully bookish witch and loved nothing more than spending an evening poring over a new textbook or a fictional epic she'd discovered at one of the many book fairs and shows she attended.

"Do you know what's wrong with her?" I asked.

"She hasn't said, but when she thinks no one is watching, she gets sad. She sighs and paces around muttering to herself."

I twitched my booping snooter. "Vorana would say if she were unhappy about me and Zandra staying in the basement, wouldn't she? If we've overstayed our welcome, let us know and we'll find a new home." I didn't want to leave our cozy basement dwelling. It was warm, safe, and was exactly what my witch needed as she found her feet in this complicated world of magic.

"You aren't the issue. If it was as simple as that, I'd have told you to sling your hooks ages ago."

"Always nice to have a friend who speaks her mind."

Sage snorted. "When you get to my age, there's no point in beating around the bush. You never know when you'll take your last breath, so I'm not wasting mine by being fake nice. Vorana enjoys having you around. She loves to cook for you and gets pleasure in making people happy with her food."

"We take great pleasure in eating it. Every scrap." Zandra and I had developed deliciously round bellies since moving into Vorana's basement. She never let us leave the house on an empty stomach and always made wonderful home-cooked dinners for us. She was like the mother Zandra had never had, although younger. Maybe more like a slightly older sister with incredible cooking skills.

"Could Vorana be stressed about work?" I said. "You don't think she's getting bored with owning the bookstore, do you? She works long hours."

"Impossible. Vorana lives for those bits of dead trees stuck together with glue." Sage huffed at the window some more. "She's not sleeping."

I rested a paw on top of Sage's flexed murder mitten. "When Vorana's ready, she'll tell you what's troubling her. Maybe she's thinking of expanding the store but doesn't have the finances. Or she wants to take a vacation and isn't sure how she'll keep the bookstore open. It doesn't have to be anything bad."

"We don't keep secrets." Sage glanced at me and wrinkled her booping snooter.

I shrugged off the comment. Maybe I kept one or two secrets from my witch, but it was in her best interest. Sage didn't agree. "Vorana is only not telling you because she doesn't want to worry you."

"That's what we're here for! We take the burden off our witches. We're their sounding board and their guidance when they get stuck. Besides, Vorana wouldn't hide anything from me."

"She's doing it because she loves you, not because she wants to exclude you. Take it as a compliment that she's working through this issue on her own."

Sage grumbled to herself as she continued to stare through the window. There were several customers inside, browsing the stacks, but they appeared to be passing the time rather than serious book buyers.

Vorana was always generous with allowing people into her store to while away an hour. She even provided free coffee and cookies, which were always popular.

I cringed as a group of non-magicals brushed past, chattering excitedly about the scarab performance. Their energy felt hot and disconnected, but I shared their sense of excitement over the event.

Scarabs were an incredibly powerful, ancient species and came with a range of talents, from performance art to singing. I'd encountered a few scarabs over the years and always enjoyed their exhibitions. The scarabs giving today's performance were aerial dancers. They'd visited Crimson Cove before, but an angel being murdered had overshadowed their event.

Now, the scarabs were back to give the performance they'd promised without the encore of a murder. But with so many non-magicals in town, they were vulnerable if those scarabs did anything slippery. And knowing scarabs, they most likely would. There'd be no malice behind it, but there could be a whole lot of trouble to clean up once they were gone.

"Three dead mice did nothing to improve Vorana's mood," Sage said.

I turned back to her. "You presented her with three wonderful gifts all at once?"

"I got lucky. Found a nest. She simply groaned, grabbed the brush and dustpan, swept them up, and tossed them in the trash. Not even a thank you. And no smile. I haven't heard her belly laugh in days."

"Have you tried vole? They have wonderfully soft fur. And those adorable little snouts. That would raise a smile."

"I want a squirrel."

"A... squirrel?" The monstrous tree rats of this universe had been my nemesis since I'd been turned into a cat. They loved nothing more than hurling acorns, insults, and kicking bark in my face every time I tried to grab one and teach it a lesson in how to behave around an ancient, once-powerful demigoddess.

"Yep. That would make Vorana smile."

"I could help you catch one." The thought of taking down a troublesome tree rat made my toe beans tingle.

"Juno! There you are." The most incredible witch to grace my company stepped out of the bookstore. Zandra Crypt was tall, dark-haired, and pale, and when she smiled, my worries went away. We were the perfectly bonded pair.

"I was keeping Sage company while we watched the crowds walk to the stage. It'll be a packed show."

Her gaze flicked to the chewed white feathers on the ground and she smirked. "Of course you were. Not getting up to too much mischief, I hope."

"Never. I'm surprised you've been so long in the bookstore." As perfect as my witch was, she'd never developed a love of reading and claimed book dust made her sneeze.

Sorcha Creer came out of the store next, covered her nose and mouth with a large red hankie, and gave an almighty sneeze. "Zandra was helping me. I still can't get over this flu or whatever is making me look like the Bride of Chucky and feel like Frankenstein's monster. We were flicking through spell books to find a cure or at least something to relieve the symptoms."

Sorcha was an impressive part vampire who ran the best café in Crimson Cove, Bites and Delights. She always had a sunny smile and a kind word and was one of the best individuals to go to for the latest gossip. But recently, she'd struggled with a malingering illness that had gotten its claws into her and refused to let go.

"Any joy in finding something to help you?" I asked.

"There are some tinctures I want to try." Sorcha looked over her shoulder back into the store. "Is everything okay with Vorana? She seemed gloomy."

"She is gloomy. There's something very wrong with her. What did she say to you?" Sage's eyes were narrowed, and her accusatory stare latched onto Sorcha.

"Um... she said it was all good, and she was just busy. But I don't know..." Sorcha sneezed loudly again.

"We even had to twist her arm to come to the scarab performance," Zandra said. "And Vorana is usually the first one to suggest a social event. She loves to mingle."

"Perhaps the scarab dance will improve her mood. We should hurry and join the others," I said. "Otherwise, we'll miss the start."

"We're still waiting for Vorana," Zandra said. "She didn't want to hustle her customers out and lose a sale."

We lingered for another five minutes while more people hurried past. The customers left, and a sulky-looking Vorana emerged from the store. She locked up and turned, her arms crossed over her chest.

Sorcha chuckled and linked her arm through Vorana's elbow. "This is just what you need. Time away from work."

"Time is money."

"It's also a chance to hang out with your bestest friends in the whole world. I've barely seen you at the café this week."

"Because you're sick, and I don't want whatever it is you've got."

I glanced up at Vorana as we walked along the busy street toward the temporary stage set up for the scarabs. I'd never heard her speak so sharply to anyone. Even when people were rude to her face, Vorana was always sweet.

Sage bumped me with her shoulder. "Told you something was wrong with her."

The witches continued to chat, Vorana somewhat grudgingly, as we dodged and weaved through the crowd and got closer to the stage set up on the green space in the center of town.

"There's seating set aside for magic users," Sorcha said. "The angels thought it best if we didn't mingle with the non-magicals. So much power concentrated in one place could get sticky." She yawned and blinked several times. "I hope I can stay awake. Even though I've had Elijah, Sammy, and Tinkerbell on my bed keeping an eye on me, I still don't feel rested."

That got my attention. Tinkerbell cared about no one but herself, but if she was watching over Sorcha, she must be worried about her. Tinkerbell was usually rude, dismissive, and pretended Sorcha hadn't provided her with a free place to live, all the food she could eat, and a soft bed when she'd had nowhere else to turn.

Their sort of bond was odd. But given Sorcha was part vampire, she'd never have a full bond with any familiar. It wasn't important. Sorcha loved Tinkerbell, no matter what she did. That was the sign of a true cat lover.

"Have you patched things up with Sammy yet?" Sage said.

I lifted my booping snooter, my gut tightening. "Not yet."

We'd barely spoken in weeks. Sammy had become a different cat for some reason and preferred Tinkerbell's company to mine. And although I hid it well, I grieved his loss.

Things had never officially ended between us, but he'd made it clear he was no longer interested in being a part of my life. He'd stopped calling at the house, dropping by animal control to see if he could help on jobs, and he spent all his time with Tinkerbell and any other random pretty female who took his eye.

I wish I knew why he'd changed and why he felt he didn't need to tell me things were over between us. I was hurt, angry, and embarrassed by the situation. I should have stuck to my values and not dated anything with fur. But Sammy's personality had shone through, so I'd ignored his fluffiness and found joy. Not anymore.

"You're better off without him blundering around in your life," Sage said. "Relationships are hard work. Why bother? You'll eventually get chucked away for a younger model or one with better teeth." She exposed her yellowed, nubbed teeth.

"We'll focus on our witches. They're the most important people in our lives." I was happy with Zandra, but our love was different from the warm snuggles I used to enjoy with Sammy. "Let's just enjoy today."

The green space that was the venue for the scarabs' performance had been transformed by a raised stage, rows of seating in front of it. A sign only visible to those with magic revealed the righthand side seats were reserved for us. The rest were for the non-magicals.

I hissed as a non-magical got too close to my tail, almost squishing me with his clod-hopper boots.

"Let's get you out of the way of the clumsies." Zandra lifted me onto her shoulder, while Vorana scooped Sage into her arms and cradled her.

As soon as I was up high, Cythera, head of the local branch of Angel Force, was easy to spot as she strode around barking orders at her angels. Every angel under her command was on duty, watching the non-magicals and making sure everyone behaved. The angels were on strict instruction not to display their wings and to keep flying to a minimum. Although from the amount of feathers I'd been catching with Sage, they were taking to the wing as often as they liked. It was much faster than walking.

"There's Torrin and Voss," Sorcha said. "Let's go sit with them."

Torrin Conner was a rough-around-the-edges part dragon, who ran a successful repair business on the edge of Crimson Cove. Voss Black was one of my new favorite people since he'd opened an artisan pizza parlor and made an incredible seafood medley pizza. The prawns he used were so large, I couldn't fit a whole one into my mouth.

There was a round of greetings then we settled into seats to wait for the performance to begin. The air was pleasantly warm, and the atmosphere tinged with excitement.

"Juno! Meet again, we do."

Amenia fluttered into my line of sight and swirled around my head, leaving a scatter of green sparkle. She was a stunning jade scarab with a feathered antenna.

"We do. Greetings! I'm surprised you're back so soon." I watched the non-magicals to see their reaction to the sparkling scarab flitting close to my booping snooter, but they didn't appear to see her. Amenia was most likely magically cloaked until the performance started.

"Intrigued, we were by our last visit to this odd little town. And a promise is a promise. A performance you require. This time, no murder. Yes?"

"That would be agreeable. As you can see, you've drawn a crowd. We're all looking forward to it."

"As are we. So many simple minds, there are. Not just among the non-magicals." She tittered a laugh. "Fun, we shall have."

I narrowed my eyes at her. "Don't do anything you shouldn't."

She tinkled another laugh as she dashed away. "Enjoy, enjoy. And don't blink, or miss it, you will."

Scarabs were so frustratingly elusive. I'd need to keep an eye on that one if she had plans for mischief making. No one made mischief in Crimson Cove without my permission.

Chapter 2

Dancing queen

Sorcha had tears in her eyes as the scarabs weaved around the stage, every movement leaving a small trail of light and sparkles. The non-magicals oohed and aahed as if watching a firework display and not the enchanting twists and turns of ancient magical beings.

I found the swirling movements enchanting, but I wasn't letting my guard down and tracked the three scarabs' movements in case they did anything sneaky. And I was right to keep a watchful eye on them because I'd spotted a flash of magic that made my hackles rise and my claws extend.

The two smallest scarabs, Amenia's children, Loris and Saphic, performed dazzling figure eight moves, their trails hanging in the air and laced with an iridescent sparkle. That sparkle lingered and then drifted toward the non-magicals.

"Did you see that?" Zandra whispered. "What are they playing at?"

"Nothing good. Scarabs are sneaky." I had to keep my voice down to ensure the non-magicals didn't notice a talking cat.

Zandra stared at the angels, who hovered around the stage. "Angel Force hasn't noticed anything wrong, and I don't see Finn anywhere to tell him what's happening. He's the only one who'll listen to us."

There were only three feet separating the drift of magic and the first row of non-magicals.

Zandra stood, flicked out her hands, and a gust of strong wind blasted away the scarabs' magic.

The fur on the back of my neck prickled, and I turned to see Cythera glowering at us. "Hide! Cythera saw you."

"I had to use a spell. That magic could have turned the non-magicals into dancing chimps." Zandra tugged on her hair. "I'll speak to Cythera and let her know they're up to something."

"You're a better witch than me," Vorana said from her seat, her gaze not leaving the stage. "Whenever I speak to her, she makes me think I've done something wrong."

Zandra grimaced. "Me, too. Wish me luck." She edged along the row of seats with me on her shoulder, almost tripping over Barney Hoffman as we got to the end.

He looked up and smiled. "Sorry, Zandra. Not much room here." Barney was a big old grizzly bear of a man who'd have been more comfortable if he'd had two of the tiny plastic seats to settle his generous form in.

"Hey, Barney. We're worried about the scarabs." Zandra crouched beside him and kept her voice low. "Did you see that wave of magic they sent out?"

"I saw something, but then saw you disperse it." Barney looked at Cythera and winced. "Ah. I see the problem. Let me come with you. Cythera needs to be handled in a certain way."

"I'm happy to handle her in a very particular way if she keeps glaring like that," I said. "Zandra was helping. Cythera never appreciates us."

"Softly, softly is the best way to go with that angel." Barney heaved himself out of the seat. "And she'll understand we need to be involved. Scarabs are magical creatures, so they fall under the jurisdiction of animal control. We're the experts, and I'm happy to make her aware of that if she has an issue with you protecting the town."

Zandra grinned at him. "Have I ever told you that you're an incredible boss?"

His cheeks flushed bright pink. "Let's go make sure Cythera understands what's going on."

As we walked over to confront the still glowering Cythera, a painful sensation yanked at my stomach. It had better not be my seafood special returning to haunt me. Maybe I should have gone with the chicken for lunch.

"I'd love to welcome an extra special guest to the stage." Amenia's silken voice reverberated with power. "Delighted, we are, to be graced with a unique individual. Someone whose dancing prowess will put us to shame."

There was another hard yank on my gut. What was going on? Perhaps I should leap off Zandra's shoulder just in case the worst happened, and I lost my delicious food.

"You okay?" Zandra rested a hand against my side.

"I feel odd."

"Ladies and gentlemen, creatures of all realms and abilities, I'd like to welcome Juno Avalon Soulkeeper the Third."

"Did Amenia just say your name?" Zandra said.

"Ignore her. It's another of her tricks," I snarled from between gritted teeth. "She's probably annoyed because we stopped the scarab magic from hitting home."

"Amenia's gesturing at you. Juno! She wants you to dance."

The pain in my gut intensified. This was Amenia's revenge for preventing whatever dastardly plan they'd been attempting.

"Do you even dance?" Zandra said.

"Of course I dance! Madam Tatiana Nectar trained me."

"Another cat taught you to dance?" Zandra didn't know everything about my colorful past. The past when I wasn't a cat.

"Long story. If Amenia wants a performance, I'll give her one." I leaped off Zandra's shoulder and landed nimbly on the stage.

The non-magicals applauded, excited to watch a cat dance.

"Here she is! This miraculous creature moves in ways you've never seen before. Telling your friends stories, you will, of the amazing Juno for months."

The crowd went wild, clapping and wolf whistling.

I hissed quietly at Amenia. I still had that ache in my gut from whatever spell she'd slunk over me. It was her attempt to make me look foolish. But I'd beat her. One thing Amenia didn't know about me was I was a trained dancer. Of course, I trained when I had two legs, but I remembered every move. And I'd put their trite, over-the-top, sparkly performance to shame.

"Juno, waiting we are." Amenia hovered at the side of the stage with her children.

"Is that an actual cat or a puppet like the bugs?" someone from the audience said.

"Shush! Let's see what it does."

I inhaled, centered myself, and began a series of ballet moves. A grand jete, en pointe, a series of lightning-fast pirouettes, a fouette, and a grand adage. Did it feel comfortable on four paws? Not always. But I was swift, sleek, and stunning.

Until I stumbled and splatted onto my belly, my side throbbing.

My gaze landed on Sammy and Tinkerbell, who sat side-by-side watching and laughing. Tinkerbell blew me a kiss. Wretched creature. She'd whacked me with a spell to knock me off balance and make me look incompetent.

I rolled onto my paws, shook off the pain, and performed a spectacular grand jete finale to enormous applause. Even though my thigh ached and my ego was bruised, I'd salvaged the situation.

Amenia and her children flitted down and joined me, soaking in the applause, too, bowing and waving their feathery antennae.

"Enemies you have," Amenia whispered. "Be careful of them."

"Should I include you as an enemy?" I asked. "I saw what you tried to do to the non-magicals. Was it a beguilement spell?"

"Perhaps. I wanted to see what I could achieve with an army of non-magicals under my command. Entertaining, it would be."

"Deadly, it would be, for them. You're too powerful. You can't use your magic on them. We've all had to be careful since they began visiting the town."

Amenia blew out sparkling kisses to the delighted audience. "Their risk, it is. They choose to come here. You're not forcing them." She twirled around her children as the applause slowly died.

"For whatever reason they're coming here, we respect the rules."

"Rules! To be bent or broken."

"Not if it means people die." I gestured her away from the front of the stage. "It's time you left."

Amenia's expression hardened before she laughed. "Leave, we will. Obligation fulfilled. Be well, Juno." She flitted away with her children beside her.

Zandra hurried over and lifted me off the stage just before I was swamped by non-magicals who wanted to pet and cuddle the amazing dancing cat and have their picture taken with her. "Hey, dancing queen. I figured you wouldn't want your super fans to get too touchy-feely."

I snuggled against her chest as she strode away, ignoring people's pleas for pictures. "Much appreciated. I told Amenia to take her children and go. She'll only keep causing trouble if she stays longer."

"Good move. And I put Cythera in her place, with Barney's help, so we're not in trouble. Come on, there's a free food and drinks reception getting started. We'll find you something deliciously fishy to take your mind off your belly flop."

"All that twirling has worked up an appetite." And food would take my mind off my tender side and belly.

"What happened up there? You were doing so well, although cat ballet is weird to watch, but a good weird." She kissed the top of my head.

"An unnecessary unkindness." I searched the crowd for Sammy and Tinkerbell, but they were nowhere to be seen. As hard as it was to accept, we weren't friends, but there was no need for cruelty.

Zandra gently elbowed her way to the buffet table, found me some overly processed fish sticks and a sad-looking array of sandwiches for herself, and we joined a worried-looking Vorana, who stood with Sorcha and an older, refined-looking woman I wasn't familiar with.

"I'm surprised you can take the time to be here," the woman said to Vorana. "Business is that good you can close for the afternoon?"

"I'm only closing for this performance. I'll re-open again soon." Vorana's hand trembled as she held her plastic cup of lemonade.

"You can't afford to turn away business. If you do, someone else will take your customers." She glanced at us as we arrived and flicked what looked like a real fur stole over one shoulder. "Oh! The performing cat. How adorably quaint."

"Greetings. I'm Juno. This is my wonderful witch, Zandra Crypt."

"Magdalena Persephone Splinter." She shook Zandra's hand and nodded at me. "Everyone calls me Old Mother Splinter behind my back, although that was my mother's nickname. I prefer Persephone."

"The late Mrs. Splinter was always kind to her clients," Vorana murmured.

A bitter smile settled on Old Mother Splinter's face. "My mother was weak, and she let people run rings around her. She also undercharged on the rent."

"Everyone thought highly of her."

Old Mother Splinter arched an eyebrow. "Those who weren't raised by her, perhaps." She lifted a champagne flute to her lips and frowned. "Harlan! My drink needs replenishing. Where are you?"

A gorgeous man of around thirty with brilliant green eyes and a smile that exposed two perfect dimples stepped forward, a chilled bottle of champagne in one hand. "My apologies. I can't have my queen going thirsty." He filled the glass with an expert twist of his wrist so not a drop was spilled.

"Stay close. And be careful who you mingle with. There are a worrying number of non-magicals here." Old Mother Splinter sniffed. "It wasn't like this the last time I visited to check on my businesses. Whatever has happened to Crimson Cove?"

"It's just a blip," Vorana said. "We're figuring out why they keep coming to town."

"If they keep showing up like unwanted bugs at a picnic, Crimson Cove will go into a rapid decline. I'll have to sell some assets and invest my money elsewhere."

Vorana's hand tightened around her plastic cup. "Angel Force is working on a solution. We think it's something to do with the magic wards."

"Then fix your wards. You can't have undesirables creeping in. Before you know it, this place will be a no-go zone, and no one will visit. You won't be able to keep your little bookstore going then."

"What business are you in?" I didn't like Old Mother Splinter's superior tone or the way she looked down her nose at Vorana.

Old Mother Splinter barely spared me a glance. "Real estate. Mainly commercial properties."

"I lease the store from Old Mother... I mean, Mrs. Splinter," Vorana said.

"Persephone, sorry to intrude, but I've had an update on that estate you're interested in." A refined man in his mid-fifties with slicked-back dark hair and perfect teeth appeared beside Old Mother Splinter. His suit was designer, and his shoes were highly polished. He nodded at everyone in the group.

"Excellent. Is the price agreeable?" she asked.

"They've accepted your terms. Shall I go ahead with the purchase?"

Old Mother Splinter inhaled deeply. "We've got them on the hook. Offer them ten percent less than the original asking price. If they're desperate, they'll go for it. Let's see how little we can get this for." She breathed out through her nose, a gleam in her eyes.

The guy nodded, turned, and dashed through the crowd.

"A business associate of yours?" I said. "Surely you don't need to work all the time."

"My assistant. And why should I stop working? I enjoy amassing assets."

It sounded to me like Old Mother Splinter enjoyed exploiting people in desperate situations. And from the way Vorana's hand still shook, she didn't enjoy doing business with her.

As Old Mother Splinter continued to disparage Crimson Cove and the non-magicals, a group of older ladies bustled past, being herded by the tired-looking tour guide, Gus Bainbridge. That guy couldn't keep away. They were chatting excitedly about the scarabs' performance, several of them commenting about what special effects were used and if they were puppets or battery-operated.

A group of non-magicals whooped and danced around, and several bottles of alcohol were being passed between them. So much for a refined end to a sophisticated afternoon of magical dancing.

"Let's get out of here," Zandra whispered to me. "It was fun to see the performance, but I'm not down to party with this lot."

It seemed everyone felt the same, and after saying goodbye to Vorana and Old Mother Splinter, leaving her with the delectable Harlan to ensure her champagne never ran out, we left the buffet.

I hopped off Zandra's shoulder and joined Sage on the ground as we ambled home. "I know what's wrong with your witch. It's Old Mother Splinter."

Sage snorted. "She's a real piece of work, that one. But I don't think it's her making Vorana miserable."

"Maybe they had an argument about the business. Old Mother Splinter didn't seem impressed by Vorana's bookstore."

"It takes a lot to impress that crone. Vorana always stresses when she comes for her annual visit, but this is a different kind of worry."

"So, how will you cheer her up?"

"By going squirrel hunting."

A high-pitched scream, followed by a thump, jerked me awake.

Zandra shot up in her bed and dragged her tangled hair off her face. "Was that Vorana?"

"Stay here! I'll check it out." I shook the last of the sleep away and dashed up the basement stairs. Every nerve ending tingled with the remnants of that scream.

A pair of eyes gleamed from the bottom of the stairs leading up to the bedrooms. It was Sage! Her fur stood on end, and her stubby tail was fluffed to maximum.

"Was that Vorana?" I glanced over my shoulder as Zandra scrambled up the basement steps. I knew she wouldn't wait anywhere safe while I dealt with this problem.

"I couldn't get a squirrel. I tried, but I got bit. Those tree rats have sharp teeth. So I went with your suggestion, and I found a vole. A big fat one with a limp."

Zandra rubbed her eyes. "What are you talking about?"

"Juno thought Vorana needed a treat. A special one. Something she'd never forget."

"Sage! Get up here and remove this disgusting thing from my pillow." Vorana's tone ensured there'd be no debating the subject.

Sage sighed. "They don't get how special these gifts are. We must hunt for them because they're so incapable. This is us showing them how much we care. We don't want our witches to perish."

"Juno! Have you been teaching Sage bad habits?" Zandra tied her robe then set her hands on her hips. "Did Vorana find a dead rodent on her pillow?"

"Sage had all the bad habits she needed before I came along," I said. "I simply suggested which kind of rodent would be the ideal gift to make Vorana happy again."

"Sage! I'm waiting. And this thing isn't getting any prettier."

Sage heaved out another sigh. She lifted a paw and a sparkle of magic slid underneath her, allowing her to float up the stairs with her harness behind her.

"We'd better stay up and make sure Vorana isn't too angry with Sage." Zandra peered up the stairs.

"She'll be fine once she calms down."

Zandra arched an eyebrow. "After that earsplitting scream, I don't think I'll get back to sleep, anyway. I'm too tense. I thought something was being murdered in its bed."

We headed into the kitchen, and Zandra filled the kettle and fished out some valerian and chamomile herbal teas to aid sleep.

Footsteps stomped down the main staircase, and a few seconds later, Vorana marched in, Sage behind her, holding something dark and furry in her mouth.

"Take it outside! And stay outside. Think about what you've done." Vorana yanked open the back door. "You, too, Juno."

"I didn't leave a gift on your pillow. Why must I leave the building?"

"You encouraged Sage. It took me years to train her out of that awful habit of killing everything small and furry. Now, she's doing it again. She told me she wanted a squirrel. Who gave her that idea?"

"I made a simple suggestion. Sage didn't have to follow it." I looked at Zandra, hoping to have an ally in my corner.

She shrugged and shook her head. "You know my feelings about the dead rodent gifts. You brought this on yourself."

My wonderful witch was kicking me out, too! It was unthinkable.

"Off you go. And don't come back until you've had a good think about what you've done and how wrong it was," Vorana said. "I turned over in my sleep and laid my cheek on a dead thing! And I'll have to burn that pillow. Maybe the whole bed." She stood by the open door, her lips pressed together.

Sage looked at me, rolled her eyes, and then wheeled outside. I followed, and the door slammed behind us.

"At least the surprise vole gift took Vorana's mind off of being sad," I said.

Sage chewed on her unwanted gift. "Looks like it. Shall we go for a walk until she cools off and lets us back in?"

I nodded, waiting for Sage to eat her late supper. She left the tail and the kidney on the doorstep, then we wandered into the gloom.

"I should have stuck to chocolates and flowers," Sage said.

"Those gifts are boring. Anyone can purchase those. It takes talent to do what we do. And Vorana will never forget that special gift."

"We're unappreciated." She glanced at me. "I've been meaning to ask. What was with the dance routine?"

I huffed out a breath, the unpleasant memory forcing its way back into my head. "I'm uncertain what magic Amenia used on me, but it felt icky. Then she challenged me to dance, so I accepted."

"It was a good routine until you belly-flopped. You lose your balance?" Sage meandered along the street, taking us away from town and toward the beach.

"I was pushed. I'm not sure which one of them did it, but Tinkerbell or Sammy whacked me with a painful spell. They were laughing when I got up."

"Not Sammy. He'd never hurt anyone."

"In the past, I'd have agreed with you, but since he's made a new best friend, he's different. Less kind."

"I get it. You two have issues now you're not dating."

"Because of Sammy! He ditched me and forgot to let me know. It makes no sense."

"Why would anyone want to ditch someone as perfect as you?"

"Exactly!" I slid her a glare, not missing the sarcasm. "I deserve the courtesy of knowing why he lost interest. We were friends before we dated."

"He's a jerk. They both need dealing with. Tinkerbell is a troubled cat, but she has to know her limits."

I glanced at Sage as we reached the outskirts of Crimson Cove. "I've heard before Tinkerbell had a troubled past. How troubled are we talking?"

"You weren't around when she first showed up. It was a while back. This poor, wretched creature dragged itself through the streets, stinking of dark magic and disease."

"Tinkerbell?"

"The very same. She got herself in deep with a chaos demon called Padma. They were into dark stuff. Rumor has it this demon went on a murder spree, and Tinkerbell helped."

"She willingly joined with this chaos demon?"

"She never talks about it, so I've only got the rumors to go on. Maybe she did, but maybe she made a mistake. Demons can be charming when they want something. Once you're in their thrall, it's hard to get away."

I nodded thoughtfully. I knew about that. Zandra had found me when I was at my lowest, ensnared by a powerful succubus with dark witch undertones. I'd been shattered and had morphed into something bitter. It was only when Zandra came into my life that I saw a chink of light and discovered there could be a different way of living. A way that would bring me happiness and ensure I did good for others.

"Sorcha, being Sorcha, did everything to heal Tinkerbell. And it kind of worked. Sometimes, you see the old Tinkerbell. She can be funny and smart, and she's got some sass in her. But sometimes, familiars get so broken they can't be repaired. I reckon Tinkerbell is one such case," Sage said.

"Sorcha can't believe that, since Tinkerbell still has a home with her."

"She feels sorry for her. But Tinkerbell must have relapsed. She used to have a decent bond with Sorcha, but it's been going wonky for ages. Sorcha hates to admit she failed Tinkerbell, but this might be one familiar she has to let go."

"Tinkerbell must have power if she's able to turn someone as sweet as Sammy into a cold, indifferent creature who laughs at another cat's misfortune."

"I'm surprised about Sammy. Ever since I've known him, he's been a decent cat. Uncomplicated. And he's been around Tinkerbell plenty of times. I don't see how things could have changed so much between them."

"It makes no sense. Tinkerbell used to bully him," I said. "Now, they're best buddies."

Sage slowed and sniffed the air. "Yeah, he was terrified of her. You think she did something to him to change him so dramatically?"

Although it hurt my heart, it felt good to talk about Sammy. "It's the only thing that makes sense. The change wasn't overnight. It came on gradually. We were still spending time together, and everything seemed fine, but he pulled back as if he'd lost interest in me."

Sage grunted. "No offence, but maybe he did. You're not the easiest cat to be around."

My heart hit an unhappy rhythm that made my chest ache. "You don't want to be my friend, either?"

"Can it with the poor me act. I didn't say that. But you keep secrets and that's sneaky."

"For the good of others. Not because it benefits me."

"If you say so." Sage lifted her booping snooter again and looked around. "You smell burning wood?"

I slowed and sniffed the air. We were close to the beach, and there was a sharp tang of salt in the air. Mingled in with the salt was smoke. "It's late for anyone to be partying on the beach."

"Let's go take a look and see who's out so late. Maybe they're up to no good."

As we drew nearer, rounding a gentle curve in the path, I could see the flickering light of a bonfire. Dancing around the flames were dozens of drunk non-magicals.

"Uh-oh. You see what I see?" Sage said. "Those pesky scarabs are here."

Amenia and her children hovered over the flames, hurling tiny blasts of magic at the dancing non-magicals.

"They've bespelled them! That magic could kill them." I was already dashing across the pebbles. Music throbbed around us, although I couldn't see the source. "Amenia! Stop!"

"Hey! What a cutie. Come here, baby."

I was hauled off my paws and into the sweaty embrace of a large bosomed non-magical wearing a slip of a dress. She smacked an alcohol-soaked kiss on top of my fluffy head.

"What are you doing out here at this time of night? You lost, baby?" She danced around with me clasped to her chest, my head at risk of being enveloped by the bouncing bosoms.

"Juno! Come to join in the fun, you have," Amenia called from over the flames. "Party with the non-magicals."

I squirmed against the non-magical's chest, but she wouldn't loosen her grip. I dug my claws into the fleshy part of her arm until she squeaked and dropped me.

Amenia blasted out more magic, her tinkling laughter raining around me. The non-magicals danced and swayed, blissfully oblivious to the danger.

Sage caught up with me and looked around, shaking her head. "This won't end well. We should leave."

"We can't. Amenia! Draw back your magic," I ordered.

"Why? Just having fun, we are. No harm done."

"Your version of fun will lead to death. Quit it."

"Help! I need help."

I turned to see Gus, the coach tour guy, struggling out of the sea. He was dragging a naked body behind him.

Chapter 3

Night swimming

Everyone ignored Gus as he fell into the shallow water and went under with the person he carried.

"Sage! Follow me." I ran across the pebbles, and we waited impatiently at the water's edge for Gus to appear. I'd go into the water if I had to, but I loathed the sea.

He coughed and spluttered his way closer, dropped the body face-first onto the pebbles, and sank to his knees. He looked around, but no one came to help with his waterlogged load.

"You kept going under. I think you swallowed water. Are you breathing?" Gus turned over the body as he talked to himself.

I remained a few paw steps back as I looked down at a pale, very soggy, very bare, Old Mother Splinter.

Gus pulled his phone from his pocket and shook it. "Someone call for help!" He waved an arm over his head. "We need an ambulance. Why isn't anyone listening?"

I listened, along with a grumpy Sage, but we could offer no helpful suggestions since talking cats would cause a stir. As frustrating as the situation was, there was nothing I could do, since Gus couldn't know magic was real.

But I also couldn't let Old Mother Splinter die.

Gus dropped to his knees and checked her breathing. He started CPR, pumping her chest and then breathing into her mouth. "Come on, come on. It's not too late. You were fighting in the water."

"We have to do something," Sage whispered to me. "I'll distract him. You check on the crone. Old Mother Splinter has power. She's a truth seer, and they don't die easy. And I think I just saw her chest move. We can save her."

"What are you—"

Sage yelled an otherworldly battle cry and leaped onto Gus's back, causing him to yelp, lose his balance, and tumble into the sea, taking Sage with him.

I jumped onto Old Mother Splinter's damp chest. There were no signs of life, but since she was powerful and had only just died, I could risk a reanimation spell.

I thumped my paws on her chest and pulsed out the magic. It was a powerful spell and came with challenges if you used it on a person who'd been dead for too long. But this would work, since there were threads of active magic inside her, and they'd grab my spell and use it to bring her back to life.

The spell caught a second later, and Old Mother Splinter heaved in an enormous breath. Her eyes flicked open. She stared at me for a second before letting out a sigh and flopping back onto the wet pebbles.

She was unconscious, but at least she was breathing. We could work with that.

"Hey! Is she okay?"

"Why is she naked?"

"Has anyone got a towel?"

Several bespelled, inebriated non-magicals stumbled toward me.

I jumped away just as Gus scrambled out of the water on his hands and knees and over to Old Mother Splinter. He checked the pulse point on her neck and let out a sigh. "She's alive! I saved her."

There were several gasps then people applauded and patted Gus on the back.

I looked around for Sage. Moonlight glinted off her sinking harness! She was still in the sea. As much as I hated the water, I had to save my friend, so I waded through the cold, salty, gross muck, grabbed the harness between my teeth, and heaved her back to the beach.

She coughed and retched and muttered multiple curses before shaking out her fur. "He wasn't supposed to fall into the sea when I jumped him. Idiot."

"Sacrificing your dignity was worth it. It worked. A reanimation spell got things moving."

Sage dropped her chin and stared at me. "That was a risky move. She could have been floating in that water for hours. You could have just created a zombie."

"She came back immediately. We got to her in time. And you said you saw her chest move." I glanced at the crowd growing around Old Mother Splinter and Gus.

"Maybe I saw it move! I didn't say for definite. It could have been a trick of the firelight."

I licked my booping snooter, grimacing at the salty taste. "She's fine. Not a hint of zombie."

I turned and glanced up at Amenia and her children, who hovered close by. I pointedly turned and walked away, looking over my shoulder to see they were following.

Once we were a safe distance from the non-magicals, I faced Amenia and her children. "This is your fault. You need to fix it."

"The soggy old lady isn't our fault," Amenia said.

"That crowd of beguiled non-magicals is. Move them on. We must help Old Mother Splinter. I got her back, but I have no clue how stable she is, and I can't check on her in front of a crowd of drunken non-magicals."

"Just here to party, we are."

"Amenia! You've broken dozens of magical rules. If I were to tell Angel Force what we discovered tonight—"

"You wouldn't. Friends, we are." She twirled in the air with her children beside her.

"Prove it. If you remove the non-magicals from the scene so we can look after Old Mother Splinter, I'll forget what I just saw. And remove any spells from those non-magicals, too. Do it safely."

"Gentle magic, it is. There are limits, I know. Would never harm. Just here for fun."

I tempered my frustration after a nudge from Sage. "Non-magicals are unpredictable. We don't want a riot in Crimson Cove because your magic caused them to misbehave."

Amenia sighed, swirled around her children, then headed to the group who'd gathered around Old Mother Splinter and Gus. A few seconds later, the non-magicals drifted off, following Amenia and her children to the bonfire, where the music started again.

"We need our witches here," Sage said. "Even though Vorana is angry with me, she'll want to help Old Mother Splinter."

I couldn't agree more. And since we knew they were awake, I summoned Zandra. I gave our bond a hearty tug, and in the blink of an eye, she appeared on the beach, still in her pajamas and robe.

Vorana flashed into view a second later, her annoyed expression vanishing when she saw how bedraggled Sage was.

"What's going on?" Zandra scooped me up. "Ugh. You're soaking wet!"

"Sage needed help to get back on the beach. We have a situation. An almost dead body situation," I said.

We quickly brought them up to speed.

Vorana tugged off the oversized sweater she slept in, released Sage from her wet harness, and briskly rubbed her with the sweater. "You could have drowned if Juno hadn't saved you." She bundled her in the sweater and coddled her like a baby.

"Juno's my hero." Although Sage grumbled the whole time she was being dried, she also gently purred. That curmudgeonly old cat loved to be babied by Vorana. But only Vorana.

"Let's go check Old Mother Splinter," Zandra said. "We must be careful, though. I recognize the guy who pulled her from the water, and he has no magic."

"That's Gus Bainbridge," I said. "You remember? He brings the old ladies to town. He was at the snail spa when we raided it."

"Oh, sure. The coach guy."

We hurried over to Gus. He sat beside Old Mother Splinter, holding one of her hands. His hopeful gaze lifted when we arrived but then fell. "Oh! You're not the paramedics. I don't think anyone has called for help. They all just stood around clapping and then left. They must be on something. No one cares. And I can't move her on my own. Will you help?"

"Of course," Zandra said. "We heard there was trouble on the beach, so got here as fast as we could."

Gus tilted his head. "I know you. You work at the animal sanctuary, don't you?"

Zandra crouched beside him. "Something like that. I'm Zandra, and this is Vorana. How's Old Mother Splinter doing?"

"She's breathing, which was more than she was doing when I got her out of the sea. I did CPR. I'm amazed I remember how to do it," Gus said. "We all have to take a basic first-aid course at work because of our vulnerable clients, since not all of them have tickers in the best shape. But this is the first time I've used it. I'm glad I could help."

Zandra glanced at me and arched an eyebrow. "Yeah, that's lucky. Some training never leaves you. What were you two doing in the sea at this time of night?"

"And why is Old Mother Splinter naked?" Vorana murmured. "I've never seen her without her furs."

"I wasn't night swimming. I was on the beach with the others when I heard her cry for help. I'd noticed an old lady standing by the water's edge. I figured she was listening to the waves and never expected her to go swimming."

"Did she get in trouble?" Vorana said.

"She must have. I looked around when I heard her calling for help then went in and got her out."

Zandra shrugged off her robe and covered Old Mother Splinter's modesty. "Do you know her?"

"No, she's not one of my ladies. My old girls are sound asleep in the bed-and-breakfast we're staying in. I came here to blow off steam and have fun with people my own age." Gus wrung out his soaked shirt. "I like my old ladies, but their idea of a wild night out is a sweet sherry after eight o'clock. It gets wearing. I heard a few people were planning a party on the beach, so I tagged along. It was fun until this happened."

While Gus ran through the evening's events, I kept watch on the scarabs. They should have left hours ago. Had they done something to Old Mother Splinter to convince her to go night swimming? She was no spring chicken, even if she was a powerful magic user. What if they'd used a spell on her, and it backfired?

My brief encounter with her after their performance hadn't left the best impression. She could have insulted Amenia or her children, so they got their revenge.

"I'm worried about her," Gus said. "What did you say her name was?"

"Old Mother Splinter. That's her nickname. She prefers Persephone," Vorana said. "She's my landlady. I've never known her to visit the beach when she's been to Crimson Cove in the past. This isn't like her."

"I'm glad I could do my bit." Gus looked around and rubbed the back of his head. "Something weird happened just before you arrived. I got jumped. I was doing CPR, and this hot, fat thing with some sort of sharp metal object in its hand flew out of the darkness and knocked me into the sea."

Sage hissed softly and buried her booping snooter into Vorana's soggy sweater.

Zandra's fingers flexed around me. "Maybe someone threw a bottle at you. You know how dumb people can be when they've had a few drinks."

Gus shoved his damp hair off his face. "It could have been that. Or I imagined it. Saving someone's life is stressful. I'm not made to be a hero."

"Let's get you to the fire so you can dry off," Vorana said.

"Thanks. I'm frozen. And I'm not much of a swimmer. It was the adrenaline that kept me going when I fought the waves." Gus let Vorana take his arm and guide him toward the fire, avoiding the most boisterous non-magicals as they bounced around.

I jumped onto the pebbles, remaining by Old Mother Splinter as I watched them go.

Gus's gaze lifted, and he stared above the flames. "Those dancing creatures are incredible. I saw their performance, and I still have no idea how they're controlled. It must be a new technology I've never heard of. I can't keep up with the kids these days."

"Yeah, it's something special that's making them move so naturally and freely." Vorana glared at the scarabs. "No clue what it could be."

Zandra slid her mobile snow globe into view. "I've just messaged Angel Force. They can help clear up this mess. They'll be here soon."

Old Mother Splinter groaned, and I turned to her. Her eyes were flickering, but they wouldn't stay open.

"Don't you die on me," I hiss-whispered. "Not after all the magic I used on you. Not everyone gets one of my reanimation spells. I don't give them out every day."

She groaned. "Magic. Not good."

"My magic is excellent. It's the only reason you're alive."

"No. Bad magic. Sick."

"What's she saying?" Zandra crouched beside Old Mother Splinter.

"Hush, now. You're only stressing yourself. We'll get you to the hospital soon. They'll check you over and make sure everything is okay." I gave her a thorough sniffing, momentarily alarmed my reanimation spell may have done more harm than good. But Old Mother Splinter smelled alive dend her chest moved up and down in a comforting rhythm. There was no hint of ghoul or zombie. My magic had worked.

"Maybe she hit her head when she was in the water. She seems confused." Zandra checked Old Mother Splinter's pulse.

"I see no injuries on her body."

A flash of white shooting through the night sky caught my attention. Three angels were flying in. They were taking a risk with so many non-magicals around, but the scarabs were doing an excellent job of distracting them.

A gust of something icy cold with sharp magical edges blasted past me in an upward arc, ruffling my fur and making my teeth clench. I turned, looking for the magic-slinging culprit, but no one was focused on me. It was probably those annoying scarabs. Perhaps one of the children who thought it would be fun to play with the magical cat.

There was a yelp overhead, and the angels tumbled through the air, spiraling down in a haze of feathers, and crashed onto the beach.

Chapter 4

Angel swan dive

The angels' undignified arrival caused a commotion among the non-magicals, who raced over to see if they were okay.

Cythera, Finn, and an angel I didn't recognize attempted to look like they hadn't just descended from the heavens on giant wings, messed up the landing, and almost flattened everyone.

"Did they just... fly in?" Gus was among the stunned-looking crowd, Vorana and Sage beside him.

"That's impossible." Zandra tucked in her chin and looked at me with a *'what the heck are they doing?'* expression on her face.

"I mean, of course. But... it looked like they were flying." He shook his head and chuckled. "Maybe I'm hallucinating. It's been a tough night."

"It's the shock," Zandra said. "It makes people see strange things. Things that aren't there, or they hear noises. It's nothing to worry about. People can't fly." She glared at the flustered angels.

"I guess not." Gus looked around and rubbed his arms briskly. "Maybe I'm getting a cold. My mother always said never to go out with wet hair, or you'll get a chill. And I'll get more than a chill if I don't get dry soon."

Old Mother Splinter laughed and rolled about on the pebbles.

I rested a paw on her arm to comfort her and keep her quiet. In her confused state, she could say anything.

"Is she okay?" Gus said. "The ambulance must almost be here. One has been called, right? She doesn't look so good."

"She'll be fine," Vorana said. "Help is on its way."

I had no explanation for Old Mother Splinter's odd behavior or the equally odd Angel Force swan dive onto the beach. Maybe they'd hit a wonky air current, and it knocked them off balance. But I'd never seen them tumble from the sky like that before.

"Everybody move back and keep quiet." Although Cythera's cheeks were pink with embarrassment, she slowly restored order. "We'll need statements from all of you about this evening."

"How did you do that?" a non-magical asked. "You came out of nowhere. Did you fly?"

"Of course not. Have you been drinking?" Cythera stalked toward the crowd, causing them to shrink away. They may not recognize her true form, but they sensed her power.

"They came from the sky. I saw them."

"Where are your parachutes? They just vanished."

The non-magicals all talked at once as they tried to figure out the impossible.

"We didn't fly in on parachutes." Cythera pulled back her shoulders and glowered at the non-magicals.

The group's mutterings quietened until they stared at Cythera in obedient silence. She was good.

"Someone almost drowned tonight at this illegal gathering. Everyone stand quietly by the fire and await your turn to be spoken to. My officers will question you to see what you know about the situation."

There were more muted mutters and a few mumbled questions about parachutes and feathers, but eventually the non-magicals moved away, cowed by Cythera's impression of a school matron.

"This is Gus," Zandra said to Finn once the crowd had gone. "He pulled Old Mother Splinter out of the water. He saved her life."

Finn nodded. "We've met before. You've been to my animal rescue on the edge of town."

Recognition lit Gus's face. "I thought I knew you from somewhere. You're a busy guy."

"Tell me about it. You're quite the hero. Let me get details about what happened, so I can fill in the gaps and make sense of all of this."

"Sure. But there's not much to say." Gus looked at Old Mother Splinter. "Shouldn't you get her to the hospital?"

"We're dealing with that," Finn said. "What happened here?"

"I acted on instinct. Someone was in trouble, so I helped."

"Let's start at the beginning." Finn gently led Gus away.

"What happened to you?" Zandra said to Cythera as soon as Gus was out of earshot. "You crash landed in front of those non-magicals."

"We were pushed." Cythera jutted out her chin, her normally neat blonde hair a fluffy cloud. "It wasn't our fault."

"Were you hurt?" Vorana said. "You've left impressions in the pebbles."

"Nothing got broken."

"What pushed you?" I asked.

Cythera brushed dirt from her sleeve. "I don't know. One second, we were coming in to land, and the next, it felt like I'd been flipped. I had no control over how I landed."

I twitched my whiskers. "Did you feel anything strange? Something magical influencing you?"

Her gaze narrowed. "Why? You had nothing to do with that odd landing, did you?"

"Cythera! I'm shocked you're even thinking that. We're on the same side, even though you like to forget that. But I felt cold magic brush past me just before you crashed."

"Where did it come from?" Zandra said.

"From behind me. You didn't feel it?"

"No, but I was watching the crowd. You were closest to Old Mother Splinter. You don't think it was meant for her?"

"It's possible."

"It could have been someone around the bonfire who fired off a spell," Vorana said.

"Other than the scarabs, no one here has magic."

"It's those scarabs," Cythera said through gritted teeth. "They're nothing but trouble. They did this."

I tilted my head from side to side. That spell could have injured the angels if they weren't adept at flying. It had maliced edges. That magic didn't come from the scarabs. Unless... did they want the angels distracted because of what they did to Old Mother Splinter? They injured the angels so they lost focus?

"I believe we got away with it." Cythera straightened her crumpled white shirt. "No harm done."

I twitched my booping snooter. Nearly all the non-magicals had seen the amazing flying angels arrive. If it weren't for the scarabs doing such an excellent job of distracting them, they'd still be here, asking how the angels flew to the beach without parachutes or some kind of hover engine strapped to them.

I inhaled, meaning to bring this point to Cythera's attention, but Zandra gently tapped my head and shook her own. She was right. Cythera had already been humiliated enough for one evening.

Instead, I turned my attention to the new angel, since Cythera hadn't bothered to introduce us. "Greetings. I'm Juno, and the wonderful witch beside me is Zandra Crypt. You may bow before her."

"No bowing required." Zandra rolled her eyes. "Nice to meet you. Are you new to the job?"

The angel nodded a greeting. She was petite for an angel, standing at just under six feet tall. Her shoulders were narrower than Cythera's, and there was a faint sparkle to her skin.

"This is Acer," Cythera said. "A new recruit. On probation."

Acer nodded at us all again. "It's my first day. Nice to meet you."

Vorana smiled and shook her hand before introducing herself. "And this is Sage. My familiar."

Sage pretended to be asleep.

I tilted my head from side to side again. "Part elf and part angel?"

Acer grinned. "Good spot. I joined when Angel Force relaxed their recruitment rules. Just finished my training. My birth father was in law enforcement in the Rose Gelding realm, and I've always wanted to follow in his footsteps."

"Welcome to Crimson Cove," I said. "We're the experts Angel Force calls when they have a tricky case they're unable to solve."

"Ignore the cat," Cythera said. "Zandra and the fluffy work at animal control. When we have an issue involving an animal, we sometimes ask them for support. More often than not, their support is a hindrance. Don't let them trick you into thinking otherwise."

"There's no need to be snippy because you crash-landed on the beach and feel embarrassed about it," I said.

Acer glanced from Cythera to me. "Well, I look forward to working with you. Will you be involved in this case?" She looked at Old Mother Splinter, who seemed to be snoozing.

"They won't," Cythera said. "Check Old Mother Splinter. Make sure she's stable."

Acer crouched and began an examination of the soggy crone.

"We might need to be involved if the scarabs had something to do with this," I said. "They fall under the jurisdiction of animal control, as I believe Barney explained to you."

Cythera scowled at me. "What do you know about the individual who saved Old Mother Splinter?"

I settled back into Zandra's arms, still chilled from my unwanted sea dip. "Gus came to party on the beach with the other non-magicals. For some reason, Old Mother Splinter went night swimming and got in trouble. He dragged her out."

"This Gus is without magic?" Cythera said.

"He's not got a drop in him. He works for those coaches that ship those old ladies into town."

She wrinkled her nose. "I'll need authorization to wipe his memories. He's seen too much. We can't let him leave after everything he's witnessed."

"Like three giant angels crashing from the sky and landing on the beach, you mean?"

"Hardly anyone noticed." Cythera attempted to smooth her fluffy hair. "I meant Old Mother Splinter. She could have said anything to Gus in her confused state. And the scarabs. They've influenced him. And they're doing something to the rest of the partygoers, too."

"The scarabs have been beguiling the heck out of everyone. Their brains are probably turning into soup as we speak," I said. "You'll be fortunate if there's anything left. You could always leave them to the scarabs then scrape up the pieces in the morning."

"Juno, not nice. We can't leave them with the scarabs. They won't survive the night," Zandra said.

I'd been teasing, but Cythera seemed to consider condemning the non-magicals to the whims of the scarabs. She was in a grump this evening. Maybe she'd bruised her rump when she'd hit the pebbles.

"What are they still doing here?" Cythera turned her irritation to the scarabs. "I told them to leave after the performance."

The scarabs twirled above the fire, their magic sparkling in beautiful waves. "I did the same. I'm wondering if there's a link between Old Mother Splinter's odd behavior and our fluttering guests."

Cythera grunted a reply but didn't dismiss the possibility.

"You think Amenia beguiled her into going night swimming?" Zandra said. "Why?"

"For fun. That's what they're all about. They love to entertain and to be entertained. Perhaps Old Mother Splinter was rude to them after their performance, so they taught her a lesson."

"They could have killed her," Cythera said. "Their actions are reckless."

"Then we need to talk to them. Figure out what they're playing at," I said.

"We?" Cythera shook her head. "I'll deal with those troublemakers. You stay out of this."

Finn walked back, flicking through his notepad. "I've got all the details from Gus. If he hadn't dragged Old Mother Splinter out of the drink, she'd have floated away. Gus Bainbridge is a hero."

We all looked at Old Mother Splinter. She was stirring as Acer prodded her, but the jumbled words coming out of her mouth made no sense.

"Sorry, I couldn't help but overhear my name," Gus said as he lurked a few steps away. "And I don't feel like a hero."

"You are to us." Finn was all easy smiles as he flipped shut his notepad. "Shouldn't you be drying off by the fire like I suggested? You don't want to get sick."

"Yeah, I will." Gus peered at Old Mother Splinter.

Finn walked over and clapped Gus on the shoulder. "Drop by the station in the morning. We'll take a formal statement to get everything signed off, and then that's all we need from you."

"Oh! Sure. But I've already told you everything."

"It's for our records. This looks like an accident, though."

While Finn continued to comfort Gus and set his fears to rest, I took in the scene.

I saw nothing accidental about the situation. And the more I wondered about those scarabs, the more I believed they were up to something less than friendly. Something that had almost gotten Old Mother Splinter killed.

***

"I've heard of situations when scarabs go too far with their games." Barney Hoffman sat in his usual seat behind his desk in animal control the next morning. "I've never known them to be malicious, though. But they have an odd awareness of their environment, and forget how fragile other creatures are."

"It's an age thing." I was nestled on a pile of Barney's paperwork. "They lose sense of the fragile nature of some beings' timelines."

"True. Scarabs have been around since the dinosaurs, and they can live for up to five hundred years. They'll outlive us all. When you're that old, you lose touch with the modern day."

"The angels are bringing them in this morning to interview." Zandra sat on the other side of the desk, powdered sugar on her shirt from her recent donut consumption. "We need to know if they messed with Old Mother Splinter."

"And caused her to dive beneath the midnight waves," I said.

Barney nodded. "Does Angel Force need support from animal control?"

"Cythera didn't want us there, but Finn argued the case in our favor last night," Zandra said. "We'll sit in on the interviews and make sure the scarabs don't run rings around the angels."

"Quite right. The angels can't be experts in everything." He smiled and patted the edge of the pile of papers I sat on. "For once, I have a quiet day. All my paperwork is done. I can do your license checks for you, so you focus on the case."

"No need. I can fit them in later," Zandra said. "The interviews won't take long."

"That's kind of you, Barney. We accept." I was happy to finish early today. I'd tossed and turned, thinking about what we'd discovered on the beach.

Something about the situation didn't sit right, but I couldn't put my paw on what troubled me.

"You get going, spend time with the angels, and figure this out. And keep watch over those scarabs. I don't want any more groups being beguiled," Barney said. "Besides, it'll be a nice change for me to get out of the office."

"We're on it." I stood and did a full body stretch then hopped onto Zandra's shoulder, and we left animal control and walked the short distance to Angel Force.

I yawned in Zandra's ear. "After this, we're catching up on sleep. I want at least fifteen hours."

She grinned. "Lazy bones. You can get away with much less sleep than that."

"Why should I, when we have such a comfy bed waiting for us? We'll speak to Amenia and her children, figure this out, then head home for serious nap time. Then we can watch a movie and order in. No! Ask Vorana to make us something meaty with dumplings."

"Sounds great. So long as Vorana's up for it. She's not had much enthusiasm for cooking recently."

"Hmmm, I've noticed. We should stick to ordering in."

"We could always cook something for Vorana."

"And give her food poisoning to add to her troubles? Let's not risk it."

Zandra chuckled. "Point taken. I'll grab pizza."

The atmosphere when we entered the pristine white Angel Force building stank of tension, hummed with pressure, and roiled with worry.

"Something's happened. Hurry!" I said.

"Could just be Cythera is in another bad mood." Zandra tiptoed forward. "It's not too late to turn back. We could get Barney to do this. Cythera tolerates him."

"Let's see what's going on. If Cythera gets too shouty, I'll scratch her, and we'll make a run for it."

"That'll make everything better." Zandra smirked and pressed her cheek against my side as we walked into the main open-plan office.

Finn spotted us and hurried over. "You've heard the news?"

"No, but from everyone's expression, it's not good," I said.

"Old Mother Splinter didn't survive the night."

"What happened to her?" Zandra said. "She seemed okay on the beach. I mean, naked and soggy, but alive."

"We're not sure. They're running tests to figure out what went wrong."

"Did she have water in her lungs?" I said.

"She didn't drown. The doctor had trouble keeping her awake when we got her to the hospital. Then she slipped into a coma. A few hours later, she was gone." Finn yawned. "Sorry. Late night. Once we were done at the beach, I spent a couple of hours at the hospital. I got called back in when Old Mother Splinter died."

"What did we miss?" Zandra said. "I didn't see any injuries."

"The doctor couldn't find any external signs of trauma. It's almost as if she gave up the fight."

I cleared my throat. "I should mention something that could be significant. Old Mother Splinter was dead when Gus pulled her from the water. She hadn't been gone long, though, so I performed a reanimation spell. There's the tiniest possibility it didn't go to plan."

"Did you feel your magic go wonky when you used the spell?" Zandra said.

"I surprised myself by how smoothly it went. I don't think anything went wrong, but maybe..."

"It's a complicated spell," Finn said. "I'll make sure the doctors check, but I don't think it was that."

"She didn't exhibit ghoulish symptoms before she died?" My magic was less than perfect since most of it had been stripped from me over thirty years ago. And although I was slowly reclaiming it, I was out of practice with the trickier spells. Had I made a mistake on the beach?

"Old Mother Splinter didn't change or behave strangely," Finn said. "The doctor said she kept complaining of being intensely tired. They assumed it was the shock of almost drowning. They kept a close eye on her, but she became unresponsive. They did everything they could, but she slipped away."

Acer hurried over. "The scarabs are here for their interviews. Morning, Zandra. Juno."

"Thanks. Let's talk to them about Old Mother Splinter. Maybe they'll be so shocked when they learn she's dead, they'll reveal what they did to her on the beach," Finn said.

"We should speak to Amenia on her own," I said. "She's the family powerhouse."

"That's the plan. And she may confess if she thinks we'll pin this crime on her children."

"Finn! How wonderfully devious," I said.

"That's the demon in me." He yawned again.

A few minutes later, we were seated in an interview room. Amenia hovered in the air on one side of the table while I sat with Finn and Zandra on the other side.

"Unhappy, I am. My children shouldn't be here," Amenia said.

"This won't take long," Finn said. "And with your permission, we'd like to interview them, too."

"Have a representative, they must. Only babies."

"Of course. We'd never interview children without them having appropriate support," Finn said. "Do you have someone in mind?"

"Juno. Trust you, I do."

I nodded. "I'm honored. Of course, I'll sit in on the interview. I'll make sure they feel no pressure when they're asked questions."

Amenia bobbed her head. "Then begin."

"As you know, last night, there was an incident on the beach," Finn said.

"No apologies," Amenia said.

"Excuse me."

"Fun, we were having. So was everybody."

"We'll get to you beguiling a load of non-magicals in a moment. I'm talking about what happened to Old Mother Splinter."

Amenia tittered. "Crazy old crone. You never know what lurks in the dark waters. Dangerous."

"Did you have anything to do with her going into those dark waters?" Finn said.

"No! But amusing, it was."

"Did Old Mother Splinter speak to you after your performance earlier in the day?" I asked.

Amenia bobbed up and down in the air, her wings fluttering. "No, but heard her, I did. Proud crone. Too prideful."

"You didn't like that?" Finn said. "You wanted to bring her down a peg or two?"

"Stayed away. Want nothing to do with pride. It comes before a fall. Painful, that can be."

"So can an unplanned night swim that goes wrong," Zandra said. "Did you invite Old Mother Splinter to the beach?"

"There was no invitation. Why the interest in her?"

"She's dead," Finn said.

Amenia zoomed to the ceiling then shot around the room, leaving a trail of sparkles behind her. "Dead! But leave, she did. She was saved. The man with the straggly hair and onion breath saved her, he did."

"So we thought, but she died at the hospital," Finn said. "They're running tests to see what happened to her. What do you think they'll find?"

"Nothing from me! Never kill with malice."

"But you have killed?" I said.

She chittered at me. "Never said that. Twist my words, you do. Scarabs aren't malicious. Here for fun, not harm. Sorry I am, she is dead, but it has nothing to do with me."

"You were on the beach, wielding all kinds of spells to bedazzle non-magicals," Finn said. "Maybe a spell hit Old Mother Splinter, and she got it into her head to go swimming."

Amenia slowed her frantic fluttering. "Did she drown?"

Finn shifted in his seat and rolled his shoulders. "We don't think so. But something bad happened to her. Her death was unnatural. Will the doctors find scarab magic running through her veins when they dig deeper?"

"No! Never! With my family, I was. Just having fun."

"Where did you go after your performance?" I asked.

"We wound down. Exhausting, performances are."

"You must have gone somewhere."

"The woods. We flew, played, and ate. Not a crime. Searching for food, we were, when we were drawn to the beach by the noise and flames. A good party, we always enjoy."

"Did you see anyone while you were in the woods?" Finn said.

"Just us. Stay out of the way, we do. People think we are mischief makers."

Which meant Amenia had little in the way of an alibi.

She lowered herself to the table and perched on top of it. "Crimson Cove is troubled."

"What makes you say that?" Finn said.

"When we arrived, something oppressive, I felt. A troubling presence."

He shook his head. "There's nothing bad in Crimson Cove. We have a few dodgy magic users living here, but they're known to us."

"At first, I thought it was the non-magicals. But... No. Something bad you have, festering at your core. Causing trouble. Killing witches. Gathering mayhem."

I glanced at Zandra. What was Amenia talking about? This was a distraction technique. Wanting the focus off her so she could sneak out of Crimson Cove with her children and not be charged with Old Mother Splinter's murder.

"Where will we find this festering core of magic?" Finn said.

Amenia zoomed up to the ceiling and back down again. "I know not. Not my town. Not my problem."

"Without evidence to support this claim, there's little we can do," Finn said. "Angel Force knows all the troublemakers in town. If any of them were making a move, we'd stop it."

"Then a new troublemaker, you have. A nasty one. One who could change this place forever if you don't stop it."

A shiver ran down my spine and tickled the spot at the base of my tail. What if this presence Amenia felt had something to do with the problems we'd been experiencing? The magic wards malfunctioning and the non-magicals romping around causing trouble. Was there something dark tinkering with Crimson Cove?

There was a tap on the one-way mirror that looked in on the room. Cythera must be watching the interview. And the sharp tap suggested she wasn't amused.

"My children," Amenia said. "Would like to see them."

"Soon," Finn said. "If you wait outside, we'll interview them in here. Then you can leave."

"Juno, be here, you will?" Amenia said.

"Of course. I'll make sure the angels treat them gently. We just need to confirm your alibi and make sure your little ones didn't get up to anything they shouldn't."

"Full of fun, not malice. Trust what they tell you. Raise them well, I do." Amenia was escorted out of the room by Finn.

"What do you think about her?" Zandra said.

"I've encountered a few scarabs, and they can be sneaky, but they're not malevolent. It's always possible this family has turned bad, though. And Old Mother Splinter was a prickly character. She could have said something that offended Amenia. Maybe even insulted her children."

"It could have been fun gone wrong," Zandra said. "Amenia, or one of her children, hit Old Mother Splinter with the beguiling spell they used on the non-magicals, but it got twisted. The combination of the spell and the shock of almost drowning was too much for her."

"Old Mother Splinter wasn't a frail old crone, though. She was sure of herself because she knew her powerful worth. It would have taken more than a wonky spell to end her life." I hopped onto the table. "I wouldn't be surprised if there's darkness mingled in this mystery."

"You think the scarabs used dark magic?"

"No, well, most likely not."

Zandra puffed out a breath. "We need more information."

"Let's bring in the children. See what they can reveal." The tingle in my toe beans suggested this puzzle was far from solved.

Chapter 5

Bad angel

A tense Cythera sat next to me in the interview room. Zandra had left with Finn to talk through the interview with Amenia and to grab coffee.

I glanced at Cythera. She twitched every time one of the infant scarabs twittered out a laugh.

"Want Mama," Loris said.

"She's right outside," Cythera said. "You tell us the truth, and you can see her. You're not leaving this room until you've been honest with us. No secrets. Only naughty children have secrets."

"Gently," I murmured. "They're only young." It was clear Cythera had little experience with youngsters.

She cleared her throat, seeming unable to get comfortable in her seat as she shuffled around. "Tell us what you did after your performance yesterday afternoon."

"We played. Just like this." Saphic nudged her brother.

They shot into the air, zoomed around, giggling and shrieking.

"Less of that," Cythera said. "This situation is serious. A witch is dead."

"The witch is dead. The witch is dead. Long live the witch." There was more giggling and sparkles.

Cythera stood from her seat and extended her wings. "Be still! No more of this nonsense. You're under investigation for a possible murder. You shouldn't be laughing about it."

I winced. Way to go in terrifying the young scarabs.

They dropped from the air and bumped onto the desk.

"Murder! Who died?" Loris said.

"Better. Now I have your attention, be quiet and listen. And answer all my questions truthfully. If I think you're hiding anything, I have a right to lock you in a cell and make you think about what you've done for a very long time."

"Cythera," I hissed.

She ignored me, her wings still outstretched in a threat display.

"Who died? Who died?" Loris bounced up and down in the air, his tiny antenna quivering.

"Be still!" Cythera loomed over the scarabs' head, her fisted hands resting on the table. "You will behave."

Saphic squeaked and flew back so fast she bumped into the wall, causing her to squeak again.

I rested a paw on the back of Cythera's hand and dug in claws. "You need to behave, too, or this interview will go nowhere."

"They aren't doing what I tell them," she hissed back. "Why are they so naughty?"

I focused on the trembling baby scarabs. "There's nothing to fear. Cythera just needs to find out who hurt the witch who went swimming yesterday. You were there when she was pulled from the water, so we need to know what you saw. That's all. Cythera didn't mean to yell, did you? She's very sorry."

Cythera grunted.

I flicked an ear. "Say sorry to them."

She mumbled something unintelligible, which sounded more like a curse than an apology.

The infants' wings trembled as shimmering blobs of liquid dropped onto the table. Tiny sobs followed.

"Now look what you've done," I hiss-whispered to Cythera.

Her eyes widened. "There's no need for tears. I'm sorry! I'm sorry for shouting. You just need to be quiet and answer my questions."

"Mean angel. Mama said not to trust you," Saphic snuffled out.

"Of course you can trust the angels. We're here to protect everybody. That's our purpose."

"You shouted. Horrible angel. And you showed your wings. Only do that when angry or showing off."

"Show off! Show off!" Loris whispered.

"No! I'm not angry. I... just..." Her panicked gaze went to me. "Do something."

I took a second to enjoy Cythera's distress then tapped my paws on the table to get the youngsters' attention. "Ignore the grumpy old angel. She probably hasn't had her coffee this morning.

You know how adults need at least two caffeine shots before they come to their senses."

Saphic floated closer to me. "She's a bully."

"I'd never bully anyone! But someone is dead. I must have the information." Cythera ducked her head. "Sorry. But I need to know what you saw on the beach. It's very important."

"We'll get the answers we need. The infants will be happy to answer your questions once they settle. Then you can buy them each a donut as a reward." I nodded at the scarabs. "Or do you prefer savory treats? Maybe moist moss?"

"That's bribery," Cythera muttered.

"It's also being nice to the infants you terrified. Surely, you don't want them telling everyone about the mean angel who lives in Crimson Cove, do you?"

She tutted. "Get on with it, since you're such a natural with them."

I cat-smiled at her. "Infants, we need to know about Old Mother Splinter."

"The naked lady on the beach?" Loris giggled. "Everything, I saw."

"That's the one. What did you see her do last night at the bonfire?"

"She waddled into the water like a duck chasing treats."

They both giggled at that vivid image.

"Was anyone with her while she waddled?"

Loris shook his head. "On her own for most of the time. She stood there for a while, staring. Then took off her clothes and walked into the water."

"But there was someone else there?"

"Yeah. Some guy."

"What did he look like?"

"Don't know."

Cythera thumped a fist on the table. "Of course you do. It's only just happened. Remember."

The tears started again.

"Hush! Ignore the angel. Focus on me. What did this man look like?" I said.

"It was dark. And we were playing with the non-magicals. Such fun." Saphic poked her tiny green tongue out at Cythera.

If someone else was with Old Mother Splinter, why hadn't they helped her when she got in distress? "Did you see anyone use magic on her?"

"No! Those non-magicals are so funny when they dance," Loris said.

"Clumsy and wobbly. Like drunk elves." Saphic giggled, which set Loris off.

I flipped my tail to get their attention. "Did you use magic to make the non-magicals dance?"

"They mainly did it themselves after they'd been drinking from those tin cans with the gross smelling stuff in them. Mama told us to be careful. Non-magicals are fragile, so we could only use tiny spells."

"They danced like loosey-goosey did a poopsy." Saphic swayed in the air.

"Could one of your spells have accidentally hit Old Mother Splinter?" I asked. "Perhaps that's what made her go night swimming."

"Not our spells. She was too far away. We saw her go in then this man ran in after her."

"Yeah. He pulled her out and kissed her." Loris made a gagging noise, and they giggled again.

"He gave her the kiss of life," I said. "It's called CPR."

"CP what?"

"Children, focus," Cythera snapped.

Their laughter vanished.

"We need to know if you saw anything unusual," I said. "We don't think Old Mother Splinter willingly went into the sea. It's dangerous to night swim."

Loris flopped onto the table. "We saw nothing."

"Tell us where you went after your performance yesterday afternoon," Cythera said. "Did you see Old Mother Splinter?"

Loris raised his head. "Please."

Cythera's eyebrows flashed up. "Um... Excuse me?"

"You didn't say please. My sister's right. You're a rude bully angel. No manners."

"Please." Cythera spoke through gritted teeth.

Saphic gave a tiny, triumphant snort. "Mama says manners cost nothing."

"And she's right. They're important." I didn't look at Cythera because her expression would have made me giggle along with the children. "So, what did you do?"

"Went to the woods. Our performances are intense, so we wind down after. Mama says we get too high-spirited and must relax. Too much chaos energy gives her a headache. We did deep breathing and stretching, and then we were free to fly."

"What took you to the beach?" I said. "It's not that close to the woods."

"The noise. Those non-magicals were shouting and cheering."

"And the flames," Loris said. "We were looking for food when we saw the lights flickering in the distance, so we went to explore. We found the non-magicals and thought we'd have fun with them."

Their account tallied with Amenia's statement. But was she sneaky enough to school them into providing an alibi because she knew she'd be a suspect? Or were they telling the truth, and they had nothing to do with what happened to Old Mother Splinter?

"Did you visit the hospital to see how Old Mother Splinter was doing after the beach party ended?" I asked.

"Yuck. Only the super ill go there," Saphic said. "We're not ill. We're healthy."

"Someone here is sick." Loris's chirpy tone had gone. "When we got here, it felt icky. We wanted to leave, but Mama said we had an opportunity... No, an orangutan. What's the word?"

"Obligation, dumb-dumb! Mama said we didn't get to perform properly the last time we were here, and it was important everyone saw how amazing we were. She said we'd perform but then leave the same day."

"Yet you're still here," Cythera said. "Why stay if you don't like the feel of the place?"

Saphic fluttered in the air. "We don't run from trouble. At least, not most of the time. Mama taught us that. Do bad, pay price. We know. We aren't scared. But we didn't kill that naked witch."

"Tell me more about what you felt when you arrived in Crimson Cove?" I asked. "What was it about the place that made you uncomfortable? You said it was icky."

Neither of them spoke for a moment.

"It feels gross. Like it needs a good bath," Loris finally said.

"Our town is clean," Cythera said.

"Not the roads and houses. The air. There's something bad here. Something you need to clean out."

There was no trace of mockery from the young scarabs.

We questioned them some more to clarify what they meant, but they just kept saying Crimson Cove didn't feel nice, but they didn't know why.

Cythera ended the interview when more tears threatened and then escorted Amenia and her children out of the building.

I met Zandra in the kitchen, gave her a quick update, and was considering exploring the food options left in the fridge when Finn dashed in.

"I just got a message from the hospital. We need to get over there. Now!"

❧❧❧

"Why is this place so full?" Zandra strode beside Finn as we walked along a hospital corridor.

The hospital was normally quiet since most ailments could be treated with a spell or potion, so there was rarely a need to visit a doctor. But

69

today, the place was transformed. Every room had a patient in it, and there were beds lined up along the corridors. They were all full.

Three nurses dashed from bed to bed, checking people and casting spells. The air crackled with magic, along with a hint of panic.

"Doc!" Finn sped up when he spotted the head doctor leaning over a patient.

He lifted a finger, gesturing us to stay back while he examined the patient. Then he stood, shook his head, and walked over to us. "I thought the angels should see this situation. I have to say, I'm worried."

"Why are there so many people in here?" Finn said. "When you said there'd been admissions with symptoms like Old Mother Splinter, I didn't think you meant half the town was unwell!"

"It's not that bad, but these people are all displaying the same symptoms as Old Mother Splinter did before she died."

I stared along the corridor at the full beds. "What magic have you used to reverse these symptoms?"

The doctor rubbed the back of his neck and sighed. "Everything. They're not responding. It's as if they're wrapped in a cocoon that repels all magic."

"When did the patients start coming in?" Zandra said.

"Late last night, not long after Old Mother Splinter arrived. They were all complaining about intense tiredness and couldn't keep their eyes open for more than a few seconds."

"Did Old Mother Splinter have something contagious? Should we be here?" I nudged Zandra. Maybe the hospital wasn't a safe place to be. If there was a risk this toxic spell could damage her, we had to leave.

"Old Mother Splinter's not the cause of this. I wasn't aware at the time, but three patients had arrived before her, also complaining of extreme tiredness."

"Are they dead?" Finn said.

"No, but all of them are in comas. We're using everything we've got to keep them stable."

I kept nudging Zandra, but she waved away my concerns. "Maybe Old Mother Splinter came into contact with your first patients. She got contaminated, somehow."

"If that's the case, we can't find a connection between them," the doctor said.

"Maybe they all went to the scarab performance?" Zandra said.

"No, we checked. One of them didn't attend."

Zandra's gaze drifted along the corridor. "There must be a link."

The doctor shrugged. "Right now, we're focused on keeping everyone stable."

"So, they feel tired. Then what happens to your patients?" Finn said.

"Just when we think we've got them stable, they slip into a coma."

My heart pitter-pattered. This was serious. "How many so far?"

"Since this morning, I have admitted twenty patients. Five are in comas. We've slowed things by forcing a suspension spell around them, but we have to keep topping it up every hour because it disintegrates. My nurses are run ragged. It's as if whatever has gotten them is eating the spells we put around them."

"May I attempt some healing magic?" I asked. "I've experienced a range of plague spells and toxic potion maladies over the years."

Zandra gave me the side-eye, which I ignored.

"I'm not sure," the doctor said. "These patients are fragile."

"If everything you've tried has failed, what do you have to lose? If they remain in a coma, will they eventually die, like Old Mother Splinter?"

He sighed again. "I believe so. And my nurses can only do so much before their magic needs a recharge."

"Juno knows some interesting spells," Zandra said. "She might be able to help."

"I can vouch for Juno and Zandra," Finn said. "I'd trust them with my life."

The doctor puffed out a breath. "I'm at a loss for what to do. If you can help, let's try. This way. I'll take you to the most serious cases." He led us into one of the private rooms at the back of the hospital. There were two beds in there, both occupied.

"That's Voss Black!" Zandra hurried to one bed. "I didn't even know he was unwell."

"Voss was found passed out at the pizza parlor," the doctor said. "No one could wake him, so they brought him here."

I jumped off Zandra's shoulder and landed on Voss's chest. His eyes flickered, but that was his only response to my fluffy arrival. I pressed my paws down and pulsed out the most powerful healing spell I could conjure.

Nothing happened to him. His eyes remained closed and his breathing shallow.

"Zandra, perhaps if we combine power," I said.

"Whatever you need." She pushed up her sleeves then glanced at the doctor. "If you can't fix this, how long has Voss got?"

"It's hard to say. Old Mother Splinter died within ten hours of admittance, but I don't know how long she'd been carrying the magic on her."

"It's definitely magic doing this?" Finn said.

"Yes. There are traces of something dark, but we're still unpicking what it is." He turned back to Zandra. "Whatever the magic is, it affects people at different rates. Some fall into a coma quickly; others stay awake for longer. Several people are still lucid if you want to speak to them."

"We do. Maybe there's a link between them to show what caused this," Finn said.

"We can't let Voss die," I said. "His pizzas are epic."

"Yeah, that's the only reason we want to keep him alive." Zandra arched an eyebrow at me. "Let's see what we can do."

We spent ten minutes testing different healing spells. Although Voss looked more relaxed, his eyes still didn't open. Whatever magic had gotten him had him in a chokehold and wasn't letting go.

Zandra stepped back and wiped a hand across her brow. "Finn, maybe you could do something? Angel magic heals."

Finn had been inspecting the other person in the bed. "If you two can't heal him, I doubt I'll be any better. You're more powerful than me." He walked over and rested his hands on Voss's chest.

He grimaced and flexed his fingers. "That does not feel good."

"What do you sense?" I said.

He turned his hands over and inspected his palms. "I know this power. It's something really dark."

"If you know what it is, can you remove it?"

"I didn't say that." His tongue traced across his teeth. "It makes me want to puke, though. Kind of reminds me of the foster home I was raised in. It's got that edgy, sharp feel. You know, if you step out of line, you get in trouble."

This was the first time Finn had spoken about his upbringing. "Who raised you?"

"A couple of half-demons. They were only in it for the cash." Finn studied his boots.

I glanced at the doctor then back to Finn. "Could it be demon energy? Would you recognize that?"

He inhaled sharply. "You could be on to something. It feels like my foster dad's power. Twisted and warped into something you don't want to be around for long."

The doctor was shaking his head. "It would take a demon of immense power to reach so many people."

"Powerful demons are out there, so it's possible. They're allowed to enter Crimson Cove," I said. "The question we need answered is why is it doing this?"

"When will all the test results be back on Old Mother Splinter?" Finn said. "We need to know what's wrong with her before we can find a reversal spell."

"The initial results showed the unusual dark magic signature, but after so many more cases came in, we ran a full panel of tests. There's been a delay in getting them because we've had so many people come in that needed urgent attention."

"Make it a priority," Finn said. "We need to know if a dark demon is behind this."

The doctor nodded.

"Could it be something in the sea?" I said. "Perhaps Old Mother Splinter drank a pollutant in the water."

"And then passed it to other people?" Zandra said.

"It's worth getting tests run on the water," Finn said. "We need to consider everything."

"Can the angels help with that?" the doctor said. "I don't have enough nurses."

"Leave it to us."

As the doctor discussed getting samples of seawater, a flash of movement in the corridor caught my attention. It wasn't a nurse or a gurney being wheeled past. It was a small, dark shape, low to the floor. And that shape looked all too familiar to me.

I jumped off Voss's chest and trotted to the door. I poked my head out and looked along the corridor. Sammy was rounding the corner.

What was he doing in the hospital? Was he unwell? Could this magic harm familiars, too?

I did an internal check. I felt fine. No tiredness or overwhelming desire to sink into a bed and never wake up. I hurried along the corridor, dodging people and gurneys to reach Sammy and ask him what he was doing. When I got to the end and looked for him, he was nowhere to be seen.

Despite the problems we had in our private lives, I wanted to ensure he was okay. Even though we were no longer together, I didn't like the thought of him feeling bad because of a toxic spell.

I returned to the room to see Finn stepping back from the bed and shaking his head.

"Perhaps Old Mother Splinter had an enemy. What do we know about her?" Zandra said.

Finn lifted his shoulders, a pensive look on his face. "We've had complaints filed about her. She's not popular. She owns half a dozen buildings in Crimson Cove and is quick to evict tenants if they're late paying or disagree with her when she increases the rent."

"Maybe a disgruntled tenant did this but accidentally tainted other people with whatever magic they used," Zandra said. "She must visit all her tenants to make sure there aren't any problems. It would have been easy to slip her something toxic during one of those visits."

"If that's what happened, it must have been after the scarab performance," I said. "She seemed fine, then. Superior in attitude to everyone she spoke to but healthy."

"Unless it's slow-acting magic," Finn said. "I know she was working before she went to the performance."

"I'll chase up those tests," the doctor said. "See if they give us pointers to say when the magic was cast or ingested."

I looked up at him. "Have you had any non-magicals admitted? If this spell gets them, they won't stand a chance."

"Thankfully, not yet. I'm keeping a close eye on everyone who comes through those doors. So far, it's only those with power who've been affected."

"Let's hope, whatever it is, it only targets people with magic," Zandra said. "If we get non-magicals dropping dead, we won't be able to hide this from the outside world."

"Which will put Crimson Cove at risk," Finn said.

"That's not happening." I hopped back onto the bed. "Let's isolate all the non-magicals. And I know just how to keep them occupied and safe while we figure out who's been messing with us."

Chapter 6

Magic show

"We have dinner plans. We don't want to stay here." A disgruntled non-magical with a bushy black beard and impressively robust eyebrows glared at Zandra.

I sat close by, unable to intervene, but watching my witch to ensure she kept a grip on her sometimes fiery temper.

"This is a once-in-a-lifetime opportunity. You won't see anything like this again. Why would you want to miss out?" Zandra's smile was fake and her hands fisted behind her back.

"Because of dinner. I want my lobster."

"You really don't. The lobsters are terrible around here," Zandra said. "And it's overpriced. They always mark up prices for tourists."

"We should stay. This sounds fun," his redheaded companion said. "They've got dancing cats, a mesmerist, fire breathers, and a chance to disappear inside an ancient magic box. I don't mind missing dinner for this."

"Babe! I want my lobster."

She poked out her tongue. "It always makes my stomach churn the way you crack open those poor innocent lobsters and slurp them down."

"Not only is this a unique night of amazing free entertainment, but there's also unlimited food available at the buffet," Zandra said. "And it's amazing. Our local café, Bites and Delights, provided it all. I eat there almost every day."

"Oh! We've eaten in there. It's fantastic." The woman tugged on the guy's arm. "We'll go for overpriced lobster another time."

"But I made us a reservation."

"There's free alcohol, too," Zandra sing-songed in a most uncharacteristic tone of voice. She was playing the role of amenable hostess to perfection.

The guy grumbled as he tugged on his beard. "Fine. We'll stay. But do we have to stay the night, as well? That's kinda weird."

I twitched my whiskers. This non-magical was being surprisingly resilient to our persuasion magic. Despite the risks, we'd been gently blanketing the town with a suggestion spell, so when we announced an exclusive surprise event in the town hall, all the non-magicals would be thrilled to attend.

"It'll be like the sleepovers we had when we were in school," the woman said. "We can hang out with Richie and Rose. Talk about the old times."

"It seems odd. I've never heard of anything like this before. And why so last-minute?" the guy said.

I stood beside Zandra as she continued to debate with the stubborn-headed guy, glancing around to see Sorcha and Finn enticing the final few non-magicals into the town hall.

It had taken all afternoon and most of the evening to arrange an impromptu magic show with dancing afterward and a free buffet and bar. We'd billed it as an all-inclusive overnight experience they'd never forget. A chance to see some of the greatest magicians that ever lived.

We'd recruited several skilled spell casters to ensure this would be a show they wouldn't want to leave and accidentally get themselves whacked with demon magic they wouldn't wake up from.

The non-magicals had to be contained in one space so we could check if any of them were falling asleep when they shouldn't. So far, not a single non-magical had visited the hospital, but it was too big of a risk to let them roam freely in case they were tainted with whatever killed Old Mother Splinter.

Just as Finn joined us, Gus Bainbridge hurried over, a clipboard in one hand. "All my old ladies are in there and accounted for. And I did a headcount of everyone else, like you asked. There are four hundred and forty-two people inside. You'll have them jammed in like sardines in a tin when we all bed down for the night."

"Good job," Finn said. "Thanks for offering to help."

"It's my pleasure. It's what I do. I'm used to tackling crowds of over-excited people, so when I saw you struggling, I thought I'd lend a hand." Gus looked over his shoulder into the busy main hall. "This is such a treat for my ladies. I'm lucky I had a party here in Crimson Cove. I wouldn't have missed this for the world." He passed the clipboard to Finn, a huge smile on his face.

"It'll be a great evening," Finn said. "But you should get inside with everyone else. You don't want to miss anything. The first act starts in ten minutes."

"Of course. And my ladies have already picked out where they want to sleep. It could be a raucous night. One of them snuck in a bottle of sherry, and they've all been secretly sipping it ever since they got here." Gus chuckled. "Not that I have the heart to tell them off and take it from them. Even though they're all on so much medication, they rattle. We all deserve a little fun."

"I couldn't agree more. Enjoy your evening." Finn waited until Gus strode inside before turning to me and moving away, so none of the non-magicals could hear us. "I think this might work."

"It has to. We can't have any non-magicals wandering around and getting hit with this magic."

"It doesn't buy us much time, though. We can keep them here this evening and overnight, but then we'll have to let them out."

"By then, we'll know what's causing the sleeping sickness and if we need to worry about it getting them," I said. "You got the seawater to the doctor?"

"Acer got the samples. They're being processed as we speak."

"We'll get these last few feisty non-magicals under control then lock the doors and cast another spell to make sure they're happy and no one has any desire to leave. Then we can go to the hospital and see if the results are in."

"Cythera is less than thrilled we're using magic to keep the non-magicals in line," Finn said.

"She can argue with us about that another time. She may not approve, but she also won't want dozens of non-magicals dying on her watch. Think of the paperwork! Besides, Crimson Cove can't be exposed. And we've been careful."

He raised his hands. "I know. But she's panicking, and you know what Cythera gets like when she panics."

I wrinkled my booping snooter. "Let's get back to the others. It'll take a combined effort to cast a spell over everyone."

The bearded guy and his redheaded girlfriend had given up the fight and were walking into the hall, hand in hand.

We joined Sorcha and Zandra, watching the crowd milling about and picking seats as they waited for the first act to begin.

"We ready to do this?" Zandra cracked her knuckles.

Sorcha nodded, her pretty freckled face unusually pale. "I've never used magic on non-magicals before. I'm nervous about blowing someone up."

"Use the lightest of touch. Imagine the magic barely trickling out of you," I said. "We just need a spell that makes them happy and relaxed, so they stay inside. Once they're occupied watching the performances, we'll cover the building in a gentle containment spell. That way, if someone leaves, we'll know about it and can get them back where they belong."

"And we're sure it's a good idea to have Remus and his vampires inside?" Finn said. "I like the guy, but it must be a temptation with all that food wandering around, unaware of how tasty they look to a hive of vamps."

"Remus promised he'd be on his best behavior," I said. "And Archie is in there, too. He'll ensure Remus does the right thing, even if he's tempted to take a nibble. We can trust the vampires. They want Crimson Cove to remain safe as much as we do. If we're exposed, Remus will have to relocate his hive. That would be a massive inconvenience for him."

Everyone linked hands, and I jumped onto Zandra's shoulder. I focused on the non-magicals inside the hall, and we pulsed wave upon wave of calming, supportive magic. We let it fill the hall, touching everyone inside. It would be just enough to keep them chilled and content.

"That should do it," I said after five minutes had passed.

Finn eased the double doors closed. Then he rejoined us, and we cast a containment spell over the building. If a non-magical really wanted, they could get out, but it wouldn't feel nice fighting through the magic. And anyone who forced their way through would trigger an alert to me and Zandra to let us know the non-magicals were on the loose.

Once the spell was in place, I relaxed. With the non-magicals no longer under threat, we could focus on finding the cause of the sleeping magic and deal with it.

Sorcha yawned loudly.

I tensed and leaped onto her shoulder. "Has the spell got you?"

She reached up and petted my head. "Relax. I've been feeling rough for weeks. It's not this sleeping sickness or whatever it is."

I gave her a thorough sniffing until she giggled and gently pushed my head away. "Your whiskers tickle. Really, I feel the same as I have for weeks. I'm overworked and rundown."

"You're certain?" Zandra walked over and peered into Sorcha's face. "You don't feel different from yesterday?"

"I promise, if I start falling asleep while on the job, I'll let you know. But it's this weird flu I can't get rid of." Sorcha tilted her head as if removing a kink in her neck. "I was even thinking about closing the café for a couple of weeks and going on a restorative retreat to see if complete rest would shift this."

"You should. Don't hate me for saying this, but you don't look good," Finn said. "And get to the doctor so he can check you out. Make sure it's nothing serious."

"I've been checked out, and he couldn't find anything wrong. I was told to take it easy and try meditation." Sorcha pressed her hands together in a prayer position. "It's the stress of my business expanding and not having everything in place to deal with the increase in customers."

"Promise me, if you feel any worse, you'll come find me," Zandra said. "I don't want you being another Voss. He collapsed at work."

"You got it. Honestly, I'm going home and straight to bed. I'll get a good night's sleep, and I'll feel better. Maybe I'll only do a half-day opening at the café tomorrow, then I can help you figure out what's going on here. And I won't be so busy with all the non-magicals shut in the town hall."

"They'll be out by lunchtime," Finn said.

"You rest and look after yourself," I said. "Ask Elijah to stay with you. I trust him."

Sorcha's eyebrows flashed up. "I never thought I'd hear you say that."

"We had a rocky start, but he's more reliable than some cats I know around here."

"There's always someone about to keep an eye on me. If Elijah's not around, Sammy and Tinkerbell will be there. They've been spending loads of time with each other."

Zandra cleared her throat and shook her head.

Sorcha pressed her lips together. "Oh! Sorry. I didn't mean to put my foot in it. You and Sammy... are you done?"

"You're fine. I'm sure Sammy will help if you need him. I just think... Well, it doesn't matter. So long as there's someone with you."

"I'm never alone at the café. There's always some furry friend skulking about looking for food. Let me know what you find from the tests the hospital is running, though. I'm intrigued to know what's doing this."

"We'll keep you in the loop," Zandra said.

We said our goodbyes then headed back to the hospital.

"Cythera agreed to post two angels outside the town hall," Finn said. "They'll stay until the non-magicals go to sleep."

"We just need to keep them safe while we figure this out," I said. "As soon as we know what magic dug its claws into Old Mother Splinter, we can reverse it and stop it from ever coming back."

We walked along in silence. Crimson Cove felt strange. Word had spread there was unpleasant magic creeping through the streets, so people were keeping out of the way in case it got them.

"If the magic only affects us," Zandra said, "that suggests it's been targeted."

"Someone wants us weakened," I said

"You think they want something in Crimson Cove and think we'll stop them from getting it?" Finn said.

"Maybe. They know if they try to take it, we'll stop them. But what could it be?"

"Or it's just some low-life messing with us," Zandra said. "They'll be sorry they ever heard of Crimson Cove by the time we're done with them."

I heartily agreed with my wonderful witch.

We arrived at the hospital and had to wait several minutes before the doctor was free to see us. The atmosphere was one of contained panic as nurses bustled past, and there were soft cries for help from several rooms.

"Things don't look any better," Finn said to the doctor as soon as he arrived.

"It's getting worse. We've had another dozen patients come in."

"Anyone else died?" Zandra said.

"No. The magic we're using is slowing the spell." The doctor scrubbed at his face, exhaustion lines cut deep in his skin. "If we'd tried that on Old Mother Splinter, we'd have saved her, too."

Finn rested a hand on the doctor's shoulder. "You didn't know what this was or how bad things would get. I brought in someone who almost drowned. Why would you think there was anything else wrong with her?"

The doctor twisted his mouth to the side. "I hate losing patients. We rarely do. We can save most people." His gaze traveled along the corridor. "Although I don't know how to do it this time."

"Are the test results back?" Finn shared a worried look with me and Zandra.

The doctor rolled his shoulders. "We found nothing in the seawater samples, so the water was clear. No traces of magic or pollutants that could make anyone unwell."

"What about the additional test on Old Mother Splinter?"

"We found something interesting. And it's showed up in all the blood samples we've tested so far. There are high levels of bergamot, lavender, and ylang ylang."

"The base elements for a sleep spell," Zandra said. "No surprise there, since everyone is saying how tired they feel. But those plants aren't deadly."

"In the wrong dose, everything is a poison. Water, sunlight, even air. Same goes with these plants."

"Do you think whoever created the sleep spell went too far? It's not just sending people to sleep. It's putting them in a coma and killing them?" I said.

"I wondered about that, but the ingredients have been mixed with something dark. It's a spell I've never seen before. Whatever its elements consist of, when it's mixed with those plants, it turns into something nasty." The doctor checked a sheet of paper a nurse handed him, signed it, and gave it back. "We pulled apart the spell elements and isolated each one, but there's something in there I can't figure out. That's the cause of our problems."

"Does the magic affect everyone?" Finn said. "Or is it targeting certain types of magic user?"

"So far, it hasn't discriminated. Although the older and more powerful you are, the more likely you can resist the spell for longer. But if it's got you, you'll go down, eventually."

I jumped onto Zandra's shoulder and curled my tail around her neck. If everyone was at risk, that made my witch vulnerable. If we didn't stop this, she could die.

She rested a hand against my side. "It's okay. I feel fine. It hasn't gotten me."

My stomach fluttered, and my toe beans tingled. "Yet! It hasn't got you yet. You're one of the most powerful witches I've ever met, and if this spell is aimed at weakening the most powerful, you'll be a target."

"If it gets me, I have you around to make sure I come to no harm."

I nuzzled her ear, my heart beating a little too fast to feel comfortable. "I promise, whatever it takes, I won't lose you to this spell."

We rested our foreheads together, and I took comfort in the pulse of our strong bond. Zandra was healthy. I'd know if she was suffering and trying to hide it from me.

"I'll keep working on the results," the doctor said. "There must be a way to unpick what's in there. Then we can begin the reversal process."

"While you do that, we'll go see if any of Old Mother Splinter's tenants have the power to create such a toxic spell," Finn said. "If we find the creator, we can get the spell ingredients from them."

"Then obliterate them," I snarled.

"I'll pretend I didn't hear that," the doctor said. "Although, from the way people are dropping, I may consider helping you with that obliteration. Whoever has done this has an evil streak."

"A streak we'll stop." Finn nodded at the doctor then turned to us. "Let's go catch our killer."

Chapter 7

An unpopular witch

After leaving the hospital, we headed to Angel Force.

Finn yawned and stumbled over his feet. "Sorry. I've barely had any rest since this investigation started."

"You're sure it's just that?" I rode on Zandra's shoulder. "You don't think the magic could have gotten to you, do you?"

"Not possible. I'm an angel. Well, part angel, so I'm practically indestructible. And none of the other angels have complained of being tired. I'm fine. We're all fine. Cythera is simply pushing hard to get a result in this case. And I'm right there with her. We've already lost one person, and now we know the cause, we can stop anyone else from dying."

"I'll make you a super strong coffee when we get inside," Zandra said. "Help keep you going."

"That'll work." Finn grinned at her. "I'm happy to be a coffee addict and have no plans to stop anytime soon."

Even though it was getting late, there were plenty of angels buzzing around the office when we arrived.

Finn gave Cythera an update, while Acer dashed off to pull files on Old Mother Splinter's business connections in Crimson Cove.

I settled at a desk with my witch in a seat beside me, watching the angels. None of them seemed tired, so I was hopeful Finn was right and the angels remained unaffected. We needed them in fighting form to help bring down this monster.

Zandra leaned close to me, her warm breath huffing my ear fluff. "You're panicking."

"I'm motivated."

"I feel great. Maybe a bit tired, but that's because we've barely stopped today. I have no weird symptoms and no desire to crawl under my duvet and never get out. I'd tell you if I felt ropey."

I jumped onto her lap and pressed my head against her stomach. "I can't lose you."

"You won't. I have no plans to go anywhere."

"What if you don't have a choice? This toxic spell is fast-moving and deadly."

"The doctors know how to slow it. They'll soon figure out a treatment." She scratched her short fingernails through my fur. "This'll all be over in a day or two. You're worrying about nothing."

"You are not nothing." I kept my head pressed against her stomach. Before meeting Zandra, I'd encountered cruel and coldhearted individuals who'd exploited magic for their own gain. I'd become infected with that negativity and had only seen misery in my future. It wasn't until Zandra rescued me and showed me life could be better, and people were decent, that I recaptured joy.

She leaned down and kissed my head several times. "I love you, too. And I should be equally worried. Maybe this spell could get you."

My head shot up. "Sammy was at the hospital!"

"Oh! You think he's sick?"

"I didn't have a chance to ask him. He seemed well, though. Maybe he was curious about what was going on."

"If this spell can get you, then we must get rid of it." Zandra gave me a one-armed hug and another kiss. "We're in this for life, got it?"

I pressed my booping snooter against her cheek, my heart happier. "Got it."

Finn walked over with Acer. She carried a pile of files while he held two enormous mugs of black coffee.

He put one down for Zandra. "Since you forgot it was your turn to make coffee, I took charge."

"Ever the hero," I said. "No refreshments for me?"

He pursed his lips. "You can drink from the sink. The faucet has a leak."

Zandra chuckled. "Thanks. Perfect. That'll keep us going for a few more hours."

Acer set down the files. "I've found three complaints about Old Mother Splinter. They were to do with unfair action against her tenants and attempting to speed up an eviction without the proper paperwork in place."

"She's been involved with the family property empire for decades. She took over after her mother died, so there could be more records in storage," Finn said.

"That could mean more files with complaints." Zandra sipped her coffee.

"And more suspects," I said.

"I'll go look." Acer dashed off.

"How's Acer working out?" Zandra said.

"Good. And she seems to enjoy the work. She's also not intimidated by Cythera, which is a bonus."

"Is Cythera any less stressed now we know more about the sleep spell?" I said.

"She's simmering at an unhealthy eight on the tension-ometer and has sanctioned as much overtime as we need to get this dealt with."

"Then let's get to work." Zandra looked through the first file. "Oh, I know this guy. It's Jacob Brolinski. He owns that quirky place *Third Time's a Charm*."

Finn nodded. "The upcycling store. That guy can turn his hand to anything and make it look incredible."

"It says here, Old Mother Splinter tried to evict him three years ago when he refused to pay the ten percent increase in rent."

"Same story here." Finn looked through another file. "Eliza MacDougall protested about an unfair rent rise. In this statement, she said Old Mother Splinter sent the heavies around to threaten her."

"I don't know this guy." Zandra flicked through the final file. "Alex Pine."

"He retired years ago," Finn said. "I've heard stories about him, though. He used to own a jewelry store. I believe he shut because he couldn't afford the increases in rent."

"Could be he's holding a grudge," I said. "He learned Old Mother Splinter was in town and taught her a lesson."

Finn flipped his file shut. "We need to speak to them all. See if anyone has been in contact with Old Mother Splinter in the last couple of days."

"Hi. I'm sorry to interrupt."

"Gus!" Finn stood from his seat as Gus Bainbridge appeared in the doorway. "How are you here? I mean, what are you doing here? Is there a problem at the town hall?"

I looked up at Zandra, and she shrugged. Neither of us had gotten dinged that the containment spell had been breached. We'd need to check to ensure it wasn't malfunctioning. The last thing we needed were marauding non-magicals on the loose when there was a deadly spell floating around.

"Sorry to bother you. I can see you're busy. I should be with my old ladies, making sure they don't get too merry on the sherry, but I couldn't stop thinking about Old Mother Splinter." Gus stepped into the office, his hands shoved in his jacket pockets. "I know she didn't make it, and I keep thinking, maybe there was more I could have done to help."

"Try not to feel bad about what happened." Finn strode over to him. "You did everything you could. And you were the only one to pull her out of the water. There were dozens of people on the beach that night, and they did nothing."

He let out a sigh through his nose, his lips pressed together. "I keep thinking about that, too. There was a guy with Old Mother Splinter just before she went swimming. He didn't help her, and he must have heard her shouting. It was super high-pitched. She was really panicked."

"Do you know who it was?" Zandra said.

Gus lifted his gaze and raised a hand. "Hey! You two again. You show up everywhere."

"We're popular." Zandra lifted one shoulder.

"You must be."

There was a second of awkwardness. There was no way to explain why someone who worked in animal control was always hanging out with local law enforcement and just happened to have a stunning white cat with an incredible level of intelligence by her side.

"So, the guy on the beach?" Finn said.

"Oh! Sure. He was fairly young and handsome. Maybe her son? I didn't speak to him, but Old Mother Splinter stood by the water for ages with him, just looking out to sea. When she went in, he stood there and watched."

"What did he do when he realized she needed help?" Finn said.

"He was walking away when she called for help. You'd think if your elderly mother insisted on going night swimming, you'd watch to make sure she came back."

"I don't think that was her son," Zandra muttered.

I nodded, unable to add anything meaningful to the conversation without freaking out Gus. I'd seen Old Mother Splinter with two men at the scarab performance. An older guy who appeared to be her personal assistant and a handsome younger guy who'd called her his queen and poured the champagne. Maybe her toy boy? Was he the person Gus had seen on the beach?

"He must be so upset because of what happened," Gus said. "Maybe he's feeling guilty. If he'd stuck around, he could have gotten her out of the sea faster than me. It took me ages to drag her back to shore. If I'd had help, we could have done more. She died because I wasn't quick enough."

"I know it's hard not to ruminate on what you should have done, but you're the hero in this story," Finn said. "You stepped up when no one else did."

"Old Mother Splinter still died," Gus said. "Was it the shock that killed her? The water was cold. Maybe her heart gave out."

"The doctors are still looking into it. I assure you, it wasn't anything you did or didn't do."

"Yeah, I know. But I still can't stop thinking about her." Gus gazed at his scuffed shoes.

Finn led him to the door. "Get back to the town hall and try to enjoy yourself. How's the show so far? That should take your mind off things."

"Oh, yeah. It's great. My ladies are being thoroughly entertained." Gus's expression brightened. "This guy levitated and then flew over the audience. I have no clue how he did it. Clever wires, I guess. The performers are having a brief break, and everyone is grabbing some late supper, so I took the chance to leave."

The flying guy was most likely one of Remus's vampires. Many of them could fly, although most turned into bats or crows to do so.

"Oh, and before I forget, although you'll think this is crazy." Gus's cheeks colored.

"Go on," Finn said. "Is there a problem?"

"I dunno. But there's a weird vibe around the back door. It took me ages to get it open. When I did, I felt this strange sensation, as if I was walking through warm treacle. It only lasted for a few seconds. I can't explain it. Have you ever felt anything like that?"

"That does sound strange. Are you sure you've not been enjoying the sherry too?"

"Hah! I have had a few beers. It's just... I don't know, it didn't feel natural. I can't put my finger on it."

"Maybe get some food inside you. That'll fix things."

Gus nodded. "Sure. I'll do that. And there's so much food in there, we could stay for a week and not run out."

If we didn't fix this sleeping spell issue soon, they may have to.

"Hey! Maybe the place is haunted," Gus exclaimed. "My ladies love a haunted house tour, although their tickers aren't really up to it. But they still insist on going on a spooky trip once a year."

Finn chuckled, the sound awkward. "You never know around here. Enjoy the rest of your evening."

Gus left, and after Finn watched him go, he returned to the desk.

"We need to strengthen the magic around the town hall," Zandra said. "Gus got out without us noticing, so others could, too."

"Our magic is still working. Gus felt compelled to leave because he needed to tell us something," I said. "That would have given him a strong intent, which broke through the spell. Everyone else will be too busy enjoying the performances and free food and drink to make a concentrated effort to escape."

"Even lobster guy?" Zandra said.

"Let's hope so. Then the lobsters can live to fight another day."

"I'll make sure the angels keep an eye on all the exits," Finn said. "They shouldn't have missed Gus leaving."

"You think the guy who watched Old Mother Splinter go swimming has something to do with this sleep spell?" Zandra said.

"We're adding him to the suspect list," Finn said. "And I know who Gus was talking about. Old Mother Splinter came to town with her personal assistant, Robin DuBrec, and her partner, Harlan Scout."

"Harlan isn't a business partner, is he?" I said. "The younger guy is her boyfriend?"

"Got it in one."

"Do they know what happened to Old Mother Splinter?"

"Sure. They've been informed."

"How did they take the news?"

"They seemed shocked. Although neither of them mentioned being at the beach when she went night swimming."

"It must have been Harlan," I said. "He's the younger of the two men."

"And keeping quiet about being there is suspicious," Zandra said.

"We need to question them again. When Old Mother Splinter's death seemed like a tragic accident, we only got basic details. But now people are falling asleep, we need to revisit everyone who has a link to Old Mother Splinter."

"Let's start with the three disgruntled tenants, then we'll tackle her romantic connections," I said.

"Let's hurry. It's getting late." Finn grabbed the address details of the tenants, and we headed out of Angel Force.

We arrived at the first house, and Finn knocked. There was no answer.

I peered through the windows but saw no signs of life.

"You looking for Eliza?" A neighbor stood on her doorstep, her arms crossed over her chest.

"Yes. Have you seen her recently?" Finn said.

"Sure. She wasn't feeling well, so she went to the doctor for a checkup. She didn't come back. I wondered if she'd gone to spend time with her daughter to recover from whatever was making her feel so bad. She looked ghastly, as if she hadn't slept for a month."

I exchanged a worried glance with Zandra.

We thanked the woman and walked to the next tenant's house. After repeatedly knocking on the door, we got no response. All the lights were off, and none of the curtains were drawn.

"You're wasting your time if you're after Jacob." A man paused on the street. "He got sick earlier today. Went off to the doctor, and I haven't seen him since."

"Did he say what was wrong with him?" Finn said.

"Trouble staying awake. I told him he needed a have a few early nights, but he said he'd almost fallen walking down the stairs. That didn't sound right to me. I sat with him for a while then convinced him to get help. I even took him to the hospital." The guy scrubbed at his chin. "It sure was busy there. I hope there's not something going around."

"Thanks." Finn pursed his lips. "How are you feeling?"

The guy's eyes widened. "Same as always. I shouldn't be worried, should I?"

"Everything will be fine. But go to the doctor, too, if you get any odd symptoms or extreme tiredness."

"Is this the same thing that got Voss Black? The pizza parlor's closed, and I heard he fainted at work. Landed face-first on a pizza pie. Sauce everywhere."

"We're not sure. It's maybe nothing to worry about," Finn said.

"Maybe. I've heard other people aren't showing up for work. I figured they were keeping a low profile because of all the non-magicals around, but is it because of this sleeping thing?"

"I'm sure they're just being cautious." Although Finn was doing his best not to panic the man, he failed. The guy inched passed us, concern on his face, then dashed away.

The last house we tried was exactly the same. There was no answer, and it seemed as if no one had been home for some time, since the rooms sat in darkness.

"If all the tenants who had disputes with Old Mother Splinter are also under this sleeping spell, it can't be any of them behind it," Zandra said.

"I'll check at the hospital to see if they're there," Finn said, "but you're right. You wouldn't cast a lethal spell that got you, too. It makes no sense."

"Unless their magic backfired," I said. "Which I doubt. It takes someone with great power to wield such a potent spell. They'd know what they were doing. They wouldn't make such a rookie error."

"We should tackle Old Mother Splinter's boyfriend and her business partner next," Zandra said.

I nodded. "We could be following the wrong lead, and Old Mother Splinter's murder has nothing to do with tenant grudges, but involves an issue closer to home. Maybe an affair of the heart gone wrong."

"Or a disgruntled assistant wanting revenge on his demanding boss," Finn said.

"There you are!" Acer rushed toward us. "I found something in the old case files in storage. There was a court case involving Old Mother Splinter and an ancient tree."

I tilted my head. "A tree took her to court?"

"No! The tree had a preservation order on it. Old Mother Splinter ignored the order and had it cut down to make room for new housing."

"That would have made a few people angry," Finn said.

"So it should." I flipped my tail. "Ancient trees hold great power. They're a source of strength and renewal for many magic users."

"One family, in particular, was furious," Acer said. "The old tree was owned by Amenia's family."

Chapter 8

A fluttering killer

"I'm seeing double. I need more coffee," Finn said around a yawn as he pushed away the file he'd been looking at. "Amenia's family and Old Mother Splinter were in court for weeks over that tree."

"It must have cost a heap of money to take the case to court." I was settled on a pile of papers on Finn's desk.

We'd return to Angel Force as soon as we'd learned about the connection between Old Mother Splinter and Amenia. More coffee had been consumed, along with plenty of sugary, doughy carbohydrates, and everyone had their second wind. Or was it our third wind? It was getting so late, the edges of time felt blurry.

I did a quick physical check on myself. No, I didn't feel excessively tired. It had just been a busy day, and I was worried about my witch.

I discreetly studied her as she downed her coffee then passed the mug to Finn, so he could get her a refill from the kitchen.

"Back in a minute." He wandered away.

Zandra caught me watching her and smirked. "I'm good. Although I'm worried about Finn. He's yawning a lot, and he almost tripped over his own feet on the way back here."

"Me, too. I know he said angels are almost indestructible, but they still have weaknesses. And we know they can die. It wasn't so long ago we were searching for an angel killer. Finn has a mixture of angel and demon in him, so he could be susceptible to this sleep spell."

"We'll keep watch on him. If necessary, we can send him to the doctor if he takes a turn for the worst. They'll use magic to slow things down until we get this thing solved."

Finn returned with more coffee and continued his inspection of the case file involving Amenia's family, the Scarabetic-Greens, and Old Mother Splinter.

He settled into a seat and stifled a yawn. "I pulled the court transcripts, and they show Old Mother Splinter didn't care she'd been caught tearing down an ancient family refuge used by the scarabs for almost a hundred years. She needed the space to grow her empire, and she repeated this statement numerous times during the court proceedings. Apparently, she was moving with the times, and history needed to be confined to books and boring classes."

"What was the outcome of the court case?" I said. "If Old Mother Splinter admitted her guilt, there must have been punishment."

"She got a fine."

"That's it! For ripping down something so important?" Zandra thumped her palm on the desk.

"She knew what she was doing. Old Mother Splinter was one wealthy lady. There are millions in the bank or stashed in various assets. Most of it is in property," Finn said.

"That could be another motive," I said. "Who inherits that fortune?"

"We're waiting for details of her will from her legal team. They mentioned it going into a corporate trust, though."

"We need to check that out," I said. "If the boy toy inherits, it would give him an excellent motive for encouraging Old Mother Splinter to take a permanent nap."

Finn nodded. "First, we speak to those scarabs. Amenia failed to mention this family connection with Old Mother Splinter."

"And it's another excellent motive for murder. When she saw Old Mother Splinter in Crimson Cove, she could have acted on her long-held hatred." Zandra checked the time. "It's late. We should pick this up in the morning."

"And the scarabs will be hard to find at this time of night," I said. "They're most likely staying in the woods."

"Agreed. Let's call it a night." Finn shuffled the paperwork back into order.

I stared at him as he stifled another yawn. "You're coming home with us."

Zandra's eyebrows flashed up. "He is?"

"I am?" Finn said. "Why?"

"Because if you fall asleep, I need to make sure you'll wake up again."

"It's sweet you care, but I feel okay."

"We're still watching you. Any signs you're in distress while you sleep, and I'll wake you."

"How do you plan on doing that? I'm a sound sleeper. I once slept through a fire alarm in my old building. Almost got carried down the stairs over some burly guy's shoulder in my boxer shorts. It was humiliating."

I flashed my claws at him. "I have many ways to get you to wake."

He grimaced. "There'll be no need for murder mitten action. A simple nudge will do."

"It's not a terrible idea if you come back with us," Zandra said. "We can keep an eye on each other. I'm like you. I don't feel any different, but maybe that's how this spell gets you. It lulls you into thinking you're fine and then drags you down when your guard is lowered."

"That's a grim thought." Finn pinched his chin between his thumb and finger. "We can have a sleepover if you've got room for me."

"Vorana has an inflatable bed. You should be able to squeeze onto that," I said. "We'll tackle the scarabs at dawn."

After another flick through the file and Finn leaving an update for Cythera to read in the morning, we headed home.

Vorana and Sage were already asleep when we arrived, but we located the inflatable mattress and set it up in the basement, where it easily fit beside Zandra's bed.

"You two sleep. I'll keep guard," I said.

"You should rest, too," Zandra said. "You get mean when you're tired."

"I can go for days without sleep if I have to." I didn't like to, but since I was more than your average cat, a little sleep deprivation did me no harm now and again.

"Thanks for watching over us." Finn dropped onto the inflatable mattress, and it strained under his bulk but held. He threw a blanket over himself then linked his fingers behind his head and closed his eyes. "Don't let the sleeping bugs bite."

"Not even the tiniest bit funny," Zandra grumbled as she settled herself down.

The lights went out, and after waiting a few moments until their breathing was deep and even, I settled on Zandra's bed between them, so I could make sure my favorite witch and my favorite part angel would be safe.

⚜

Finn rolled over and fell off the mattress onto the floor with a thud. He groaned, and his eyes flicked open to meet mine.

"Greetings," I said from the edge of Zandra's bed. "I'm happy to announce you both survived the night."

"I'm not sure my back did." He groaned again as he sat and knuckled his lower back. "I don't know why I couldn't share the bed with Zandra. There's plenty of room."

107

"There wouldn't have been if you'd been in it," she mumbled. "This is my bed. No hulking angel guests allowed."

He chuckled. "You're no fun."

After some more complaints about the sleeping situation, they used the bathroom then headed up the stairs.

Vorana was in the kitchen, whipping up breakfast. Sage was settled in her seat at the table.

Vorana turned when Finn walked through the door. Her eyes widened, and her mouth dropped open. "Oh! We have company. I didn't hear the front door."

"Finn stayed the night." Zandra dropped into a chair. "And before you get any ideas, we were working late on a case, and Juno decided it was safer if we stuck together."

"Why would I think anything else was going on?" Vorana grinned. "What would you like for breakfast, Finn?"

"Whatever's going, thanks. And plenty of it." He gave an enormous yawn.

"What case are you working on that needs you to stick together? It's not something dangerous, is it?" Vorana pulled out boxed cereal and a fruit salad.

"Haven't you been listening to the gossip?" I nodded at Sage as I settled into my usual seat next to her.

"I know about Old Mother Splinter. Is that what you mean?"

"She started this case," Finn said. "But it's a lot more complicated than some dappy old girl thinking it would be fun to go night swimming and getting a cramp."

"I heard she went swimming. What was she doing on the beach so late?" Vorana set out an extra mug for Finn and poured the coffee.

"Old Mother Splinter survived her dip, thanks to Juno's intervention, but then she died at the hospital." Zandra glanced at Finn. "It's okay to share this with Vorana, isn't it?"

"You know I can be trusted." Vorana pressed her hands together. "I promise, I won't blab."

"Everyone will need to know soon," Finn said. "If there's a way to slow this thing down, we shouldn't keep it a secret."

Vorana sat in a seat. "What's going on? It sounds serious."

"There's a sleeping spell going around town," Zandra said. "We don't know where it came from or who created it, but it killed Old Mother Splinter. She went to the hospital because she almost died while swimming, and just when they thought she was recovering, she lapsed into a coma. Died a few hours later."

Vorana inhaled sharply. "You think this sleeping spell was the cause?"

"Not to begin with, but other people showed up at the hospital with the same symptoms." Finn stuck a spoon into the fruit salad and filled a bowl. "The doctors have figured out a way to slow things down, but they need to know what's causing it."

"The sleep spell is mixed with dark magic," I said. "They're not sure what it is yet."

"Is everyone vulnerable?" Sage's ears were pricked, her attention on Vorana.

"We think so. That's why I got Finn to stay here overnight. He's been worryingly sleepy."

"No sleepier than any other overworked angel," he said. "Juno made sure I was safe, though. I'm in her debt."

I batted away his sassy comment.

"What symptoms should we watch out for?" Sage stared at Vorana.

"Mainly extreme tiredness. Falling asleep at odd moments. That's about it," Finn said.

Vorana chewed on her bottom lip. "Should I keep the bookstore closed today?"

"It's not a bad idea. Just until we know what's going on," Zandra said. "We should hear more from the doctors today."

"Definitely stay here with me." Sage poked me with a paw. "How's your witch doing?"

"So far, so good. But I'm watching her every move."

"Which isn't necessary. I'll let you know if I don't feel good."

"We should make sure they do nothing foolish, like going out and saving the day," Sage said.

"I try to keep Zandra safe at all times, but she never listens. I won't be able to keep her away from this case."

"She's also right here and can speak for herself." Zandra waved at us.

"So can I," Vorana said. "Although maybe I will shut the store. I have new inventory I can work on from here. We can stay in and have some familiar-witch time. I've been meaning to try that new lavender bath soak. You love a good soak."

Sage's fur bristled. "Cats hate baths."

She was such a fibber. I'd heard her splashing around in the tub with Vorana when she thought no one was around.

We exchanged knowing glances. Our witches were wonderful, but they didn't always do the most sensible of things when staring danger in the face. That's why we were needed.

After we'd discussed the case some more and eaten breakfast, we left the house and hurried to the woods. It was the scarabs' favorite place, since they could fly free and use their magic with no one disturbing them.

"We need to be on our guard," Finn said. "If the scarabs are behind this sleep spell, they won't come quietly."

"Especially now we know Amenia concealed information," I said. "And we have her motive for wanting Old Mother Splinter dead."

Zandra tugged on the ends of her hair. "Maybe she'll open up once she knows we're on to her."

Finn stumbled over his feet and grabbed a tree to stay upright. "Who put that stump there?"

"Clumsiness is a symptom of this strange magic," I cautioned. "Do you need me to give you a friendly nip to keep you awake?"

He shied away from me. "Keep your claws and fangs away from me. I'll let you know if I plan on falling asleep."

"Maybe you won't get that option." Zandra lifted her eyebrows and nodded at me. I took it as permission to scratch Finn if he got too sleepy looking.

It took half an hour of searching and a fair amount of sniffing before I picked up the scarabs' scent. It took us to a large, ancient oak tree with a hollowed-out section several feet off the ground. It was the perfect scarab resting place.

"Should I knock?" Finn said.

"Amenia knows we're here," I said. "She also knows we won't go away until we get answers."

There was a faint scratching noise and then the sound of tiny beating wings.

"Answers, you seek, Juno. From me? Honored, I am." Amenia drifted down from the top of the tree.

"We need to talk to you about the sleeping magic in Crimson Cove," I said.

"Intriguing. What magic is this?"

"You must know what's going on."

"Keep to ourselves, we do. Don't like trouble. Performed and then left."

"This magic killed Old Mother Splinter," Finn said.

"Good news to brighten any day."

"You admit you didn't like her?"

"Didn't know her well. Only met her briefly at the performance. A proud creature."

"You're certain you had nothing to do with Old Mother Splinter when she was alive?" I said.

"Certain, I am. Any more questions? Soon, we will be leaving."

"Plenty. You're a powerful scarab. Could you cast a spell that affects everyone in Crimson Cove?"

Amenia's antenna quivered. "Too much credit, you give me. Beyond me, that power is. Although thrilled you think me so strong."

"You beguiled a beach full of non-magicals and bent them to your whims," I said.

She fluttered through the air. "No challenge, they were. Minds easy to manipulate. Crimson Cove residents are powerful. All magic, they should be able to resist."

"True. But you underplay your ability. Why do that?"

"No trouble, I want. We will leave."

"Not yet. We know about your ancestors' tree." Finn held up a hand. "The tree Old Mother Splinter had torn down to make room for new apartments."

Amenia's wings blurred, and she landed on a tree branch.

"And we know about the court battle your family went through to make her pay," I said. "She got away with just a fine for destroying something so powerful and ancient. That must have left a wound."

A hiss rattled out of Amenia's mouth. "Directly involved, I wasn't, but I know about the murdered tree. My sister loved that tree more than life. Heartbroken, she was. How did you find out?"

"We recognized your family name from the court proceedings," Finn said. "It was simple to find the connection."

Amenia nodded. "I supported my sister to take Old Mother Splinter to court. Paid most of the fees. Fighting injustice isn't cheap."

"It's no problem if you have bottomless resources like Old Mother Splinter," I said.

"Fighting over that tree's safety for almost a year, they were. She offered ridiculous sums of money to whomever she could to get the preservation order removed," Amenia said. "It was the only thing stopping her from building those ugly apartments. She'd convinced everyone who owned land around the tree to sell to her. Determined to get it, she was."

"But Old Mother Splinter didn't expect to run into resistance from your family?" Zandra said.

"Trees root us to the ground. Live comfortably in an old tree, we can. They protect us and nourish us. We gather energy from nature. Trees mean everything to us. My sister and her children used that tree as a summer base for years."

"And nothing could convince her it should be torn down?" I said.

"To tear down such an ancient tree is to rip out part of the planet's heart. Know it to be wrong, we do."

"Old Mother Splinter did it anyway."

Amenia hissed again. "Shattered was my sister's heart. So certain she was the court would put Old Mother Splinter away. A fine was all she received. Nothing to her, it meant."

"And she got to build her apartments."

"Got away with tree murder she did."

"Why didn't you tell us about this connection to Old Mother Splinter when I asked if you knew her?" Finn said.

Amenia's tiny snort rippled with sarcasm. "Suspicious, it looked. Know exactly what you angels are thinking. Old Mother Splinter I saw, so revenge, I took."

"This new information gives you a great motive for murder," I said. "You were avenging a family member. How's your sister doing since the tree disappeared?"

"Never quite been herself. For some time, she grieved. Better now. Never whole, though."

"I expect she'll fully recover when she hears the news about Old Mother Splinter," I said. "Have you already told her?"

"A quiet celebration of our own we will have when the time is right," Amenia said. "Too evil to live are some creatures."

"Did you kill Old Mother Splinter?" Finn said. "It must have been a shock to see her at the performance."

"Unhappy, I was. But the proud cold heart didn't even recognize me. Every court session, I went to. Too full of her own self-importance to notice the little creatures."

"Which would have made it even easier for you to get to her," I said. "Old Mother Splinter wouldn't have been on her guard."

"True. Hated her, I did, but I was with my children when she went swimming."

"Perhaps you visited her after she went into the hospital," Zandra said. "Cast the magic that meant she'd never wake."

"No! My children are young and cannot be left for long. Never kill in front of them, I would."

"Is that the truth? I can check to see if you visited the hospital," Finn said.

"No lies, I tell."

"You could have flown in through a window," I said. "Cast the magic and been out within a couple of minutes. Your children could have stayed outside."

"They'd have still been seen," Finn said. "The hospital wards monitor visitors, even those who stay outside the building."

"Check!" Amenia's wings whirred. "I did not do it."

"Where are your children?" I said. "It would help us if we could speak with them. Just to be sure you never went to the hospital together."

"Playing nearby. Restless they were and had nightmares. Sent them to play, I did, to regain their joy. Young ones need happiness in their lives."

While Finn continued to question Amenia, I snooped around to see where her children had gone. If they were playing close by, it was very quiet. And if there was one thing I'd learned about being around the young scarabs, they were the opposite of quiet. Giggles always filled the air, along with teasing vibes and fluttering wings.

I paced away from the tree, lifting my booping snooter and inhaling. I followed the faint trail of scarab scent. It was sort of spicy with an undertone of evening jasmine. The smell grew stronger, and I stopped.

The infant scarabs were on the ground with their tiny legs in the air.

Chapter 9

Wake up!

I ran to the infants and nudged them.

Neither stirred, but it was a relief to see their chests moving. I prodded, nipped, and gently shook them, but nothing would rouse them. The sleeping magic had gotten them.

I dashed back to the others. "Amenia, you need to see this."

She must have seen the alarm in my gaze because she didn't hesitate in following me. Finn and Zandra were close behind.

Amenia inhaled sharply and dropped to the ground beside her children. "What game is this?"

"I'm sorry. I don't think they're playing. The magic that killed Old Mother Splinter has got them," I said.

"No! They can't be magic tainted. Only babies, they are. Children, wake." Amenia fluttered around them in a rapid spiral. She dabbed their faces and pushed them with her head.

"How did you know they were in trouble?" Zandra whispered to me.

"I didn't. I thought it was odd we couldn't hear them playing, so I went to look."

"Help me!" Amenia said. "Wake them up. Full of life, they are."

"Our magic has no effect on whatever spell this is," Finn said.

"Try! Healing spells. All of you, now."

There was no point in arguing with a mother in distress, so we surrounded the small scarabs and took turns to get them to wake. None of the healing spells or revitalizing magic worked. Their little eyes remained shut.

"All together. Combine power. Heal them, you must," Amenia said.

"It'll be too much for them," Finn said. "The doctors have been treating people. They know a way to slow the effects of the spell."

"Old Mother Splinter is dead! This magic killed her?"

"We think it did," I said as gently as I could. "But the doctors didn't know what they were dealing with when she was brought in, since she was the first case they identified."

"My babies are fragile. What if they don't survive? Try again. More magic."

I walked over and rested a paw on one of her trembling wings. "We need to be careful. We don't know what magic we're dealing with. If we hit your children with a powerful spell, it could make things worse."

She shrugged off my paw and shot into Finn's face, pinging off his nose. "You! Strange powers you have. Use them. Make my babies better."

He rubbed the end of his nose, shaking his head. "You saw that my angel healing did nothing."

"Other power you must use. Call for your demon. Suck out the poison, he will."

Finn glanced our way, his hands rapidly scratching through his sandy brown hair. "Bad idea. That guy is never into helping people. He'll cause more harm if I let him loose."

Amenia pinged off his nose again. "Darkness must fight darkness."

"It isn't wise. Finn struggles to control his demon when it's free," I said. "You don't want to meet it."

"Do it! My babies must not die." Amenia blasted a spell into Finn's face.

"Hey! Stop that." He staggered back and scrubbed at his skin. "That hurt."

Amenia lunged at him and repeatedly slammed spells into Finn's eyes.

She was trying to anger him, so his demon emerged and fought back. It was a wildly dangerous game. "Amenia, stop!"

Zandra watched with wide eyes. "There's no way that'll... uh, oh. Maybe that will."

Amenia cast a spell to lift an enormous log off the ground. She slammed it against Finn's head.

"Enough!" I yelled.

Red flickers of demon energy danced across Finn's outstretched white wings. He'd covered his head with his giant wings to protect himself, and when he lowered them, his eyes were black and his teeth bared.

"Demon! Remove the darkness contained within my children," Amenia commanded. "Make them well." The log hovered by Finn's head, ready to strike if he disobeyed.

He snarled at Amenia, and she zoomed the log past his nose, brushing the tip.

"Now! Or pound you into the ground, I will."

Finn stalked over to where the children lay and loomed over them. He inhaled deeply and then laughed. "I see my brother's work here."

"You know what this is?" Zandra said.

Finn pinned her under a black, steely gaze. "You can't stop this. You're all ruined. He'll take you down and destroy you one by one until he gets what he wants."

"Who is he?" I said. "And what does he want?"

"Freedom. And he'll take whatever he needs to get it. If I didn't hate him so much, I'd congratulate him." Demon Finn's voice was a rumble of gravel across metal.

"Undo it, you can?" Amenia said. "If you know what the power is, take it away."

He stared at Amenia, unblinking for thirty seconds. "It would be my pleasure. Let me see what I can do." He ducked, and his wings covered the sleeping children.

"I don't like this," Zandra muttered. "We know how unstable Finn is when his demon comes out to play."

"Maybe we underestimated Amenia. He's doing exactly what she ordered. And if the demon version of Finn knows where this power comes from, we can remove it."

"What are you doing to them?" Amenia's voice was a high-pitched squeak. "Are they waking? Show me what you're doing."

Finn lifted his head. His cheeks were bulging, and the children had vanished.

Amenia squealed and rocketed toward him. She bounced off the wing he used as a shield and rolled antenna over tail until she slammed into a tree trunk.

I leaped onto Finn's shoulder, sinking my claws in deeply and biting the back of his neck.

He roared out his rage as I clung onto him, flooding him with positivity and reminding him who he was. Saphic and Loris popped out of his mouth and landed on the ground.

Finn reached around and grabbed my tail. My murder mittens were ready to enter this battle as he tugged, but a spell slammed into his stomach, stopping him.

Zandra had her hands outstretched as magic poured out of her. "Hurt Juno, and you'll have me to deal with."

I didn't want my witch going up against Finn while he was in demon mode, but I also didn't want to lose my tail. I wasn't letting go, though. Finn must remember who he was and that he was surrounded by people who loved him and wanted only good things for him.

"Come at me, witch. Let's do this," Finn growled out. "I've been wanting to take you down ever since my angel side wimped out on claiming you."

"You're not welcome here. Leave." More power flooded out of Zandra and smashed into Finn, forcing him back several steps.

"The scarab wanted my power, so she got it." He glanced at Amenia, who wasn't moving, and laughed. "Although she must not have realized what she was asking for."

"She didn't ask for you to eat her children," Zandra said. "Go away. Nobody wants you here."

"Finn does. He's sick of being Mr. Goody Two Shoes. He wants fun. Maybe I'll have fun with you and your weird cat."

"There's nothing weird about Juno." Zandra thrust out another spell that took Finn to his knees.

My wonderful witch had learned a few tricks from our older half-sister, Tempest, who literally ate demons for breakfast. The demon version of Finn didn't know who he was going up against.

Finn's grip loosened on my tail. I spun around and attached myself to his back, so I looked more like a fluffy backpack than a murderous fanged scarf. "Finn, listen to me. You always want to help people. You can't do that while your demon's in control."

"Shut it, fuzzball. You're one big pain in Finn's butt. When I get my hands on you, you're toast."

"Never gonna happen." Zandra slammed him with another spell. "Give us back Angel Finn."

"I'm here now, and I'm staying." Finn's wings shot out, and he attempted to take off, but a blast of magic from Amenia sent him tumbling to the ground.

I lost my grip and rolled away, tasting the sour tang of demon and the sugary undertones of angel on my tongue.

Amenia was flat on her stomach, but her antenna quivered as more magic filtered out of her, pinning Finn down.

Zandra kept her magic on him too, restraining him as he fought to get free. "Juno, we need to yank out the angel."

"Use your old power," Amenia yelled. "Call your ancient spells into being."

"Old power?" Zandra kept her focus on Finn as he bucked under the torrent of magic.

"This is all I have," I said to Amenia. "It'll work. If we combine energies, we can calm Finn enough to give him a chance to chain his demon."

Zandra looked like she had more questions for me but now wasn't the right time.

Amenia limped over and joined us. I landed on Zandra's foot while Amenia settled on my head. We cast out a combined bubble of power and circled it around Finn.

He twitched and bucked, trying to shake off the magic, but with the three of us fighting him, he stood no chance.

"I should destroy him for what he did to my children," Amenia hissed.

"You asked for a demon's help after whacking him awake with a log. What did you expect him to do?" I said.

"Desperate, I was. My poor babies."

"At least now we know you didn't cast the sleeping magic over Crimson Cove." Zandra's hands were out, and she tilted them slowly from side to side, ensuring Finn remained enclosed in the bubble of restraining power.

"Taken my word for it, you should," Amenia said. "I'd never do something so terrible to my babies."

"He's calming," I said.

The red flickering across Finn's wings faded. He hunched, his shoulders rounding as his fists rested in the dirt.

"Great power, this one has," Amenia said. "Underestimated the demon angel."

"I think we all do," Zandra said. "He rarely complains about his dark side or lets it peek out."

Behind Finn's normal cheery demeanor, he battled daily with this demon to keep it in check. He was an angel among magic users for ensuring none of us got hurt by the dangerous magic inside him.

After several minutes of surrounding him with our restraining power, positivity, and love, Finn slowly raised a hand.

"I'm good. It's me again. The demon jerk has gone."

We slowly drew back our power, but I kept mine ready to fling out if Finn even twitched the wrong way.

Amenia dashed to her children and checked them. "They're okay. Soggy but alive."

"Sorry. I don't think he'd have eaten them. It was his idea of a joke." Finn slowly raised his head. His face was drained of color and covered in sweat. "You shouldn't have messed with him, though."

"Apologize, I do. But I'd do anything to keep my children safe."

"Maybe don't summon a demon to help if you ever find yourself in a situation like this again," I said.

"Although we found out something useful," Zandra said to Finn. "You know who's behind the sleeping spell."

He sat back on his heels. "I do?"

"You don't remember what you told us?" I said.

"The memories are fuzzy when he takes over. Did he say something about a brother?"

"I'm not sure he meant your literal brother," I said. "But he confirmed demon energy is behind this sleeping magic."

"And that demon wants to be free, and he'll do anything to make sure that happens," Zandra said. "Ring any bells?"

Finn's forehead furrowed as he considered the question. "It doesn't. I try not to communicate with my demon side. It's safer that way. We don't know each other's secrets, fortunately."

"Amenia, let's take Saphic and Loris to the hospital," I said. "The doctors can help slow the magic so they remain stable while we figure out where this sleep spell demon is hiding."

"I'll do it. My responsibility, they are." Amenia gathered her children to her chest. "My apologies, again, Finn." She shot in the air and vanished.

Finn stood, rubbing the side of his head. "I feel like I've been hit by a truck."

"Try a huge log and a fury-filled magical cat," Zandra said.

Finn looked down at the fallen log and winced. "I remember that bit. What was she thinking?"

"That she had little time to save her children and thought she could control you," I said. "Just like we don't have much time to save everyone in Crimson Cove."

"What did Amenia mean about using your old magic?" Zandra said. "She seemed certain you knew some special spell or had a power that would solve this."

I glanced at Finn. Although he didn't know my full backstory, he was acute at picking up on the things I said that suggested my past was complicated.

He shook his head and looked away. This was my twisty problem to deal with, and he wasn't putting his opinion forward. I appreciated that.

"Amenia was panicked," I said to Zandra. "She must have thought I had more power than I do."

"That's it? I mean, we all have powers. Why focus on you?"

"The mind of a panicked mother is complicated."

She arched an eyebrow. "And you know that, how?"

I focused on a tiny knot in my tail and worked it loose with my teeth. "Let's focus on the problem at hand. We have to stop more people from going to sleep and reverse the spell on those who've already been caught up in the magic."

Zandra crossed her arms over her chest. "Sure. We will talk about this later, though."

I turned and scurried through the woods, Zandra and Finn following. That wasn't a conversation I was ready to have with Zandra, but I knew it was coming.

"We can take the scarabs off the suspect list," Finn said.

"Agreed. It's time to question the men in Old Mother Splinter's life," I said over my shoulder. "Did they have something to do with her death?"

Chapter 10

Too close to home

"I've never seen a queue like this at Sorcha's." Finn hopped from foot to foot. "I'll drop soon if I don't get a vat of her super strong coffee inside me."

I peered through the window into Sorcha's busy café. She was behind the counter but moving at a snail's pace as disgruntled customers waited for their orders. "She doesn't look well. We should help her."

Zandra grimaced. "I would, but you know what I'm like in the kitchen."

"You know how to brew coffee and pour it into mugs. You handle the drinks, and Finn will do the food."

He lifted his hands. "I can make a decent meal when I want to impress a lady friend."

"Then let's move. Sorcha needs us." We dodged past the grumbling queue and headed behind the counter.

Sorcha's bleary eyes widened. "Hey! Sorry for the long wait."

"We're your temporary new assistants," I said. "Zandra's on drink duty. Don't let her near any food unless you want to serve it burned. Finn will help with everything else."

"You guys! There's no need. I'm just operating at half-speed today. I'll get this crowd dealt with soon."

"Doubtful. I've been waiting twenty minutes for my club sandwich on rye bread," a guy at the counter grumbled.

"Desperate times call for desperate measures. And if you reward these two with free coffee, they'll clear the queue in no time," I said. "I'll take a bowl of oat milk."

Sorcha's eyes filled with tears, and she shut them for a few seconds. "Thanks. I was panicking, but I can't go any faster. I don't know what's wrong with me."

"We do," Zandra said. "Now, who's next?"

Half an hour later, the queue was cleared, Finn, Zandra, and Sorcha had enormous mugs of steaming coffee in their hands, and I enjoyed a delicious plate of smoked salmon and cream cheese as a reward for overseeing their tasks and making helpful suggestions when they did things wrong.

"I can't tell you how much I appreciate this," Sorcha said. "I was about to cry. Everyone was so grumpy at having to wait, and I kept getting their orders wrong. Someone would tell me what they wanted, and I'd forget. Even when I wrote it down and triple-checked it, I still gave them the wrong thing."

"It's not you," Zandra said. "Well, it is you. But it's lots of other people in Crimson Cove, too. Have you heard how busy the hospital's been?"

"I've barely been listening to the gossip. It's all I can do to focus on the task at hand. Although someone said the pizza parlor was closed because Voss is unwell. Is he in the hospital?"

Finn glanced around to make sure none of the customers were listening. "It's serious. And other people have been showing up at the hospital with similar symptoms to Old Mother Splinter."

Sorcha pressed a hand against her chest. "You really think I've been whacked with this sleeping magic? Juno sniffed me when I was at the town hall! She said I was fine."

I gulped down a piece of salmon. "I said I didn't think you'd been caught by the spell because you've been ailing for weeks."

"You make me sound like I'm on my last legs!"

"Maybe you're fighting it better than everyone else, but it could be the sleeping magic," Zandra said.

I finished the last of my salmon. "I'm still not sure. You've been unwell for some time, haven't you?"

Sorcha dropped several more pieces of salmon on my plate. "I've not been feeling amazing for a while. That's why I'm looking for an assistant for the café. I figured I was pushing myself too hard and not taking enough breaks. But when I go to bed, I worry about all the things I have to do the next day. It doesn't help."

Finn set down his coffee mug, his expression serious. "You don't think you're patient zero, do you?"

"Sorcha can't be the source of this magical sleep spell," Zandra said.

"No! Of course not. Why do you think it's me?" Sorcha squeaked. "I haven't left Crimson Cove in weeks to find a malevolent spell caster to make this spell. And I've not had the time to whisk up something so deadly. Why would I?"

"It had to start somewhere and with someone." Finn shrugged. "Sorry. Dumb idea. You'd never be involved in anything like this."

I studied Sorcha's face. "Do you feel you want to sleep all the time?"

"I try to, but I can't. When we put the non-magicals inside the town hall, I came back here and went to bed. But I couldn't sleep. I was wide awake. My body was exhausted, but my mind kept racing."

"Doesn't sound like the sleep spell to me," I said. "Have you had contact with any demons recently?"

"Demons! No!" Sorcha winced as several customers turned to look at her. "You never said a demon was behind this."

"Ah. New information, thanks to Finn and Amenia coming to blows," I said. "This power is dark and toxic, and it's not giving up easily."

"What's your next move to stop this demon from sending everyone in Crimson Cove to sleep?" Sorcha whispered.

"We've been eliminating suspects," Finn said. "We wondered if the scarabs were behind it, but we've eliminated them from the investigation."

"The sleeping magic affected Amenia's children," I said.

"Will they be okay?"

"They should be. Amenia took them to the hospital to get treatment."

"There's a cure?"

"There's a way to slow it down while we figure out what the reversal magic is. That's as good as we've got so far," Finn said. "Our next move is to speak to Old Mother Splinter's business assistant and her boyfriend."

Tinkerbell sidled out of the back room and sauntered to the counter. She didn't look at us, but she was listening to the conversation.

Sorcha busied herself by cleaning the counter of crumbs and filling the empty pastry slot with custard cream tarts. "You should speak to them. Maybe they're involved. It can't be anyone local."

"You know Harlan and Robin?" I said.

"No! Of course, I saw them with Old Mother Splinter when she was alive. Harlan ran around after her, making sure she was comfortable and had every creature comfort you could imagine. He even checked the temperature of the milk for her coffee!" Sorcha finished cleaning the work surface. "It looked like they were a couple. And Robin spent most of his time fielding messages and writing things down. They barely left her side."

"Harlan was quick enough to leave her side when she went night swimming and needed help," Finn said.

"He probably hoped she wouldn't come back if she treated him like a servant," Zandra said.

Sorcha pursed her lips. "Talk to them. It's got to be someone close to her. Like I said, no one local."

I paused in my hunt for any tiny pieces of salmon I may have neglected. Sorcha was worried about something. "Did either of them give off any weird vibes? Make you think they were plotting her death?"

"I wouldn't say that. But it must be someone Old Mother Splinter knew well. She didn't seem trusting, so she wouldn't have put her guard down and let anyone approach and whack her with a powerful spell. She even had Robin taste her sandwich."

Finn raised his eyebrows. "She thought it was poisoned?"

"Maybe. Or she was paranoid. Speak to Robin." Sorcha turned away.

"Everyone can tell you're lying." Tinkerbell hopped onto the counter.

"Not on there! Customers don't like free fur in their food." Sorcha attempted to lift Tinkerbell, but she hissed and danced out of her reach, leaving Sorcha grabbing air and sighing.

"Shouldn't you be out harassing people?" I said.

"Sammy is doing that for me. He's a wonderful sidekick. I don't know what I did before he came along. So obedient and sweet. You should never have let him go."

My hackles rose, and I stood slowly. Only Zandra's hand on my head stopped me from leaping at Tinkerbell and slashing that smug smirk off her fluffy face.

Tinkerbell ignored me and licked her paw. "It isn't Harlan or Robin you should focus on for this murder."

"Who do you think killed Old Mother Splinter?" Finn said.

"Tinkerbell! Don't spread gossip," Sorcha said. "It'll get innocent people in trouble."

"You would think she's innocent, since she's one of your closest friends."

"Who's Tinkerbell talking about?" Zandra said.

Sorcha flapped a cloth in the air. "It isn't her. She didn't do it."

"Who? Do what?" Finn said.

"Try talking to our friendly local bookstore owner if you want to find out what really happened," Tinkerbell said.

"Vorana! Why would she want Old Mother Splinter dead?" Zandra said.

"Shush! Of course she doesn't." Sorcha caught hold of Tinkerbell and placed her on the floor. "If you can't say anything nice, say nothing. I've told you that so many times."

"And keep the dirty little secret that's been keeping you awake?" Tinkerbell's tail lashed from side to side. "Don't you want justice? Isn't that what you're always bleating about, Juno? You want the bad guys caught so you can collect another gold star and get a pet."

"Vorana has goodness running through her," I growled out. "Unlike you."

Sorcha massaged her forehead with her fingers. "First off, Vorana is innocent. I'm certain of that. But there is something you should know."

"What's got you worried she might be involved with Old Mother Splinter's murder?" Finn slid his notepad out and flipped it open.

"Nothing!"

"Lies!" Tinkerbell trotted away, her tail up.

Sorcha sighed again. "It's just... well, Vorana had a fight with Old Mother Splinter about the bookstore."

Finn made a note on his pad. "What about the store?"

"Old Mother Splinter wanted to double the rent she charged Vorana. She only gave her a month's notice about the increase and said Vorana should be grateful for the warning. Most clients only get two weeks."

Finn whistled out air. "That's bad."

"Sure, but it doesn't mean Vorana killed Old Mother Splinter," Zandra said. "Vorana wouldn't have been happy about having to pay more rent, but she'd have figured something out. The store does well."

"Does it? Vorana's said a few times she's strapped for money," I said.

"It's why she rents her basement to homeless creatures she takes pity on," Tinkerbell called out from her seat on the window ledge.

"Ignore her. She's been spiteful for weeks." Sorcha shook her head.

"Spite is doing the rounds," I muttered.

Finn scribbled more notes. "Maybe Vorana's concealed how bad things have gotten at the store. She may be scared about losing her business if the rent goes up."

"That still doesn't make her a killer!" Zandra glowered at Finn. "You've known her longer than me. What does your gut tell you?"

He tipped back his head. "That there's no way she did this. Vorana saves spiders and puts them outside. She'd never kill anyone."

"You're ignoring the fact she has a motive?" Tinkerbell tutted. "No wonder the angels have such a hard time solving cases and rely on amateurs to get things done." She glanced my way, and that smirk shifted back into place.

"Vorana wouldn't kill," Sorcha said.

"We can all agree on that." I was still glaring at Tinkerbell. "And Vorana wouldn't evoke a spell that caused such chaos in Crimson Cove. She loves this place."

"It's still quite a motive," Finn said. "And I wouldn't be doing my job if I didn't speak to her."

"And ask her what? She didn't do it. It's a waste of time," Zandra said.

"To rule her out," Finn said. "How bad was the argument?"

"Nothing bad. It didn't get physical or anything like that." Sorcha twisted the cloth she held. "But there was yelling. Vorana eventually threw Old Mother Splinter out of the bookstore."

"You saw the argument?"

"No, she told me about it. She was upset and needed to calm down. You see! That makes her innocent. She'd hardly talk about the fight if she killed Old Mother Splinter."

"Don't make Vorana a suspect," Zandra said to Finn. "We have better leads to follow. Leads that don't involve our friend."

"You do? Good! That's excellent. Follow them," Sorcha said. "Is it Robin and Harlan?"

Finn tucked away his notepad. "I'll keep this information about Vorana on the back burner for now. But if Cythera gets wind—"

"She won't," Zandra said. "We'll keep this quiet and find the killer. Vorana's name doesn't need to be linked to this investigation."

I glowered at Tinkerbell. She'd deliberately dropped Vorana in it. Maybe she'd send her new sidekick, Sammy, to blab about the argument to Cythera, so Finn would have no choice but to question her.

"We should hurry this up," I said. "Let's go interrogate Harlan."

Sorcha puffed out a breath. "I'm finishing up here then shutting for the rest of the day. I couldn't handle another rush like that on my own."

"Good plan. And get to the doctor," Finn said. "Make sure there's nothing to worry about."

"I will. I promise. Let me know as soon as you have a definite lead on this case. I'm so worried about Vorana."

Zandra briefly hugged her. "You got it. And don't worry, we know she didn't do this."

After hissing at Tinkerbell, I dashed out of the store with Zandra and Finn.

"Old Mother Splinter rented a place on Golden View Lane," Finn said.

"The posh part of town," Zandra said.

"She can afford it if she's doubling everyone's rent," I said. "Vorana must be so stressed about the situation. And it doesn't help Tinkerbell is spreading malicious gossip. Why does she have to be so mean?"

"You think we should be worried about Tinkerbell blabbing?" Zandra said.

"She'll cause trouble if she can." I swished my tail from side to side. "Let's find out who really did it and stop her vicious lies from causing any damage."

We made the ten-minute walk to Golden View Lane. The streets were quieter than usual, which suggested word was spreading about the mysterious sleeping spell.

When we got close to the detached house with a pillared entrance and extravagant floral window displays, we discovered Harlan on a bench out the front with a mug in his hand and an empty plate covered in toast crumbs. Losing his significant other hadn't diminished his appetite.

Harlan lifted his head and raised a hand to shield his eyes. He was casually dressed in jeans and a pale blue shirt, but none of it looked cheap. His hair was casually messy, but most likely took him half an hour to sculpt into place. He was lean, tall, and his dimples popped when he recognized Finn.

"Hi, Harlan," Finn said. "Got a few minutes?"

"Of course. Finn, isn't it?" He stood and shook Finn's hand. "I spoke to you at the hospital."

"That's right. I've got follow-up questions about what happened on the beach." Finn nodded our way and made the introductions.

"Sorry for your loss," Zandra said. "How long were you involved with Old Mother Splinter?"

He smiled. "Almost two years. And although everyone else called her that, I preferred Persephone. It was such a pretty name."

I imagined he would, since calling your significant other 'old mother' anything must have taken the romance out of any situation. But I doubted Harlan had been involved with Old Mother Splinter because his heart had called to the obscenely rich dead crone.

"Can I offer anyone coffee? Or water?" He looked at me.

"No, thank you," Finn said. "We won't stay long."

"I understand." Harlan remained standing, his posture relaxed and hands in his jeans pockets. "Is there any word when Persephone's body will be released? She left exacting plans in the event of her death, and I want to make sure they're followed. She wanted an extravagant sendoff. My Persephone did nothing by halves."

"There's been a delay in releasing her body," Finn said.

"Sorry to hear that. There's so much to do. Persephone's estate is huge, and the business needs looking after. Of course, that's not my area of expertise, but I want nothing overlooked."

"I'm sure Old Mother... Persephone would have appreciated you being thorough," Finn said.

A half-smile lifted one side of Harlan's face. "She'd have appreciated it in her unique way."

Finn pulled out his notepad and opened it. "Could you remind me where you were when you heard about what happened to her?"

"Here. On my own."

"Did Old Mother Splinter tell you she was going to the beach that night?" Zandra said.

Harlan's full lips pursed several times. "I don't remember if she did. It wasn't uncommon for her to go on an evening stroll, though. It cleared her head and helped her to sleep. She sometimes found it hard to relax."

"It was late to be out on her own," Finn said. "You didn't go with her?"

"Persephone was fearless. And Crimson Cove is such a peaceful little place. She had no reason to worry."

"You definitely didn't go with her?"

Harlan's amiable smile remained in place. "No, I stayed here."

"And you were alone?"

He nodded. "Just me and a bubble bath."

"You're staying here with Robin?" Finn said.

"That's right. There are plenty of rooms, so it's no problem to share a house. We usually do that when we travel."

"How would you describe your relationship with Persephone?" I said.

Harlan chuckled and glanced at the sky. "I know what you're thinking. She was older than me, so what was I doing with her? After all, I have this." He spread his arms. "I could have anyone I wanted."

Zandra softly snorted.

"You don't think it's true?"

She crossed her arms over her chest. "You're not my type."

"Let's try an experiment." Harlan focused on her, and his eyes sparkled with an unnatural luminance. "How about we grab a drink sometime? Just you and me. You could tell me about your dreams. I always love listening to beautiful women."

Rather than issuing another snort of derision, Zandra giggled. "Sounds fun. You're cute."

"I'm sure your boyfriend won't mind us hanging out together, will he?"

"There's no one special. I'm not interested in anyone. You?"

Harlan chuckled again and blinked, breaking eye contact. "You see. I could be with whoever I wanted, but I chose to stay with Persephone."

"How did you do that to my witch?" I moved in front of Zandra, my hackles lifted.

Zandra was slowly blinking, as if her senses were taking their time to click into place. "What just happened?"

"My apologies. But you challenged me," Harlan said. "I'm an incubus crossed with a nymph. When I choose to be, I can be irresistible to anybody."

"Not me," Finn said.

"Oh, why not? I love a test." Harlan's eyes sparkled again. "You look like you work out. And there's something more to you than just that gorgeous shiny angel exterior. Why don't I take you to dinner, so I can learn all about you? I imagine we'd have a fascinating night."

Finn blushed, and his gaze went to the ground. "I'd love that."

Harlan exhaled noisily. "How dull! You're no challenge. I was barely trying with you, and you succumbed immediately."

Finn straightened and rubbed the back of his neck. "Huh. You're good at that."

"I know. I'm excellent. My good looks get me what I want." Harlan smoothed a hand down the front of his shirt. "I accepted Persephone didn't keep me around for my brains or business acumen. She wanted someone who looked incredible on her arm and charmed anyone who caused her a problem."

"Your romantic relationship was a front?" Finn looked flustered from being so easily influenced by Harlan.

"No, we were blissfully happy. We never argued and enjoyed each other's company. Persephone was an experienced older woman with a wealth of knowledge about the world. I enjoyed spending time with her."

"Did she enjoy spending time with you?" I maintained my guard position in front of Zandra. "Since you can easily turn on your charm, perhaps you were manipulating her."

"Not possible. That was the unique thing about Persephone. Her ability meant my talents didn't work on her."

"You couldn't glamor her?" I said.

"Juno! I'm disappointed. My power is much more sophisticated than a mere glamor. I focus on what makes people tick and bring that out of them. I make people happy."

"You use magic to manipulate," I said. "I've been involved with a twisted succubus, so I know what they're like."

"I'm sorry if you've been mistreated," Harlan said. "Succubus have a habit of losing control and letting themselves get too big for their beautiful boots. It was never my intention to misuse Persephone. And even if I'd wanted to manipulate her, she'd have seen straight through me."

"Because she was a truth seer," Finn said.

"If anyone lied to her, she knew about it. She'd get this feeling in her stomach that told her she was being deceived. Glamors, disguises, misinformation, she saw straight through it."

"That's a handy talent to have when running a successful business," Zandra said.

"It was handy in all areas of her life. There was no point in me lying to her because she always knew the truth. She told me what she wanted, and we came to an arrangement. It worked."

Finn nodded slowly. "You never argued?"

"We had the occasional dispute, but I wanted to stay with her, so I adapted. It wasn't a hardship. She looked after me extremely well."

"Yet you aren't grief-stricken she's gone," I said.

Harlan lifted one shoulder. "All good things come to an end. I had fun with Persephone, but I was ready for a change."

"Ready enough to hurry up her demise?" Finn said.

For the first time since we'd met, Harlan looked surprised. "I never said that. I was as stunned as everyone as to why she went swimming and then didn't recover. Is that why you're here? Have you found something?"

"Persephone was hit with a sleep spell. The doctors thought she was recovering, but then she slipped into a coma. It's happening to other people, too."

A shaky breath shot from Harlan's mouth. "I had no idea. The spell killed Persephone?"

"Her death wasn't an accident," Finn said. "We're looking into reasons someone wanted her dead."

"Of course, of course." He chewed on his bottom lip. "And you think I'm a suspect?"

"We're looking into everyone who was close to her."

"It wasn't me! Why would I kill the woman who took care of me?"

"You gave us your motive," I said. "You're ready for change."

"Not ready enough to kill!" Harlan rapidly shook his head, his fingers messing up his styled hair. "Persephone always insisted on the truth. Why bother with anything else, when she could see through a lie? She always told me, if I ever got bored or needed a change, to be upfront with her."

"Did you ever need a break from her demands?" Finn said. "I imagine she wasn't always easy to be around."

"No! I was thinking about moving on and trying something new, but I was at the thoughts stage. I hadn't talked to Persephone. If I'd wanted out, I could have gone. She wouldn't have stopped me."

"And lose your luxurious lifestyle?" Zandra said. "Why do that?"

"I didn't want that! I wasn't finished with Persephone." Harlan tugged on his shirt sleeves. "I'm stunned she died from a sleep spell, though. It must be powerful magic to have hurt her."

Harlan's shock seemed genuine, but maybe he'd rolled out some of his charm power so we wouldn't suspect him.

"Can you think of anyone Persephone was close to that could have used such damaging magic on her?" Finn said.

His forehead furrowed. "She owned property in half a dozen towns, not just Crimson Cove. They're all leased to magic users, so, technically, any of them could have cast the spell. But I guess it must have been someone here, since she got into trouble after we arrived. And you say it's spreading?"

"It is. We've figured out how to slow it down, but until we find who cast the spell, there's not much more we can do."

"I'll keep thinking. And I'll speak to Robin. He knows all the business contacts since that's his area of expertise. I'm so sorry this is happening. If there's anything I can do, just let me know."

"Stay around and answer any more questions we may have," Finn said.

"Whatever you need, I'm here."

After a few more platitudes, we left Harlan to his cold mug of coffee and his tousled hair and walked back toward the center of town.

"Was he being genuine at the end, or had he turned on the charm again to lull us into thinking he was innocent?" Zandra said.

"That was so humiliating," Finn said. "But it proved he's a powerful magic user."

"Harlan beguiles and excites. His magic wouldn't send people to sleep," I said.

"He has no alibi." Finn studied the notes he made. "And he lied about being at the beach when Old Mother Splinter went swimming."

"Harlan has a decent motive, too," Zandra said. "Despite what he told us, he wanted out of the relationship. Maybe Old Mother Splinter said no."

"And since he can charm anyone, what's to say he didn't charm a powerful magic user into casting this sleep spell?" Finn said. "He's still on the suspect list."

"There's not enough evidence to charge him." Harlan was smooth, but I was uncertain if he was the smooth criminal we were looking for.

"On to question Robin?" Zandra said.

Finn glanced over his shoulder. "I should have asked. I'm off my game today. I'll be back in a moment. Harlan should know where we can find Robin." He dashed back to the house.

"You giggled when Harlan charmed you," I said to Zandra.

Her nose twitched, and she stared at the house. "I don't remember doing that."

"You only ever giggle around Randal."

"I won't be giggling at all until this case is solved." She glanced down at me. "And I don't giggle around Randal."

Finn jogged back to us. "How's this for weird. Harlan said Robin is most likely sniffing old books."

Chapter 11

Booked!

There were three thrift stores in Crimson Cove, one of which specialized in old books and crumbling maps of long-expired magical realms. That was where we found Robin.

He had several hardback books tucked under one arm and was flicking through another with his free hand. Robin wore a tailored navy-blue suit with a white shirt underneath. He looked professional and in-charge handsome if you enjoyed admiring the clean-cut business type.

"Old Mother Splinter liked her hotties." I was perched on Zandra's shoulder as we stood outside the store, watching Robin browse.

"Juno, I'm certain that's not politically correct," Finn murmured.

"I'm making an observation. I doubt she'd have been seen with a man who had an excellent personality but a face like a squashed turnip."

"He's model good-looking," Zandra said. "So is Harlan. And Old Mother Splinter..."

"Was an aging crone?" I said.

"Well... she could have been Harlan's mother. The age gap was huge."

"It's a power thing," Finn said. "A woman with influence is super attractive."

"And the money. Let's not forget the oodles of cash." I tucked my tail around Zandra's neck to keep her warm.

"Let's go see what Robin has to tell us." Finn yawned as he pushed open the door into the thrift store, and we headed over to Robin.

An enormous wicker basket containing balls of wool momentarily distracted me, and I felt the urge to dive into it and roll around. I gently hissed at myself. I had to get my cat urges under control. When I had a moment, I'd tackle the elusive bangle I'd recently discovered that had, so far, refused to release my magic back to me. Once I had that missing part back, I'd feel more in control and less likely to want to shred a ball of wool to pieces. The thought of wool clamped between my teeth made me drool. How humiliating.

Robin looked up as we drew near. "Finn! I was planning on visiting Angel Force this afternoon to get an update on the investigation."

"Then I've saved you a journey. I've got more questions about Old Mother Splinter." Finn made the introductions.

Robin set down the books he held. "Of course. Anything to help."

He sounded just like Harlan. Old Mother Splinter had her boys well trained.

Finn glanced around, but other than us, the place was empty, although noises from the back room revealed the owner's location. "We have concerns that her death wasn't an accident."

Robin's expression grew serious. "So I understand. I went to the hospital first thing and got an update from the doctor who treated her."

"How could you do that?" Zandra said. "You only worked for Old Mother Splinter."

"True. But we used to be married." Robin examined his bare ring finger. "Well, we still are. We never got around to the divorce."

"Why didn't I know about this connection?" Finn said.

"You never asked. But it's no secret. She always called me her assistant, but I was more of a business partner. When we were officially together as husband and wife, I'd help on the business side. Running a property empire is stressful, so I took the load off."

"And when you split, you kept working for her?" Zandra said.

"Yes. I know what I'm doing in the business, and Persephone trusted me. Even though the marriage didn't work, we worked well together. She was a Type A person. So am I." He rubbed his palms together. "No messing around when a job needed doing."

"Didn't things get awkward when Harlan came on the scene?" I said. "He must have been jealous you were still around. Wasn't he worried you might get back together, and he'd be kicked out?"

Robin smiled and gently shrugged. "I wasn't able to make Persephone happy in our marriage, but I still wanted her to find joy."

"That's decent of you. Harlan made her happy?" Zandra's acerbic tone revealed exactly what she thought of his smooth line.

Robin raised his hands. "From the outside, I see how strange this would look, but it worked. When they got together and things grew serious, we had dinner and talked about how we'd fit in around each other. Persephone insisted I had to stay." He smiled broadly, not a trace of annoyance on his face. "I even remained at the house. Well, it's a mansion, so there's plenty of space. I could go days without seeing either of them. Although I'd always catch up with Persephone at the end of every day to give her an update."

"You weren't jealous she'd found another guy?" I said.

"I wasn't interested in Persephone romantically anymore. But we made a go of things for almost six years. It was a lively marriage. She had a strong will and knew what she wanted, and in the end, that wasn't me. We were unhappy and wanted more out of life."

I glanced at Finn when he didn't pose a follow-up question. We usually tag-teamed well. He swayed on his feet, his eyes half closed. I hurried over and swiped his calf with my claws.

"Ouch! Juno! Why did you do that?" Finn leaped away and grabbed his leg.

"To keep you awake. Focus."

"Oh!" He rubbed his eyes. "Sorry. I didn't realize I was falling asleep on my feet."

"I'll happily sit on your shoulder and chew an ear to keep you awake."

Finn pressed a hand over one ear. "I like my ears unchewed. Sorry, Robin, you were saying?"

"I was done." Robin extended a hand as if to help keep Finn on his feet. "Are you feeling okay? You look pale."

"I've been better." Finn drew in a deep breath then let it out slowly. "How long had you been separated from Old Mother Splinter before she started dating?"

"About a month before she met Harlan."

"That's fast, especially since you were married for such a long time."

"Like I said, Persephone was Type A. She went after what she wanted and made it happen. She hated being alone, so she found someone to be her new companion." Robin shrugged again. "We remained friends. And Persephone was an excellent employer. She had high standards and demanded a lot, but the pay was excellent. Plus, I could stay in the house I'd grown to love. It worked well for all of us."

"You never found it claustrophobic?" I stayed close to Finn, in case I needed to bring my murder mittens back into play. "Maybe you wanted out, but she wouldn't let you go because you were too useful to her business."

"Nothing like that." Robin hesitated. "I mean, we all think about trying new things from time to time, don't we?"

"What were you considering trying?" Zandra leaned closer to him.

Robin rested his hand on the pile of books he'd set down. "I'm a bibliophile. I adore books. My main hobby is searching for old and rare texts. That's why you caught me in here. I was having a stroll during my lunch break and couldn't resist having a snoop. You find all sorts of treasures in thrift stores. People give away books and have no idea of their value."

"That's a different line of work to helping run a property empire," Finn said.

"We don't always follow our passions. I was told from a young age, there was no money in books and it was a foolish dream. I should get a business degree. People always say there's money in property. So that's what I did. I bought commercial properties and rented them out." His gaze turned wistful as he looked at the book pile. "I met Persephone at the start of her empire building. Her ambition outshone mine, so I sold my small portfolio and joined her. Still, I always had a dream that, one day, I'd get back to my books."

"And now you can," I said. "There's no one to stop you."

"I was the only one stopping myself. It's a pity Persephone is dead, but her death gave me the nudge I needed to move on and take a few risks." Robin inhaled deeply as he looked at a stuffed bookcase of secondhand reads.

My booping snooter twitched. Maybe Robin was the one to nudge Old Mother Splinter into the sea. He was done being her assistant and wanted more. If she'd refused him, he'd have been miserable. Miserable enough to kill?

"You're giving up working in the property business?" Zandra said.

"Soon. It'll take time to sort out Persephone's estate. I know she had everything figured out, though. The business will be passed on, and life will go on."

"You don't inherit the business?" I said.

"No, she knew my passion didn't lie in property. She wanted her empire to continue, not be sold off, which is what I'd do to it. It's being transferred to a group of expert investors she'd worked with for years. They'll maximize the profits and cut out anything that makes a loss."

That didn't sound good for Vorana's bookstore. What if these investors sold it? Vorana would lose the thing she was most passionate about. She'd be heartbroken.

"Working with Persephone was only ever meant to be temporary," Robin said. "But I ended up staying for two years. I am sorry she's gone, but I was taking the easy route with my life by staying with her. I'd always have a job and a home, so long as I played by her rules. But I wanted more. Now, I can have it."

"Do you know what she's left you in her will?" Finn said.

"There's a small settlement but nothing significant." His eyes narrowed. "Do you know who cast the sleeping spell over Persephone?"

Finn stifled a yawn. "Sorry. We're still looking for the spellcaster. And she wasn't the only one affected, so we need to find whoever did this so we can reverse the magic as soon as possible."

Robin's tongue traced across his bottom lip. "I'm not at risk, am I?"

"We don't know if the spell is targeting particular people," I said. "So far, there's no pattern. Those who are more powerful can fight off the effects of the sleep spell for longer." I glanced at Finn.

Robin patted his chest as if checking his heart still beat. "I feel fine. I don't think whoever did this to Persephone would come after me. I get on with everyone I meet."

"What powers do you have?" Zandra said.

"Oh! You're looking at me as the spell caster?" He shook his head. "Sorry to disappoint, but I'm your less-than-average nymph. My father fell in love with someone with no power. He even moved to a town with no magic."

"How unfortunate," I murmured.

"The marriage didn't work, as they so rarely do, but I was the result. I have half the power I should, so I stick to basic spells. Anything else, and I'm wiped out for days. I promise I had nothing to do with this. And what would I gain by killing my former wife and employer, who I was friends with?"

"You'd be free," I said. "You could follow your passion for books without judgment from Old Mother Splinter."

He nodded slowly. "There is that. But like I said, I was comfortable. I made an excellent living, had a beautiful home, and no complicated relationship issues."

"Or looking at this situation another way, you were a kept man, working in a business you cared nothing about, dealing with a woman who'd tossed you away for a younger model."

His cheeks flushed. "That's not how I see this."

I did. And they were decent motives for getting rid of Old Mother Splinter.

"You must have been around Harlan and Old Mother Splinter all the time," Finn said.

Robin dragged his annoyed gaze from me. "I saw Persephone more than Harlan. But I've gotten to know him well over the time we lived together."

"What can you tell us about their relationship?"

"Why? I don't want to get Harlan in trouble. He's a decent guy. Not the smartest guy in the world but not a problem."

"If he's innocent, then there'll be no trouble coming his way," Finn said. "But he was close to Old Mother Splinter. Someone would need to get near her to cast the sleep spell."

"Sure. But I don't think it was Harlan."

"Their relationship was good?"

"It was... complicated. I'll leave it there."

"Don't. Tell us everything you know," Zandra said. "If Harlan is behind the sleep spell, then we need to know so we can stop him."

Robin flipped open a book then shut it. "On the outside, their relationship looked fun. They'd go to parties, go shopping, and out to dinner. But I could tell Harlan was frustrated. He wanted out."

"He told you that?" Finn said.

"No. Our relationship was surface-level chats about sports over a beer when Persephone was in bed. We never talked about anything meaningful. It was easier that way." Robin toyed with the book, turning it slowly with his finger. "But there were little things, like the way he'd look at Persephone when her back was turned. He wasn't getting what he wanted from the relationship, and it was a problem for him."

Finn pulled out his pad and made a few quick notes. "We've already spoken to Harlan. He claims they had an idyllic relationship."

"That's what everyone on the outside was supposed to think. They were the perfect couple. The rich, older woman and the younger playboy finding true happiness together. I mean, come on! That only happens in fiction. Real life is more black-and-white. Besides, Harlan doesn't have that kind of power."

"You know how he uses his abilities?"

"You only have to be around him for a few minutes to know where his skills lie. He's a consummate charmer. And I should know, because I'm the same, just with a tenth of the power. Harlan takes things to the next level with his silken words. If he wanted, he could get any woman he desired."

"And does he?" I said.

Robin arched an eyebrow. "You do know what Persephone's ability was?"

"A truth seer."

"Exactly. If Harlan gadded about town, bedding every woman he wanted, she'd get the truth out of him."

"Did he ever stray?" Finn said.

Robin winced. "You didn't hear this from me, but I heard a few rumors he entertained other women, but he never formed a commitment. It was always one night and then over."

"How did he hide that from Old Mother Splinter?"

"He'd spend at least three days away from her, usually doing charity work. When he returned, all thoughts of the other woman were gone, and he'd be enthused about what he'd done. Persephone didn't delve with too many questions about what else he'd been up to."

"Because she didn't think he'd been unfaithful or because she didn't want to know the truth?" I said.

"Perhaps both. What she didn't want to know didn't harm her." Robin clasped his hands together. "Was it a healthy way to deal with a relationship? Of course not. But that's how things worked for them. And most of the time, it did work. They got what they wanted."

"Harlan was unhappy, and now Old Mother Splinter is dead," Finn said. "Maybe things were more toxic than you realized."

Robin hummed under his breath for a second. "Perhaps. I didn't delve into their relationship issues. I knew Harlan was unhappy at times, and I should have supported him more. After all, I've been in that situation. But I've moved on."

I tilted my head. Had he? Until Old Mother Splinter died, Robin had seen her every day, worked for the same company, and lived in the same house as her. Little had changed in his life.

"Could you tell me where you were when you heard the news about Old Mother Splinter being taken to the hospital?" Finn said.

"I've already told you, haven't I?"

"No. We weren't collecting alibis when I first spoke to you. We assumed Old Mother Splinter's death was an accident, linked to her night swim, so there was no need to check where everyone was."

"Oh! Of course. Well, I had a late-night meeting with the local bookstore owner, Vorana Stowell. Do you know her?"

Chapter 12

Landlady lies

After our conversation with Robin, we needed to speak to Vorana ASAP.

"How do you want to handle this?" Finn stumbled beside Zandra as we walked away from the thrift store.

"I'd like to speak to Vorana without you lurking." Zandra's tone left no room for debate. "We know she didn't do it, but I don't want her panicked."

"We can keep things informal for now. Although, just so you know, I never lurk." He scrubbed his eyes with the back of his hands. "I need to get back and give Cythera an update, anyway."

"Don't fall asleep," I said.

Finn's shoulders sank. "I don't want to admit it, but I reckon the sleeping spell has gotten me. I was standing in the thrift store, and all the voices got fuzzy, and I couldn't focus. My eyes grew heavy, and I wanted to drop to the floor. If you hadn't scratched me..."

"Don't go anywhere that'll encourage you to sleep," Zandra said. "Stay on your feet and keep downing coffee."

"I'll fight this for as long as I can," Finn said. "How are you both feeling?"

"No problems here," Zandra said. "Juno?"

I hopped onto her shoulder. "As bright as a polished silver coin sitting in the blazing sun."

"I'll catch up with you soon. Hope things go well with Vorana." Finn hurried away, although his movements were worryingly sluggish.

"Maybe one of us should go with him," I said.

"Even though Cythera can be a moron of epic proportions with the small stuff, she cares about her angels. She won't let anything bad happen to Finn."

"We'll check on him if he doesn't come back soon."

"Agreed. And this meeting with Vorana will be fine," Zandra said. "She isn't involved in killing Old Mother Splinter."

"Then stop sounding so worried if you think she's innocent."

"It's just weird." Zandra pressed a hand against my side. "Vorana hasn't mentioned any problem with Old Mother Splinter increasing her rent. And now she's having a late-night rendezvous with a murder suspect."

"We've barely seen her to ask about any issues with the store," I said. "Ever since the scarabs' performance, it's been non-stop because of this sleep spell issue."

"But why meet with Robin so late? And it was right around the time someone whacked Old Mother

Splinter with the sleep spell before she took her naked dip. It seems too convenient to be a coincidence."

"Maybe that was the only time they could meet," I said. "She didn't mention it to you because it was a business meeting about books, and you always make it clear what you think about books."

She rolled her eyes. "I don't hate them that much. But I could never get as passionate about dead trees and ink as Vorana does. Or Robin."

"Which was why she didn't mention her meeting with Robin. Why would she, when you'd only yawn and change the subject?"

"Hey! I'm not that bad, am I?"

"You're like a petulant school child who's been told she needs to read the complete works of Chaucer three times in a row in the original English language transcription."

"Yeah, no idea who or what that is."

"You're a heathen."

"What I am is worried about my friend. Even though I have no love for books, I don't want Vorana's business at risk. Did you hear Robin talking about her empire being passed to cutthroat investors? Vorana's store is hardly a goldmine. They could close it and convert it into apartments. That would leave Vorana broken."

"I thought the same thing. Which is why we won't let it happen. We'll get to the bottom of this mystery and make sure her bookstore is the most amazing place in Crimson Cove. Everyone will visit and buy something."

Zandra wrinkled her nose. "Sounds like a lot of work."

"Even if it is, you'd do it. She's your friend."

"It won't mean having to spend a lot of time with books, will it?"

I gently bit her ear, making her squeak. "I'm sure I can find you something to occupy your time without getting too close to the books."

"No Chaucer?"

"No Chaucer. No one needs him in their lives."

We arrived at the bookstore to discover it shut.

Zandra rattled the handle. "Vorana rarely shuts early. She even debated closing for an hour to see the scarabs' show."

My heart thudded as I peered through the window into the darkened store.

"You don't think the sleeping spell has gotten her, do you?" Zandra said.

"No. She was thinking of keeping the store shut until the sleeping magic has been dealt with. Or maybe she got a call about an amazing deal on discounted stock and has gone to collect it. Sometimes, she's gone for hours when she's bargain hunting for books."

We tried around the back of the store, but the door was bolted from the inside.

"Let's try the house," I said. "Maybe she's there doing paperwork so she wouldn't get distracted by an exciting new read. Or she could be figuring out how to pay the increased rent and needed a neutral space to think."

Zandra broke into an uncharacteristic jog, demonstrating her concern for her friend. I jumped off her shoulder, since the movement made me queasy, and we dashed along the quiet streets, back to the house. We reached the front door and headed inside.

"Vorana! You here?" Zandra poked her head into each room, and I followed. They were all empty.

"I don't smell her," I said. "No fresh scent, anyway. Sage isn't here, either."

"You take the basement. I'll go upstairs." Zandra dashed up the stairs two at a time.

I rocketed down to the basement. The place was quiet. There was no sign anyone had been down here since we'd gotten up that morning.

On impulse, I grabbed the bangle containing my suppressed magic and tugged it over my head. If I got this power free, I should be able to help with this pesky sleep spell. When I was at full strength, there were few spells that defeated me.

I closed my eyes and breathed in deeply. The magic was there, sitting beneath the surface of some blockage. "Don't you remember me, old friend? It's been a while, but it's really me. We need to reunite. We have to defeat this evil magic that's hurting the people I care about."

The bangle grew warm against my skin, but the magic stayed stubbornly silent.

Zandra's footsteps thudded down the stairs. "She's not up there."

"She's not down here." I rejoined her in the hallway. "We could try the café."

"Let's go back to the bookstore." Zandra's brow furrowed. "What have you got around your neck?"

"A magic aid. It could help with the sleep spell if I can get it working."

"I'm willing to try anything. Hurry!"

We left the house and ran back to the bookstore.

Zandra cast an unlock spell to get through the front door. We'd taken two steps inside when the air crackled with power and a sparking ball of fluffy rage charged toward us.

"Sage! It's us." I threw up a shield spell to protect Zandra.

Sage hissed, then her rage magic faded to be replaced with terror that filled the air like noxious gas from the rear end of a sick dragon. "Vorana! I can't help her. Follow me." She turned and dashed back through the bookstore, her harness clacking as it whacked a bookcase.

We followed her into the storeroom, which was lined with metal shelving covered in books and paper. Vorana was on her knees, head down, as she leaned on a book stack.

Sage nudged her with her booping snooter. "I've tried everything, but I can't keep her awake. Nothing I do works."

"And you thought blasting us with magic would help this situation?" Zandra was beside me as I hurried over to Vorana.

"I panicked. I thought someone was breaking into the store to hurt Vorana. I can't keep her safe. I'm failing her. My witch... I can't fail her. She's my everything."

I rested a paw against my friend's side, her magic spiking against my toe beans like tiny, hot daggers. "I'd be the same if Zandra was distressed.

Fortunately, the sleeping spell doesn't seem to affect her."

"Lucky you. Our bond is dying, and I'm not strong enough to do anything about it. I'm a worthless familiar." Sage's pupils were dilated, and her breath rasped out of her.

"Vorana's still awake." Zandra inspected her friend's face. "Only just, but at least we have something to work with. Let's get you up. You need to get walking and talking."

Vorana muttered something unintelligible as Zandra dragged her to her feet.

"It's dark in here. Let's go into the bookstore where there's more natural light. That could help," I said.

Zandra grunted as she tugged her sleepy friend along beside her, one arm wrapped around her waist. "Once we get you forming sentences, we can try other things to get you wide-eyed again."

"I even gave her a couple of painful zaps to get her moving, but it didn't have any effect." Sage was right behind Vorana, so close her booping snooter touched her heels. "She just kept saying she needed to sleep."

"When did this start?" I said.

"Just after breakfast. She made another coffee and then sat at the kitchen table. If I hadn't jumped on her stomach and whacked her thigh with my harness, she may have gone to sleep then." Sage nudged Vorana's calf with a paw. "It was enough to jerk her awake. Vorana decided to open the store but couldn't get going. Every movement seemed an effort."

"What have you tried to keep her awake?"

"Any revitalizing spell I can think of. I've shouted in her face, begged for her help, and jumped on her. I even bit one of her fingers. She's going. Our bond is fading. That means she's dying." A strangled sob choked out of Sage.

I yanked on her tail to stop her walking and then stood in front of her.

She bared her blunt teeth and swiped at my face. "Get out of my way. I must be with Vorana."

"Zandra is taking care of her, and my witch always takes the best care of people she loves. You have nothing to fear."

"I have everything to fear. She may need me."

"And when she does, you'll know. Your bond is still strong. It's why she's still alive." I pressed a paw on Sage's hot, fluffy head. "My friend, you're more than enough for Vorana. You're her best friend and ally in all situations. You'd even stand beside her when she's wrong about something."

"My incredible witch is never wrong." She shoved at my paw.

"Exactly. We all feel the same way about our witches. You're an incredible familiar."

Sage snorted. "I'm a damaged mess. Vorana keeps me around because she feels sorry for me."

"Not true. She loves you with every fiber of her being."

"She should replace me. I'm old and broken. I've never been the same since I lost the use of my legs."

"Also not true. Physically, you're different, but you're still the same wholehearted, brave, loyal familiar you've always been. Those are the most important traits."

"It's not enough, though. If I was younger and faster, my magic would be better. I could have stopped this without your help." Defeat washed over Sage, and her shoulders sagged.

"Wisdom comes with age. As we mature, we grow in confidence. We have life experience behind us that teaches us how to better protect those who need support." I glanced over my shoulder. Zandra was talking to Vorana. "If some whippersnapper of a familiar had been brought in to replace you, Vorana would lose that wisdom. That's what she values. She doesn't care only your front legs work, your teeth are yellowed nubs, and you sometimes smell strange."

"I smell strange?"

"You and Vorana are bonded for life. She wouldn't pick anyone else to have beside her in a moment of crisis."

"This is a moment of crisis! And I've failed her."

"You kept her going long enough for us to assist you. That's what counts."

Sage hadn't taken her eyes off Vorana as Zandra dragged her around the store. "I'll talk to Vorana when she's better. Maybe I can mentor someone younger and then step aside when Vorana wants me to."

"I mean, you could offer that ridiculous idea, but she'd never agree to it. You're her perfect familiar, and she's your perfect witch. We lucked out by finding our ideal witches. It doesn't happen with every familiar." I donked my forehead against

Sage's. "I understand why you're doubting yourself but stay strong. You're more than enough for Vorana. We'll get her moving and then figure things out. Just promise me you'll go nowhere."

"I'll go if she wants me to."

"Then it's sorted. Vorana will never tell you to leave. So, we're stuck with you. Funny smell and all." I lowered my paw. "This sleeping spell isn't affecting familiars. That's our superpower. We must use it to protect our magic users."

"You sure?"

"I feel fine. And I've not seen any familiars struggling. How about you?"

"I... no, I'm good. What does that mean?"

I didn't know, but I took it as a positive sign. It meant I'd keep fighting if Zandra got sleepy.

"I'll go brew extra strong coffee for Vorana," Zandra said. "Can you two keep an eye on her?"

"Sage will make sure she doesn't go to sleep, won't you?"

Sage's gaze dropped to the floor and slid from side to side. "I'd never let my witch down."

"Sit on this wooden stool. It's the most uncomfortable seat you have in this place." Zandra perched Vorana on a polished, wooden, backless stool in the corner. "And keep your eyes open. Don't make me smack you to get those eyes working."

While Zandra dashed to the kitchen, we ran to Vorana. Sage stood with her front paws resting on Vorana's knee, while I jumped on her shoulder.

I tapped Vorana's cheek with my paw. "Stay with us. You don't want me and Sage to use our murder mittens on you."

"I'd never hurt my witch."

"You'd scratch her until she was bloody if it kept her eyes open," I said. "And it might be what she needs. Pain makes people focus."

Sage softly hissed at me, but when Vorana's eyelids lowered, she dug her claws into Vorana's knee, making her squeal.

"That's it! We just need to keep her going until the coffee arrives. Zandra brews coffee so strong, the spoon stands up in it."

We spent the next few minutes donking Vorana's nose with hard paws and digging our claws into her knee.

Vorana kept yelping and grumbling complaints but didn't have the strength to move us. And it was keeping her awake, so we kept doing it.

"Coffee is here. I brought in the pot." Zandra hurried over and kneeled beside Vorana. She placed a mug in Vorana's hands and held it to her lips.

It took effort, but Vorana inhaled deeply and drank the black, restorative liquid. It took the best part of a full mug before she became responsive.

Zandra peered into her face. "How are you doing? Back with us?"

"About fifty percent of me is back." Vorana grimaced. "What am I drinking?"

"Magic potion juice." Zandra grinned. "A triple shot of that Panhandler's Blend you've got in the back of your pantry. I've been meaning to try it for ages."

"Urgh! That stuff is nasty. It's why it got shoved to the back."

"It's also strong enough to wake the dead." Zandra's grin slipped as she helped hold the mug steady. "You had us worried."

Vorana slowly blinked. "What happened to me?"

"It's the sleeping spell," Sage said, her chin resting on Vorana's knee.

"Oh! Oooh! I sort of remember. I felt so odd this morning, and it took me ages to get ready. Normally, I'm a morning person."

As Zandra poured coffee for both of them, the bangle around my neck grew uncomfortably warm. It became so hot I couldn't keep it against my skin anymore. I used a paw to tug it over my ears, and it dropped onto Vorana's arm.

She jerked as if she'd received an electric shock. "What was that?"

I went to take back the bangle, but a warning spark shot from it. I studied it. The magic wanted to come out but not for me. Did it want to help Vorana? "It's my bangle, but it wants to be your bangle for a short time. The magic must sense your distress and want to help."

"There's so much energy coming off it." Vorana hovered a finger above it, and the bangle crackled. "Where'd you get it?"

"I've had it a while. I didn't think it worked, though."

"It's helping my witch," Sage said. "Vorana must keep it."

"Not forever," I said swiftly. "It's important to me."

Sage snarled at me. "If it's keeping her awake, she keeps it. I'll fight anyone who says otherwise."

Zandra rested a hand on my head. "If it's helping Vorana to stay awake, we won't take it from her, will we?"

I gritted my teeth and huffed out a breath. "You can keep it for now. But I will want it back. Soon." Without all my magic where it needed to be, I'd never be complete. I'd never get back what I lost.

"I definitely feel better while holding it." Vorana slid the bangle onto one wrist and held it up. "I've never felt power like this before. Is it yours?"

I glanced at Zandra. "It's very old. You must be careful with it." I adored Vorana, but I couldn't lose that piece of my power.

"I'll treat it like a newborn kitten familiar." Vorana let out a sigh. "I feel so much better."

"Drink more coffee, and then we'll find some potions to add to the mix," Zandra said. "As many rejuvenating spells as you can handle. We don't want the sleep spell getting you again."

"It was so weird. I felt like I had no choice but to sleep. But I didn't want to go back to bed. Lately, whenever I close my eyes, I've been having terrifying dreams."

"You have been restless at night," Sage said.

"No matter how many positive affirmations I chant, the dream comes back. It's about a red-eyed monster creeping through town and hurting everybody."

Zandra's mug stopped midair. "A red-eyed monster?"

"I figured it was all the myths and legends books I've been looking through. I got a stack in from a dealer, and some of those stories are dark, so my subconscious has been having a field day with the information and giving me nightmares."

Zandra set down her mug and chewed on her bottom lip. "I've been having the same dream, too."

"You didn't tell me." I turned to face Zandra.

"It was a dumb nightmare, so I thought nothing of it. But if Vorana is having the same dream..."

"There's a connection," I said. "Could it have something to do with the sleep spell? It hasn't gotten you, too, has it?"

"I'm good. You don't need to keep worrying about me."

"It's my job. How long have you been having these nightmares?"

"A few weeks? I can't remember when they first started. But it's always the same red-eyed creature skulking about."

"Yeah, he's always lurking around," Vorana said. "And my dream always takes place in Crimson Cove. It's as if this creature is waiting in the shadows for the right time to strike. That's why I didn't want to go to sleep. He's always there, waiting."

"I already hate this creature," Sage muttered. "If I could go into your dreams and destroy it, I would."

"Could it be real?" I said.

Zandra sat back on her heels. "In one of the urban legend books Adrienne gave me, there's a section on shared dreams. They're important. Maybe this thing is sending us a warning while we sleep."

Vorana drank more coffee. "A warning?"

"Or a prediction," Sage said. "Letting us know trouble is on its way. Maybe it's teasing us because it thinks we won't be able to stop it."

"If the thing is real, we must obliterate it," I said.

"Normally, I'm no fan of your obliteration plans, but in this case, if this is the thing messing with the town, then it must be dealt with," Zandra said.

Vorana almost slipped off the stool, spilling her coffee across the back of her hand. I leaped away and landed on the floor, avoiding the warm puddles of pungent coffee.

"On your feet. Let's get you marching." Zandra dragged her up.

Vorana protested but staggered to her feet and clumsily marched on the spot. "I feel ridiculous."

"Better to feel ridiculous than fall asleep with no hope of ever waking up." Sage marched along with her, her stubby front legs flipping up and down. "Keep moving. Get those knees higher."

She grumbled and huffed, but the marching kept her eyes open and the blood pumping.

"Vorana, while we're here, we've got a few questions about Old Mother Splinter." Zandra gripped her mug and glanced at me.

"What about her?" Vorana swung her arms.

"Um... Have you had any problems with her recently?"

Vorana punched the air. "She could be intimidating, and I never looked forward to her visits. I felt like I wasn't good enough to rent this store from her. She always looked down her nose at me."

"This bookstore is the best place in the world," Sage said. "Old Mother Splinter had no taste."

"We know that." Vorana paused to pet Sage, but a paw swipe got her moving again. "Old Mother Splinter thought the store was dull. She even told me that. She said the books made the place gloomy. Books are life!"

Zandra pressed her lips together but made no comment.

"Anything other than you feeling intimidated by her?" I said.

"I'm not sure what you mean."

"Did she do anything to make you angry?" Zandra said.

"Um... No?"

"Was that a question?" I stepped closer to Vorana and peered up at her. "You're among friends, so we won't judge. If there's been trouble between you, we need to know."

"Why?" Sage said.

I spared my fluffy friend a gentle look of reproach. "You know why. Angel Force is looking for the person responsible for this sleeping spell."

Sage stopped marching. "It's not Vorana!"

"We know it isn't," Zandra said. "But Angel Force will investigate all avenues. If you're concealing anything that makes it look like you could be involved, and we know you're not, you must tell us, so we can fix things."

Vorana started doing jumping jacks, her breath puffing out of her. "There is one thing they might be suspicious about. Before Old Mother Splinter visited, she let me know there was something important she had to tell me. I was expecting a new building code or dull extra insurance paperwork to deal with. But it wasn't that. It had to do with the rent on this place."

"What about it?"

A pained look crossed Vorana's face. "Old Mother Splinter wanted to double it."

"Which has nothing to do with the sleeping spell in Crimson Cove," Sage said.

"Why didn't you say anything to us?" Zandra said. "If you need extra cash to cover the increase, charge us more rent. What we pay you for the basement apartment is criminally low."

"No, no! I'd never do that. Besides, I planned on fighting it. I accept the rent has to go up a small amount every few years, but there was no reason to double it." Vorana's sad gaze went around the store. "Old Mother Splinter sees little value in books, though, and she thought she could make more money by having a different business in here."

"She told you that?" I said.

"She was thinking it. She always had a disdainful look on her face when she visited. And she'd make comments about the place being old-fashioned and cluttered. It's a bookstore! The place is full of books, so it'll always look a little messy. People don't always re-shelf things neatly after browsing."

"The store is perfection," Sage said. "Don't change a thing."

Zandra looked around. "There are a lot of books in here. Maybe it could be neater."

Sage hissed at her.

I leaned against Zandra's leg. "What my wonderful witch meant was people have different aesthetic tastes. Old Mother Splinter didn't appreciate the beauty of your books. That doesn't mean they aren't important."

"She wanted them gone," Vorana said. "This was her final attempt to get me out and have some soulless little chain store in its place."

"You couldn't afford the rent hike?" Zandra said.

Vorana stop doing her jumping jacks and refilled her coffee mug. She took a long sip and grimaced. "I made a bad investment a few months ago. Lost a lot of money. Someone claimed to have a ton of old books they were offering at a discount. They said they were clearing a relative's house after they died and discovered them. They couldn't be bothered to get them all valued, so I got the first refusal. They listed some titles and their editions, and I knew how rare they were. And valuable."

"They weren't legitimate?" I said.

"The deal seemed aboveboard. We met, and I looked through a box of books. They were all incredible quality, and I was so excited. I love contemporary books, but there's nothing better than getting your hands on something rare." Vorana gently touched the spine of a book. "Anyway, we made a deal, and I paid fifty percent of the money upfront, and the guy delivered them here. I checked the boxes, and the books were in them, so I paid him the rest of the money."

"What went wrong?" Zandra said.

"I was naïve. I'd opened each box but only looked at the top layer of books. I didn't register it at the time, but they were the ones I'd seen the first time we met." She sighed. "Only the top layer of books were legitimate, and I ended up paying a lot of money for paperbacks I can only sell for peanuts."

I swished my tail to show my annoyance at how someone could swindle sweet Vorana. "You got some books that are worth something, though?"

"Sure. But even if I resell them all, I won't make half my money back." Vorana lowered her gaze. "I lost most of my savings. Not that I had much to begin with."

"I've pledged to find this con artist and destroy him," Sage said.

"Not if I do, first." Zandra thumped down her mug. "Vorana, I'm so sorry. Why didn't you tell us about this when it happened? Maybe we could have helped."

"By finding the thief and carving him into tiny pieces." Sage slashed a paw through the air.

Vorana shrugged. "I was embarrassed. And I felt lousy. I couldn't believe someone cheated me out of all that money."

"Was it a lot?"

She ducked her head. "Thousands. If the deal had been legit, I'd have made three times that money back. But now I'm struggling. I've got other businesses I owe money to, and I'm having to figure out repayment plans to pay off a minimum monthly amount. Then Old Mother Splinter came along and wanted to double the rent. It felt like I was losing my business piece by piece."

"Vorana is still innocent of murder," Sage said. "This information doesn't make her guilty."

"It doesn't." There was a note of caution in Zandra's voice. "But if the angels find out about this, it gives you a motive for murder."

Vorana was quiet for a moment. "You don't think I did it, do you?"

"We don't," I said. "But if you could tell us your alibi—"

"What kind of friend are you?" Sage punched a murder mitten at me, claws out. "My witch said she's innocent, so that's an end to this."

Vorana sat back on the stool and lifted Sage onto her lap. "It's fine. Even though I've got nothing to hide, I have an alibi for that night. I was meeting a new book friend, Robin DuBrec."

I breathed a sigh of relief at the same time as Zandra.

"You don't seem surprised," Vorana said. "You already knew my alibi?"

"We've spoken to Robin. He said you were his alibi, but we had to check that out," Zandra said.

"Oh! Of course. You're speaking to everyone close to Old Mother Splinter." Vorana shook her head. "I feel like such a fool. I hid things from you, I've made a mess of my business, and now I'm a murder suspect. And I'm fighting this sleeping spell that wants to drag me into an eternal slumber."

"You're not a fool. I get why you tried to tackle this alone," Zandra said.

"Vorana is never alone," I said. "She'll always have Sage by her side. Isn't that right?"

Sage narrowed her eyes as she leaned against Vorana's belly. "Always."

"And if Angel Force has trouble getting their heads around Vorana's innocence, I'll whack sense into them," I said.

"I told you my witch was innocent." Sage snuggled against Vorana's stomach.

I nodded. "We didn't doubt you for a second. But we have a problem. Since Vorana, Robin, the scarabs, and Harlan are innocent, who does that leave us with as a murder suspect?"

Chapter 13

Angel down

"It's too quiet." I stopped by the reception desk as we entered Angel Force. Usually, there was a steady hum of activity from the back office as angels bustled around, keeping busy. But this afternoon, it was worryingly quiet.

"Maybe they're chasing leads and figuring out who cast the sleep spell," Zandra said. "We need to update Finn about what Vorana told us. He's already on her side, but we'll make sure Cythera understands Vorana isn't a suspect in this investigation."

I lifted my booping snooter and inhaled. The air was too still, and there was a lack of food smells. Angels loved their treats, so you could guarantee someone had a plate of cookies or a tasty meat sandwich close at hand.

We headed into the main office, and the sight that greeted me sent a shiver down my spine and tingled my toe beans. Three angels were asleep at their desks.

Zandra hurried to the first one and checked her. "She's alive but fast asleep."

I jumped on the angel's back and bit her ear until I drew blood. She didn't stir. I bit both wings and gave her a hard paw slap across the cheek. Nothing.

"We should get them to the hospital," Zandra said.

"I'll check the other two. You move this one."

While I dashed to the other angels, giving them bites and paw slaps, Zandra translocated the first sleeping angel to the hospital. She'd just returned when Finn staggered out of Cythera's office. Deep purple bags sat under his eyes, and his face was ghost white.

"You're awake!" Zandra ran over and caught hold of his arm. "You look terrible."

"It's got us all." Finn's words were slurred. "Every angel started dropping. They were all awake when I got here, but I could tell things weren't good. Everyone was working at half-speed. And you should see what it's done to Cythera."

"She's still awake?" Zandra said.

"Yeah. But I kind of wish she wasn't."

"Finn! Where is that long ruler? These files aren't straight. I must have them straight. Where are you? Wretched angel." Cythera's unnaturally shrill voice blasted out of her office like jagged spears of ice.

"Why does Cythera need to measure her files?" I took a step toward her office, but Finn shook his head.

"I wouldn't bother her. Cythera's always been particular about things, but the sleeping spell has tipped her into full-blown OCD. She panics if she sees anything out of line and has been doing this tapping routine every time she leaves her office."

"Is she doing it to help herself stay awake?"

He scraped a hand through his hair. "Maybe. I dunno. But it's getting worse. She's out of control."

"I'll take the other sleeping angels to the hospital," Zandra said.

Finn nodded. "Thanks. I'd fly them there, but I don't trust myself. My power feels scattered, and I can't concentrate on anything."

"I'll stay with Finn," I said. "Make sure he doesn't fall asleep."

"Finn! Ruler! Now!" Cythera bellowed from her office.

Zandra touched both angels, and they disappeared.

I jumped on Finn's shoulder and dug my claws in.

He winced. "Got to love the pain, since it's keeping me going. Let's go tackle the boss."

We entered Cythera's office. Her desk looked like a military general with a desire to be the most minimalistic creature on the planet had set it up. Everything was lined up at sharp angles. There wasn't a piece of paper out of place or a rogue paperclip anywhere.

"Give it to me." Cythera held out her hand. "This binder is in the wrong place, and the pen angles are incorrectly aligned. I shall have to start again if I can't get it right."

"It looks perfect to me," Finn said.

Cythera's wings flared out. "It's not! Help me, or you're fired."

"How about a strong coffee?" I said. "It'll keep you going without you having to measure everything."

Cythera didn't look at me. "I must have everything perfect. An untidy office makes for an untidy mind. I must get my focus back. There's so much to do." She stood and paced, her fingers tapping against her arm.

"It's the sleep spell doing this to you. It's affecting people in different ways and at different speeds. This is a side effect," I said. "You can fight this."

She waved a hand at me. "I'm too powerful to be affected by a spell. Get me that ruler, Finn."

"I'd better do what she says," he whispered to me. "Her measuring and tidying obsessions are keeping her occupied."

"Stop wasting time talking to that creature," Cythera said. "Its angles are wrong, and it looks like a trodden-on pillow."

I hissed at Cythera over Finn's shoulder as he dashed off to find a ruler.

Several minutes later, we were in the kitchen, far away from Cythera and her measuring obsession. I refused to let Finn sit, so he stood drinking an espresso while gnawing on a bar of extra dark chocolate we'd found in the cupboard.

Zandra reappeared and joined us. "The hospital is overrun. I grabbed the doctor for a few seconds, and he said ten more people are critical."

"They're unable to slow the sleep spell anymore?" I asked.

"They don't have enough staff. Even if they did, he said it feels as if the spell is becoming stronger.

It's as if it's figuring out a way around the magic they're using to keep people alive."

I wrinkled my booping snooter. "Whatever malevolent demon has cast this spell, it wants people to die. It's not content to put them into an eternal slumber."

"You think it'll benefit from people dying?" Finn said.

Zandra grimaced, grabbed her own coffee, and stole a chunk of Finn's chocolate. "Maybe. Or with fewer magic users to defeat, this demon can finish what it started."

"Which is what?"

No one spoke. We didn't yet have that answer.

"How's everyone else doing at Angel Force?" Zandra said.

"Me and Cythera are the last angels standing."

"There are no other active angels?" That wasn't acceptable. "Can't you call in reinforcements?"

"Before Cythera got all ruler happy, we talked about requesting backup. It can't happen. What if they get hit by the sleeping spell, too?" Finn shook his head. "It's too risky. We need to contain this to Crimson Cove."

As frustrating as that was, Finn made a valid point. I hopped onto the kitchen table. "Let's review where we are. We've discounted the scarabs. We all agree Amenia wouldn't use a sleep spell that harmed her children."

"It's clear she loves them," Zandra said. "Unless her magic backfired, she's not involved."

"Amenia holds great power, so she could create such a spell, but it's a stable power," I said. "She didn't do this. I believe she's innocent. And so are her children. Scarabs use magic for fun. If one of their spells misfired, they'd have fixed things. They can be mischievous and occasionally badly behaved, but they wouldn't destroy a town for entertainment."

"And she was broken up when she realized her children had been hit with the sleeping magic," Zandra said. "You can't fake grief like that. If she'd spun out this spell, she'd have destroyed it to ensure Saphic and Loris were safe."

"The scarabs are in the clear. How did your chat with Vorana go?" Finn said.

"She was in a bad way when we found her. Almost unconscious. Sage had kept her going, but she was losing the fight," I said.

"Vorana's doing okay now?"

"Better. Sage is working her magic on her, and Juno gave her a boost." Zandra raised her eyebrows and looked at me.

I didn't elaborate. "Sage will protect her."

"Which means we rule Vorana out, too," Finn said. "Not that I thought she was ever guilty."

"None of us did," I said. "She also has an alibi. She confirmed she was with Robin DuBrec when Old Mother Splinter went swimming."

Finn scrubbed his chin. "Could Robin have cast the spell on Old Mother Splinter earlier that day? We've seen people react to it differently."

"Someone with such diluted power wouldn't be able to cast such an immense spell over an entire town. Robin only has one parent with any magic," I said.

"Let me check to be sure he was telling the truth about his parents." Finn headed back into the office, and we followed him. It took him ten minutes to muster the energy to press the right buttons and get the information churning on Robin.

While we waited, Cythera's ruler kept slapping down. Then she'd mutter, and there'd be a frantic shuffling of objects.

Finn tapped the screen in front of him. "This confirms it. Robin's mother is a non-magical. He's definitely out of the picture for this spell."

"And when we spoke to him, I detected no dislike of Old Mother Splinter," I said. "Their relationship ended civilly, and he continued working for her. Even living with her. He couldn't have done that for long if there was any resentment or ill will."

"Then we have Harlan," Zandra said. "We know what his power is."

"He doesn't have an alibi," Finn said. "And he lied about being on the beach when Old Mother Splinter went swimming."

"Robin also told us Harlan wanted out of the relationship."

"Maybe he paid someone," I said. "Old Mother Splinter had immense wealth. Could Harlan have gotten his hands on some of that money and used it to pay a skilled magic user to get rid of his problem older woman?"

"I did a financial check on everyone close to Old Mother Splinter to see if anything unusual stood out." Finn pulled up a file. "She held on tight to her money. Harlan got an allowance from her, but it wasn't huge, and he spent it on clothing and partying. There was never anything left at the end of the month."

"Could Harlan have charmed extra out of Old Mother Splinter?" Zandra said. "He easily influenced us."

"She was a truth seer," I said. "If money vanished, she could have asked if he took it. Harlan wouldn't have gotten away with it."

Finn's yawn was so wide, his jaw cracked. "I don't see how he'd have gotten enough cash to pay for this spell."

"Magic like this wouldn't come cheap," I said. "It would take a small fortune to get someone to devise such a potent, wicked spell and then keep quiet about it."

"What are we missing?" Zandra settled into a seat. "Or who are we missing? We've looked at everyone close to Old Mother Splinter for her murder, and they've been discounted."

"Why does the killer want everyone in Crimson Cove to fall under a sleep spell anyway?" Finn said.

"So we're left vulnerable," I muttered.

Finn shrugged. "Why? What does the demon want?"

No one had an answer to that troubling question.

"We have a murder, no suspects, and people dropping by the hour with no way to help them." Finn grabbed a seat, but I jumped on it so he couldn't get comfy.

He rolled his eyes at me. "Thanks, Juno. I'll stay on my feet."

"We have another problem we can't keep ignoring," I said. "The non-magicals are still in the town hall, right?"

Finn sucked in a breath. "I forgot! We should have let them out at noon. We said it was an overnight stay with a free breakfast. They must be wondering what's going on."

Zandra yawned.

I leaped onto her shoulder and peered into her face, my heart tippy-tapping a fear rhythm. "Not you, too?"

She wriggled her nose. "I... I'm not sure. I do feel tired."

"Fight it!" Finn passed her more dark chocolate. "You're stronger than me."

"Of course, I won't sit here and let it take me." Zandra swayed in her seat.

My stomach flipped-flopped, and I booped her cheek. "A cold shower. That'll get you going. Both of you get in the shower. Now!"

"We have an on-site shower," Finn said. "We could use it together to save time."

Zandra grimaced. "I'll pass. Unless things get terminal, there's no way I'm doing that."

He grinned at her. "We could try a tepid shower to start. I'd even keep my clothes on. Yours are optional."

"Still a no."

I urgently nudged Zandra with my booping snooter. "On a scale of one to ten, how sleepy are you?"

"Two. Maybe three."

"You always hide when you're not feeling right. It must be at least a six. Finn, help me drag her to the shower. Set it to freezing."

"Juno! Stop! I'm doing okay. Yeah, I think the spell has got me, but I'll fight it. And you'll let nothing bad happen to me. If I doze off, you know what you have to do."

"Put you out of your misery?" Finn chuckled when I hissed at him. "Sorry. We'll stick together. Watch for signs of excessive sleepiness."

"Since this spell seems to be growing in power, we've gotta get the most vulnerable out of Crimson Cove," Zandra said. "That means releasing the non-magicals as soon as possible. We can't let this magic touch them, or they'll die."

"I haven't heard from the angels guarding them. At least, I don't think I have." Finn's wings fluttered. "I've dropped the ball on this. The non-magicals slipped from my mind. How could I do such a dumb thing?"

"Haven't you checked on them at least once?" I studied Zandra's face, looking for any sign she might nod off.

Finn scrubbed at his forehead. "I meant to, but I'm struggling to keep thoughts in my head. I know I was supposed to talk to the guard angels a couple of hours ago."

"And did you?"

"I don't remember. Maybe? Or maybe I tried and got no response. Did I go there? Did I send them a message? Sorry, Juno. I'm being no help."

"So, the non-magicals could already be under the influence of the spell?" Zandra tugged on the ends of her hair. "What if we open the door and find them... gone?"

I looked around the empty office. "We need more support. Individuals who aren't affected by the sleeping spell."

"Everyone is affected," Finn said.

I flicked my tail. "Do you see me getting sleepy?"

"Huh. Actually, no. Hey! Maybe you're behind this. You have a secret plot with all the other cat familiars to take over Crimson Cove and turn it into an all-you-can-eat fish buffet."

I bared my teeth at Finn. "No time for jokes. Familiars don't seem to be affected. You stay here. I'll get someone to watch over you."

"What will you do while we wait here?" Exhaustion slid through Zandra's tone.

"Rally the troops. It's time to defeat this sleep spell, find the demon behind it, and take it down."

Chapter 14

Magical mission

"I hate this plan. Vorana needs to keep your bangle on her wrist. She'll fall asleep without its power." Sage guarded Vorana, her hackles raised.

"You kept her going without the bangle before I arrived. And I only need its power for a short time. We have to get the non-magicals safely out of Crimson Cove." I kept my posture neutral, so as not to antagonize an already panicked cat.

After leaving Angel Force, I'd dashed back to the bookstore to get my bangle. I needed more power for this kitten impossible mission. But a spiky black cat stood in my way. And I understood why. I'd be the same if it was Zandra in such a vulnerable position.

Well, she would be soon if I didn't max out my power, so I could slay the sneaky demon messing with the town and return things to normal.

"It's okay," Vorana said. "I'll do more jumping jacks and stay on my feet. And I'll brew more of that gross coffee."

"What if it's not enough? You can't fall asleep!" Sage said. "The bangle stays with you."

"I know you want to protect your witch, but the whole town is vulnerable. We deal with those most at risk first and then help everyone else. Once the non-magicals have been taken care of, there'll be less pressure."

"There'll only be less pressure if they take the sleep spell with them. Maybe it was one of them. Everything's gone wrong since the non-magical infestation began. It's all their fault."

"Sage, they're not termites. And they've spent plenty of money in this store. I kinda like them," Vorana said.

"They still shouldn't be here!"

"We always welcome travelers who get lost." She gently petted Sage until her hackles lowered.

"If you ask me, too many of them are getting lost," Sage grumbled.

"Calm yourself, my friend," I said. "We all take a pledge to protect the vulnerable. And to do that, I must have the magic in that bangle."

"Take it." Vorana peeled the bangle off her wrist. "I do feel better. And I know what to do to keep myself going without it."

Sage snarled at me as I took the bangle.

"I promise, I'll give it back as soon as I can. Thank you." I slipped the bangle over my neck. The magic had better cooperate, or I was risking Vorana's life for nothing. "Sage, I also need your help. We've got to get to the town hall and clear everybody out."

"No way. I'm staying with Vorana."

Vorana marched on the spot, swinging her arms. "I can do this alone."

I watched Vorana for a few seconds. "No, Sage stays with you. She's right. She'll protect you if you get too sleepy. Maybe you should go to the hospital, though."

"From what I've heard, the doctors and nurses are running around not knowing what to do," Sage said. "It's riskier going there than staying where we are. There are too many distractions and sleepy idiots at the hospital. I can give Vorana my undivided attention if we stay in the store."

"Your choice. But they have spells."

"So do I. Painful ones that'll whack you if my witch doesn't make it."

"Hush! So dramatic. From the way you hiss and snarl, you'd think I was a witchling who had no skills of her own." Vorana lifted Sage and danced her around the store. "Juno, how are you getting the non-magicals out of the town hall?" She planted a loud smacker on Sage's head.

"With help from magic and old friends. Stay safe." I dashed out of the bookstore and almost collided with Sammy. "Oh! It's... it's been a while."

He blinked at me several times. I'd missed that adorably chubby, fluffy face. "Yeah. I guess so. What's got you in a hurry?"

I stepped from paw to paw. "A little magic problem. How have you been?"

"I've been around."

I huffed out a breath. "I know we aren't on the best of terms, but I need help with something. You know about the sleeping spell that's messing with everyone?"

"Sure. It's done a number on some people. Lucky for me, I'm not affected."

"Lucky for all familiars," I said. "I don't know why, but none of us have been affected. Our bonded magic users haven't been so fortunate."

"Not something I need to worry about." He sniffed. "So, what do you want?"

I wanted my adorable, fluffy snuggle partner back. I wanted Sammy not to snap at me and look like he wanted to be anywhere but here.

"I have a plan to help the non-magicals. They're in the town hall, but I need to get them out of Crimson Cove in case the magic hurts them."

"What a waste of time. They're not of any value. So what if the magic gets them?"

My mouth dropped open. This wasn't the Sammy I knew and adored.

"Leave them there to rot. We could always burn down the town hall when the smell gets too much."

"Sammy! That's a terrible thing to say. Why don't you want to help? You were always happy to help when I had a mission to complete."

He sneered at me. "Oh, right. Your dumb kitten impossible missions. They always turned out so well for me."

My claws extended an inch. "Most of the time, they did. And those missions always work better when I have a team with me."

"More like servants. You're so full of yourself, you think you can do anything. But you haven't thought this through. How will you get those dumb dumbs in the town hall to listen to you? You're just a cat to them."

"I have a plan, but I can see you're not interested in helping, so I won't tell you what it is." I sounded petulant, but Sammy was being rude.

"Why should I help? You dragged me from one stupid mission to the next when we were together. It was always about you. You never asked if I was having fun. It was always the Juno Show."

"If you had a problem, you should have said. Stood up for yourself. Been less of a wet weekend."

"I'm doing it now. I'm happy I cut you out of my life."

My heart felt like someone had punched it. "Well, so long as you're content. I didn't realize being with me made you miserable."

A weird light lit his eyes for a second. He shook his head, blinked, and stepped back. "I need to go."

I lifted a paw. "Wait! Are you okay?"

"Better now I don't have you in my life." He trotted away.

I could do nothing but watch him go, his fluffy hindquarters jiggling as he sped up. How had I gotten things so wrong with Sammy?

No, not now. My bruised heart would have to be examined later.

I probed the magic in the bangle, and it throbbed back a response. "Please work. This isn't about me. This is about saving other people. If you cooperate, it'll help many lives."

Warmth trickled through me, and I let out a sigh of relief. My magic would cooperate. Maybe only temporarily, but that was all I needed to make this mission a success.

I started at the Gingerbread Bakery. The door was open, but there was no sign of Tia Starbow or Binky, her cougar familiar.

The smell of burning led me to the kitchen, where smoke billowed from an oven. I hopped on the counter and flipped off the power then opened a window using my paws and booping snooter to let the smoke out.

Something heavy hit the floor above me. I dashed up the stairs to discover Binky standing over Tia.

Binky snarled, but then her eyes widened with recognition. "Juno! Help! Why is everyone falling asleep?"

I sniffed Tia. She was still breathing. "Short explanation. A demon cast a sleeping spell over the town. Zandra's been hit by it, and most of Angel Force is down. I need your help to stop this spell from killing anyone else."

"Tia's gonna die? No! I can't leave her."

"You won't be able to wake her. Believe me, I've seen how this spell messes with magic users."

"So... what do I do? I won't give up on her." Binky rested a giant paw on Tia's chest.

"Never! Take her to the hospital. They're using magic to slow the progression of the spell. That'll buy her time while we find this demon and stop its evil games once and for all. You in?"

"Give me five minutes." Binky vanished, leaving me pacing the apartment, the smell of burned cake filling my booping snooter and anxiety churning my stomach.

I still had no clue how to find this tricky demon or how it had hidden itself so well in the town. Why had no one spotted it?

Binky flashed back into view. "It's busy at the hospital. I almost had to bite a nurse to get her to look at Tia."

"Can they help her?"

"Yes. As soon as they cast spells over Tia, she was calmer. I didn't want to leave her, though. Our bond feels weird. Kinda broken. Will it always be like that?"

"No. And you can get back to her soon. But we need to clear the non-magicals out of Crimson Cove first, so they aren't at risk when we expose the demon and destroy it."

Binky tilted her head from side to side. "I mean, sure, I can do that. I can chase them to the town border, but it'll terrify them."

"I'm thinking something subtler. How would you like to have two legs and no tail?"

Binky poked out her tongue. "Sounds like a nightmare."

"Follow me. I need more recruits to make this work."

Ten minutes later, I was back at Angel Force with a grumbling Elijah beside me.

"Why do I have to be the babysitter for a bunch of tedious sleeping angels?"

"Because I can't risk turning you human. You already have complicated magic running through you to prevent you from turning full ghoul." I tapped the charm on the collar he wore. "If I blast you with more powerful magic, it might be too much."

He puffed out his furless chest. "I can handle anything."

"If we had the time, we could experiment and test that theory, but I need someone to watch the angels and Zandra. I won't be able to focus if I'm worrying about her. This is a crucial part of our mission."

"I'm doing okay." Zandra's expression was tight as she gripped her mug of coffee.

"Okay isn't good enough. Elijah will watch you, Finn, and Cythera. Any signs of sleepiness, and he has my authorization to use his teeth and claws to get you moving."

"Always happy to bite an angel," Elijah said. "A feisty witch, too, if she misbehaves."

"You're too late for Cythera," Finn said. "She went to sleep a few minutes ago. Sat in her chair, closed her eyes, and I couldn't get her to move. I tried everything. Even threw water on her face."

"Which shows this magic is speeding up. The demon is pulling out all the stops to get what it wants. Elijah, I'm trusting you with my most valuable person. Zandra means the world to me. You must keep her safe." I met his gaze, unblinking.

He flipped his tail in the air. "Sure, sure. It's not as if I had anything else to do."

"Sorcha was okay with you leaving her?" Zandra said.

"Asleep, same as everyone else."

"Hurry!" Zandra said to me. "If this magic gets to the people in the town hall, it'll be a disaster. Crimson Cove will be over."

"I need one more recruit." I touched foreheads with Zandra. "Stay safe. And stay awake." I dashed out of Angel Force, where Binky was waiting outside. I looked around. "He's not here? Is he coming?"

"Archie is on his way. I can smell him."

An intense whiff of patchouli and sandalwood hit me, mixed with a little sulfur, just as Archie rounded a corner and blasted toward us, smoke streaming behind him.

He skidded to a halt, his tail wagging, and hit me with an enormous, slobbery tongue greeting. He tried to do the same to Binky, but she batted his head away with a huge paw and issued a warning growl.

"Greetings, Archie." I scrubbed hellhound spittle off my ears. "Did Binky tell you everything about our mission?"

"Evil demon. Sleep spell. Vulnerable non-magicals need shifting. Oh, and we get to be human. How cool is that?"

"Very cool. We have to disguise ourselves before we tackle the non-magicals. Human form is the safest, so we don't scare them."

He bobbed his head. "Can't wait! Can I have a skinhead? No! A long black braid down my back. Ooh! How about a mullet?"

I sniffed a patch of dried blood on his fur. "How are the vampires managing with the sleep spell?"

"Um... They're having trouble controlling their urges. Remus tried to bite me. I pinned him down for half an hour before he stopped snapping his fangs at me. He kept saying sorry then lunging at my throat. It's definitely messing with them."

I shuddered. "The last thing we need is out-of-control vampires romping around Crimson Cove taking a bite out of anything juicy."

"Maybe the demon wants the place in chaos so it can finish what it's started," Binky said. "Nothing spells chaos better than hungry vampires on a hunt."

"What does this demon want?" Archie said.

"When we find the monstrous thing, we'll ask it before taking off its head." I drew in a breath and centered myself. "Are you ready? This'll feel strange. Your center of balance will change, so don't be surprised if you feel dizzy."

"Bring on the two legs and no tail," Archie said.

I took several deep breaths and closed my eyes. I drew on the ancient well of power inside me and attached it to the magic in the bangle around my neck. The powers recognized each other, but there was resistance before they merged.

"Everything working okay?" Archie whispered.

"The transformation spell is ready." I pulsed magic over Archie and Binky. It flooded through me too, warming my toe beans and making my ear tips tingle.

I opened my eyes. Archie had transformed into a tall, Viking-like blond with a cheery smile and blue eyes. Binky was an auburn-haired temptress with violet eyes. They looked very human. Unfortunately, I hadn't considered clothing in this transformation, so they were naked. And so was I.

"Whoa! You've made us look like gods." Binky patted herself. "Check out these curves!"

"You both look magnificent. Naked but magnificent. How do I look?" I swayed on the strangeness of two feet. After all these years, it felt bizarre to have an actual body.

"Like an ice queen. White-blonde hair, piercing blue eyes. You look hot," Binky said. "Almost as good as me. I'm not sure about losing my tail, though. I feel bare without it. Everyone can see my butt."

Archie grinned and kept forcing his gaze away from our chests. "I promise, I'm being a good boy, but man, it's tricky when you both look so pretty."

"Let's grab clothes then deal with the non-magicals. And dress down. We don't want to be a distraction to them," I said.

The nearest place that had clothes was the *Whimsical Wonders* thrift store. No one was inside when we entered, so we had time to search for suitable tops, pants, and shoes.

Once dressed in the plainest clothes we could find, and I'd tucked my glorious pale hair under a hat, we ran to the town hall.

"How will you get all the non-magicals out of there?" Binky said.

"I don't mind chasing them," Archie said. "I love chasing things."

"No chasing. Remember what you look like," I cautioned.

Binky touched my arm. "You can't march them out of town in a long line. It would be weird. They won't agree to it."

I slowed. In my haste, I hadn't thought about the mechanism of moving so many people in one go.

Then, I spotted Gus Bainbridge standing outside the town hall and smiled. "I know just the man who loves to herd non-magicals."

Chapter 15

Coach party

Gus raised a hand when he saw us. "Morning. Or should I say afternoon? Are you our release party?"

"That's us," I said brightly. "This is Archie and Binky. I'm Ju — Juniper. Sorry for the delay in getting you out. You know how the day can get away with you."

He tilted his head. "Gus Bainbridge. Have we met before? You sound familiar."

I cleared my throat. I looked different, but my voice was still the same. Magic doesn't work miracles. "I don't think so. If everyone is ready to leave, we can get you on the road."

Gus nodded. "I've got three coachloads of people inside who belong to me."

"Three!" Archie said. "How are you able to look after so many?"

"Oh, you know, cutbacks. Honestly, and don't tell my boss this, but I've found this trip a bit much. When I get back to the head office, I'll ask for an assistant. The last one never came back from sick leave. I love my old ladies, but they can try the patience of a saint." He raised a hand, his fingers splayed. "They need comfort breaks, cushions for piles, rest stops to take their pills. And don't get me started on their obsession with discussing their ailments and who's just died. And then there's—"

"Gus, I'm glad we met you. Could you help get everyone else out of town, too? Not just the parties you're looking after?" I fluttered my newly long eyelashes at him.

He grinned. "You sure we've never met before? I swear I know you from somewhere."

"No. And I always remember a handsome face." I looped an arm around his shoulders and walked him a few steps from the town hall. "The thing is, there's been a serious gas leak in town. We're evacuating."

"Again! You have the worst luck with gas."

I gritted my teeth then forced a smile. "You were here the last time we had a leak?"

"Sure was. We spent the day at the animal sanctuary on the edge of town, instead of coming here. If you keep getting problems, get your underground pipes checked. Could be a serious fracture. That's an explosion risk. The whole town could go up in flames."

"We know. I'll speak to the people in charge, but we need everyone to leave until we find the source of the leak."

He pursed his lips, his gaze cutting along the street. "You'll need a specialist. That won't be cheap. I know a few people. They'd give you a friend's discount."

"I'll bear that in mind. Can you help us get the non-mag... I mean, the rest of the visitors out of here?"

"This sounds like the kind of thing they did on island nations during the war. You know, shipping people off to the countryside, so they wouldn't get hurt by bombs. Of course, this isn't a bomb, just a gas leak, but it's still dangerous. It makes sense to move people out of danger."

"It's kind of like that," I said. "And I need everyone out of here as soon as possible. The gas leak is a health risk as well as an explosion risk."

"That serious? Say no more. My coaches weren't full, so I can take some people when we go. How about I make a call and get some extra coaches shipped in? They can pick up the slack, so we can all leave at once."

"That's perfect. I'll cover the costs and pay for your time."

"I'd appreciate that. This job doesn't pay much. I mainly do it because I adore my golden oldies."

"Gus, you're an angel."

"Just trying to help. Give me an hour. Oh, and a word to the wise, you need to lay on food for everyone inside. It's weird. People say they want to leave but then go to the door and change their mind. It's as if something is forcing them to stay."

"That is strange," I said. "Can't imagine what it could be."

"Sometimes, people love to complain just to hear their own voice. And we had a great time last night. The entertainment was out of this world incredible. We were talking for hours about how they managed those tricks. It convinced more than a few magic is real."

"We all know magic isn't real." I laughed, and Gus joined in.

"I'll get to work on those extra coaches for you."

I fluttered my lashes some more. "Would you mind letting people know what's happening? No need to alarm anyone, just so they know how important it is they don't stay."

"Leave it with me. I know how to handle fragile souls."

I could have kissed him. "Meet you back here in an hour?"

Gus saluted me then dashed inside the town hall.

"Mission is a go?" Binky said as I rejoined my companions.

"Thanks to Gus. He's getting extra coaches and telling everyone about the gas leak."

"What if they don't want to go? How will you get them out of here?"

"I have a plan for that. Archie, you're on a food-buying mission. Get as much food as you can carry and bring it back here. All the delicious junk food a non-magical can dream about."

He waggled his butt, which I imagined was his version of a tailless wag. "That's my kind of mission."

"Once they're fed, stay here and keep an eye on things. And make sure they know they can't walk around on their own because of the dangerous gas leak."

"Cool. Junk food, fake gas leak, watch the non-magicals. Got it." Archie raced away, running too fast for your average human, but there was only so much I could do to conceal our magical awesomeness.

"What will we do?" Binky said.

"We're making a gas leak with specialist help. This way."

I was relieved to find Randal Nix still awake when we got to animal control. I tapped on his door.

He turned in his seat, his appearance disheveled and tiredness sitting under his eyes. "Um, hi. Can I help you?"

"It's me. Juno. I look a little different from the last time you saw me, huh?"

Randal's eyebrows shot up. "I thought I recognized the voice. Why do you look like that? And who is this?"

"This is Binky. Tia's familiar. We're on a vital mission, and we need your help."

He rubbed his eyes. "Doing what? How's Zandra?"

"That's sweet of you to ask. Are you concerned about my witch?"

He ducked his head. "I haven't seen her around. Wanted to make sure the sleep magic hadn't gotten her."

"Sorry to say it has, but she's holding up. I'm looking after her."

"Good. I keep zapping myself to stop from nodding off. The pain keeps me alert."

"That's exactly how you need to stay. We're removing all non-magicals from Crimson Cove. Someone is arranging transport, but we need to create an impressive gas leak situation. Something that smells so noxious, no one will want to stay."

Randal's forehead furrowed. "And you want me to do that?"

"Yes! We need to get them out of here as quickly as possible."

He picked up a small metal object and held it in his hand for a second. It bounced, and he jumped in his seat before hissing and dropping the item. "I can help, but I'm working flat out to keep the wards active."

"They're still malfunctioning?" Binky had been sniffing around the room. It was an odd thing to watch since she looked human. She came over and joined us, holding an empty carton of takeout in one hand.

"Malfunctioning and getting worse. Because everyone's magic is wonky due to this sleep spell, it's distorting the wards. I stabilize one, and another goes down."

"We believe a demon is behind this chaos. Maybe they're tampering with the wards, too," I said.

"You think they want to let something in?" Randal said.

"Or expose our magic to the world," Binky said. "There are weird groups who hate hiding their magic. Tia often complains about how irresponsible they are."

"It happens," I said. "If that's what this demon is doing, it's even more important we stop it. They're not just messing with us. They could have plans that extend farther. Plans that destabilize other magic communities. Lives will be lost."

Randal yawned. "Then let's do this. I need an Odorous Potion, a Linger Potion, and a pile of sulfur dirt. That'll create a foul stench that'll be hard to escape. And anyone who smells it will instantly feel sick."

"Sounds perfectly nasty. We'll focus most of the potion at the town hall and use the air-con system to waft it inside," I said. "They'll start feeling bad, and when they get outside, they'll smell more foul air and know we're not messing around."

"Then they'll jump on the coaches and leave," Binky said.

"Randal, you've got less than an hour to work your stinky magic."

He drew in a breath. "Then let's get to work."

While I monitored the magical wards with Binky and we made tweaks to the remote signaling system to keep them going, Randal worked feverishly to generate the noxious potion. In between yawns and coffee refills, he let me know everyone at animal control was asleep, and he'd taken them to the hospital. Barney had been the last one on the team to drop.

"I gotta say, I was terrified when it all started," Randal said. "No one knew what was going on."

"We're still figuring out the finer details." I nudged a dial and watched the magic ward flicker back to life.

"And you're sure Zandra is doing okay?"

The sweet look of concern on his face made me smile. "She's battling the spell tooth and nail. She's at Angel Force, and Elijah is watching over her."

"Good. That's good. Maybe you should get her to the hospital."

"Elijah will let me know if things take a turn for the worst." I slid Randal a glance. "Perhaps when this is over, you can take Zandra out and celebrate us defeating the demon and saving the town?"

He blushed. "Maybe. I value Zandra's friendship."

"She does yours. But you could be so much more than friends."

He shrugged. "You think?"

"I know. But first, let's get this gas leak on the move and deal with the demon."

It took another fifteen minutes of tweaking the potion, but we soon had twenty vials to distribute around town. Five would go into the town hall air conditioning system, and the rest would be placed at strategic points around Crimson Cove.

Randal secured the potions into two bags and handed them to us. "I'd come with you, but I've got to monitor the wards. If they go down, we'll be too exposed. Magic will drift out, and unwanted attention will seep in."

"Understood. Stay here. And stay awake." I had the urge to head-butt his calf but settled for a fist bump. It was so weird being back in a body that had two arms and two legs. I'd almost forgotten how to show my appreciation without using my head or tongue.

As we returned to the town hall, we placed the stinky potion around Crimson Cove. The smell that followed us was reminiscent of rotting fish and eggs. It turned my stomach, so I hoped it would have a violent impact on the non-magicals.

As we approached the town hall, Archie gave us a cheery wave. He held a gigantic bag of nachos, and his mouth was full.

"You'll want to stop eating in about five seconds," I said.

"Nothing puts me off my food. I can eat—" His eyes watered, and his nose wrinkled. "What the heck is that?"

"The fake gas leak. Randal conjured a miracle."

"Oh! Yeah, it's nasty." He dumped the nachos in the trash and wiped his hands on his second-hand pair of jeans.

"How have the non-magicals been behaving?"

"Some have been jerks, but Gus helped keep them calm. They all know about the gas leak."

"And here come the coaches," Binky said. "Right on time."

Three large coaches lurched into view, their engines groaning as the messed up magic prodded at the electrical circuits.

"Let's get the potion sprinkled around the town hall. That'll encourage any lurkers to leave," I said.

We'd just finished ensuring the town hall stank like a rotten egg fiesta when Gus hurried out. His skin was waxy yellow, and he held a hand over his mouth. "The leak is getting worse. There must be a problem with a nearby pipe because it's seeping into the hall. What kind of gas do you use to power this town?"

"All sorts. Most of it is renewable. Some of it is farm waste. And you're right. We just had word another pipe cracked, so I'm glad your coaches are here," I said.

"My boss was happy to make extra money by hiring them to you. I'll get people moving."

While Gus rallied the crowd, I batted aside the magic keeping everyone inside, so there'd be no excuse for them to resist leaving.

We stood back, happy to watch the crowd of non-magicals surge from the town hall. Many clutched their stomachs or had their hands over their mouths and noses. We didn't hear a single complaint that they had to leave Crimson Cove so swiftly.

"This is really working," Binky muttered.

"Did you doubt my genius? And once they're gone, we can focus on finding the demon who did this to our town."

"And punish it?" Archie whispered.

"It's threatened the lives of the people we love. Tia is out cold, the vampires are dangerous, and Zandra is struggling. This ends now."

"What's that word you always use?" Archie said. "We'll observe them? No, that's not right. We're going to oblige them?"

"Obliterate. We'll obliterate this demon for what it's done to our beloved town. No one messes with Crimson Cove or our magic users and gets away with it."

"Count me in on some obliterating," Binky said. "I nearly died of fright when Tia collapsed. And our bond got all weird and distorted. It reminded me of the time that guy stole me and messed with my magic."

"You can join in the obliterating, too," I said. "The more murder mittens in the mix, the better."

I inspected the coaches and nodded. They looked full.

Gus strode over. "Just need to check that no one got left behind. Sometimes, my old ladies take forever powdering their noses. Something to do with weak bladders. I don't ask questions."

"Thanks for helping," I said.

"No worries. It's been an eventful stay. Although there are complaints from people on the coaches. I don't think you'll get any five-star reviews for the town."

"They're welcome never to come back."

"What was that?"

I smiled at him. "I said they're welcome to come back any time."

"Thanks. My golden oldies love it here. We'll be back. Although we'll wait until you get this gas problem fixed. Back in a minute." Gus strode into the town hall, a large hankie over his mouth and nose.

"If you don't need me anymore, I'll go to the hospital to check on Tia," Binky said. "Any chance you could turn me back?"

"Of course." I walked Binky around the side of the building out of everyone's view and rested my hands on her shoulders.

She shuddered as my magic flooded out of her and into the bangle before turning her back into her magnificent cougar form, with thick pale brown fur and a black stripe running up her nose.

Binky huffed out several breaths and shook her fur. "That feels better. Much more natural."

"I appreciate the help."

"Let me know when you want that demon obliterated, and I'm all yours." Binky sped off toward the hospital.

"Archie! You're next. Ready to get back on four paws?" I called.

He poked his head around the side of the building. "You betcha."

After I'd transformed Archie, and he'd bounded off to check on his vampires, I cast more magic and turned myself back into my glorious white cat form. As fun as transformation magic was, it was exhausting. I'd said nothing to the others, but keeping those disguises in place had been an effort.

The bangle sat heavily around my neck. When I had a moment, I'd test how willing the magic was to join with me for good. I'd be stronger then and capable of performing dozens of spells before needing a recharge.

I raced to the front of the town hall, and my booping snooter wrinkled. It really was the most disgusting smell Randal had created. He was a mastermind.

Gus hadn't returned, and the coaches idled, full of passengers. Maybe he'd gotten sick. We'd used a lot of the stinky potion to encourage people to leave.

I ducked my head into the entrance. Sammy was passing through a door at the end of the corridor.

What was he doing here? Had he had a change of heart and decided to help, after all? If he'd seen me in my two-legged form, he wouldn't have known it was me. He must be trying to find me and apologize for his off-handishness.

I hurried after him, hope making my heart pitter-patter. I knew my old Sammy was in there somewhere. He'd just gotten on the wrong path. Once he came to his senses and realized Tinkerbell was bad for him, we'd be back together. We could have snuggle times and grooming sessions and overindulge on the finest smoked salmon like we used to.

I rounded the corner and slowed. Gus was crouching and petting Sammy. How adorable. Sammy had a new friend.

Gus stood and walked away. He shoved his hand into his jacket pocket then tossed something to Sammy. He caught it in midair and ate it.

That was the way to Sammy's heart. Feed him well, give him tail base rubs, and he'd soon be purring.

Then Gus did something odd. He gestured for Sammy to follow him.

I snorted. Anyone who knew cats knew they were impossible to train. They'd create the illusion you had them under your control, but they knew what they were doing. A cat couldn't be trained unless it wanted to be.

So, I was surprised when Sammy stood and trotted after Gus into a small side room.

Curious, I followed them.

Chapter 16

Goodbye, good guy

Gus clicked the door shut behind Sammy, so I had no way of getting into the room without making it obvious. The blinds were down on the windows, so I couldn't see inside. I pressed flat to the floor and shoved my ear against a small gap at the bottom of the door.

"We're almost there. Not much longer. Everything is poised to collapse." Gus was talking to himself.

"You've worked so hard."

I jerked back. Sammy was talking to Gus! He knew the rules. We never engaged with non-magicals unless it was an emergency. Were the treats Gus fed him really that good?

"There's barely any resistance left. A few loose ends, but I'm unconcerned about them."

"Be careful of Juno," Sammy said. "She's clever and has more power than she lets on."

"She'll be too worried about her wounded witch to concern herself with my plans. And when she does, it'll be too late to make any difference."

My eyes widened, and I blinked at the door. Gus knew about witches? How was that possible? And why wasn't he freaking out that a cat was talking to him?

"Juno has support, though. She's always bragging about her magical misfits and dragging them on ridiculous missions." Sammy snorted. "I'm amazed she hasn't gotten anyone killed. I've had a few near misses because of her recklessness."

Those words wounded me. I never put my friends in direct harm. They sometimes brushed up against it in times of crisis, but I never enjoyed risking their lives.

"Her friends are also occupied by protecting those they care about," Gus said. "That's what makes this so perfect. I only needed half the magic to disarm all the residents."

"The vampires aren't asleep. I thought that was part of the plan."

"True. But they're unstable and on the verge of tipping into out-of-control killers. Once that happens, all eyes will be diverted from what I'm about to do."

I couldn't believe it! Gus was involved in this shady business. It made no sense.

"You'll keep me once the job's done?" Sammy's voice was pitched with uncertainty.

"Of course! You've been helpful, and I couldn't have done this without all of you."

There was a chewing noise, and Sammy gulped something down.

"I need to contact the others. Make sure they're in place." Footsteps headed away from the door, and I could only hear murmuring as Gus spoke to someone.

This was too much. Gus shouldn't know about witches, magic, vampires, and talking cats. Was someone in Crimson Cove controlling him? I drew in a breath. Or had he been playing a nice guy role all this time? And how did Old Mother Splinter's death fit into this?

No! This was Gus Bainbridge. Mildly incompetent, yet always cheery, non-magical. He didn't have his sights set on ruining Crimson Cove. He didn't have any power.

I strained to hear who he spoke to but couldn't get any coherent words. There had to be an explanation. Maybe Gus touched a magical object, and it had warped his mind. It could have temporarily given him powers or opened his eyes to the world of magic.

I'd been around him plenty of times, and he was your typical, bumbling, non-magical. There was nothing special about Gus.

"What's the situation with the angels?" Gus said.

"Nearly all out," Sammy said. "There's one stubborn one left. The spell's taking its time to work on him because he's a mix of demon and angel."

"Of course. Finn. I should have recruited him to our side. I hear that one has power."

"When he's not suppressing it," Sammy said. "He'll always be on Zandra and Juno's side, though, so it's a waste of time trying to bring him over to join us."

"It would be a shame to kill him if he has potential. Maybe when he sees the fight is lost, he'll join the winning side."

"You're the boss. What's next?"

"I'll make a show of taking the non-magicals to the border then leave them there. I'll have to subdue them so they don't bother me. I'll leave them in the coaches then come back and destroy the last of the resistance."

I swallowed my panic several times, but it remained lodged in my throat like an unwanted splinter of chicken bone. Gus was behind this chaos. That was why he'd killed Old Mother Splinter. She must have met Gus and seen what he was. He'd have had no choice but to kill her, to stop her from revealing his true form.

And Gus had been popping up everywhere. He'd shown up at the animal sanctuary then the snail spa, and the beach, pretending to save Old Mother Splinter, when in all likelihood, he'd beguiled her into taking that night swim in the hope she'd drown.

Something must have gone wrong that night. Perhaps he realized someone else would save her, so he dragged her out and played the hero role so no one would suspect him.

And Gus must have done something to Sammy, too. This demon in disguise had corrupted my sweet, innocent Sammy. There was never anything wrong between us. It was all this monster's fault.

I inched away from the door. I needed backup. If Gus was strong enough to conceal his magic and do all this damage right under our booping snooters, he was immensely powerful. I couldn't tackle him alone and expect to survive.

But who could I call on? Zandra was under the effects of the sleep spell, so was Finn, and the rest of the angels were in slumber town. Sorcha was asleep, and I couldn't risk exposing Vorana to this malice.

I could try the vampires. A bunch of dangerous vampires would be ideal weapons to take down a demon. But what if they lost control? Crimson Cove would be destroyed while they drank everyone dry.

It had to be the other familiars. I needed to round them up again and come back in force to take down Gus. That was the safest option.

I turned to leave and found Tinkerbell behind me.

She snarled and slashed a murder mitten through the air. I sprang over her head and dashed away, my heart a thunderous mess in my chest. I'd been so focused that I'd missed her sneaking up on me.

"Stay where you are, you little snoop." Tinkerbell was hot on my fluffy heels.

I sprang along the corridor, heading toward the exit. I was a dozen steps from freedom when the doors burst open and the non-magicals bundled in.

"Get that cat!" Tinkerbell yelled. "Stop it from getting away. Kill it if you must."

The non-magicals surged toward me, their eyes glazed, jaws slack, and mouths open. They looked more like an army of fresh zombies than a gaggle of silver-haired grannies on a fun day trip.

I scuttled back, my gaze flashing to the high windows.

"You're not getting away," Tinkerbell said.

"Stop using your magic on them," I said. "You'll kill them."

"They'd die willingly for us. They believe in the cause."

"They don't have the free will to believe anything with you controlling them. Let them go."

"They were all willing to accept magic into their hearts. It's hardly my fault if they have trouble containing it in their weak bodies."

I leaped up a wall, my claws digging into the concrete, attempting to grab the window ledge, but the windows were too high. I crashed onto the floor, landing on my paws with a bone-jarring thud.

"Get it!" Tinkerbell shrieked.

An elderly guy with a long, grey beard and an enormous beer belly attempted to flop on top of me. I dodged away and crashed into the chino-clad legs of a middle-aged woman who smelled of sugar and flowers.

She lunged at me. I slashed her hands with my claws, causing her to recoil. I couldn't use my power to defend myself when the non-magicals were already under the influence of a strong mind control spell, but I could legitimately use my other weapons. My murder mittens and fangs were primed and ready.

Every time a hand or leg got too near, the claws shot out and sank into flesh, causing squeals and grunts. But they kept coming. I slashed and snarled, bit and tore, but no matter how much blood I drew, nothing would slow them.

I tried to reach a window again but missed the ledge by inches. And I was tiring. Using magic to transform the others, and now this physical fight, made my muscles shake and my chest ache.

"Give up, loser." Tinkerbell sat at the back of the room, a smug expression on her furry face as she watched me get cornered. "Gus won't be happy you've injured his minions. And you don't want to be around him when he gets angry."

My sides heaved in and out as I backed away from a group of non-magicals with murder gleaming in their glazed eyes. "These people aren't yours to control. Tinkerbell, I know we've had our differences, but you must see how wrong this is."

"All I see is you interfering, as usual. You can never leave things alone. Now look where it's got you?"

I slashed at a grasping hand. "Why are you doing this? People have looked after you since you came to Crimson Cove."

"Because I can. Because I should. Why must we hide our natural ability? Gus believes it's time to shake things up."

"That never ends well for us. Read the history books." I bit a flabby calf and jumped away from a sweaty, grabby hand. The non-magicals were edging me into a corner.

"We want a new way of living."

"This isn't you," I said. "I know things in your past weren't good—"

"What do you know about my past?" Her hard gaze narrowed.

"You got in with a dark magic user. They forced you to deal with dangerously unstable power. That changes a cat."

Sparks of magic flared around her. "Keep your nose out of my past and my business. You know nothing about me. And it's a waste of time appealing to my kind side. I haven't had one of those for a long time."

"You could if you wanted." I shrieked as someone caught me by the tail and lifted me into the air.

"Finish it! Destroy that cat." Tinkerbell jumped to her paws, hatred blazing in her eyes.

"That's enough." Gus strolled into the room, Sammy on his shoulder. "Well done, Tinkerbell. Hold Juno but don't hurt her."

"You can't trust her," Tinkerbell snarled out. "You must destroy her."

"I'd never say that about you." I swung in the air, my spine complaining.

Tinkerbell tilted her head. "Even if I killed your witch?"

"Maybe then. But I'd give you a chance to plead your case. Nothing about this situation is fair." I scrabbled in the air, but the burly non-magical who'd caught me held me at arm's length. My claws had shredded his forearm, so he knew not to get too close.

Gus crouched and petted Tinkerbell then fed her a treat from his pocket. "I'm almost sad you've been captured, Juno. I hoped you'd stay out of my way. I've grown to like you and your witch. You were annoyingly good, but I had a feeling you could be turned."

I glowered at him. "Sammy, you must see supporting Gus is wrong."

"There's nothing wrong about no longer being held back," Sammy said. "That's what you did to me."

"Never! I encouraged you."

"When it suited you," Tinkerbell said. "I watched you lead Sammy around like a prize. You made him look like a lovesick fool."

I ignored Tinkerbell's jibe. "This must feel wrong to you. You have goodness running through you."

"Where did that goodness get me? The witch I was bonded with was killed because I couldn't keep her safe. And I haven't found anyone else to join with. Your pathetic attempt to bond me with the boring Barney Hoffman ended in disaster."

"I chose the wrong magic user for you, but there'll be others. When you find the right one, you'll be happy."

"I'm happy now. I've come into my true power, thanks to Gus." Sammy's eyes glowed an unnatural dull red.

"Don't feel bad you've lost Sammy to us." Gus petted Sammy's rump like he was a flea-riddled mutt. "He wasn't living up to his true potential while saddled with you. Now, he knows what he can really be, he'll become a new creature. I may even gift him some horns."

My heart broke as Sammy leaned against Gus's head. Seeing him perched on that monster's shoulder made me even more determined to break free and defeat Gus. As soon as I figured out how to get this brute's hand off of my tail without killing him or getting my tail yanked off.

"All this time, you were playing the good guy," I said to Gus. "What do you really want with Crimson Cove?"

He smiled. "For it to be mine."

"What do you need in our town that's so important to you?" I needed to stall Gus for as long as possible, while I worked on a plan to get free.

"Power. Isn't that what people always crave? And Crimson Cove is full of it."

"It's not yours to take."

"I'll take it if I want. And I do." Gus grimaced at the lingering non-magicals. "I wouldn't have put up with those things if it weren't for a juicy payoff. Now, the town is weak enough to succumb to me, and I can have what I want."

"Which is?"

His laugh was laced with ice-cold darkness. "You'll see. Take Juno and lock her in an empty coach."

I squirmed in the man's hot hand as he strode toward the door. Several more hands grabbed me, and my mouth was clamped shut by a stinky palm with long, red fingernails that dug into my skin.

Magic simmered on my toe beans, but I held it back. I should blast them with a spell and get free. But what if my magic tipped them over the edge? I couldn't be responsible for killing these non-magicals. They needed help, not more manipulation.

One coach was empty, and I was shoved inside it, the door slamming behind me.

I thrust out a spell to blast through a window, but my magic ricocheted off the glass and hit me in the side. I yelped out my discomfort, my skin stinging and the stench of burning fur flooding my booping snooter.

Knuckles rapped on the window, and Gus's face appeared. "This coach is covered in my protection spell. If you do anything to get out, I'll send it right back to you and make you sorry."

Magic flared on my paws as my anger got the better of me. "You'll regret this."

"No threats," Tinkerbell said in her most mocking tone. "Or I'll find your witch and ask her what she wants on her headstone."

"If you hurt her, I'll hunt you for the rest of time."

"That'll be fun. Enjoy what's left of your miserable life." Tinkerbell laughed, and Sammy joined in.

Footsteps drifted away, leaving me stewing in a mixture of rage, frustration, and an unhealthy splatter of fear. Tinkerbell would be sly enough to tackle Zandra, but if she did, she'd better be prepared. Even though my witch was under the influence of the sleep spell, she wouldn't go down without a vicious fight.

I hunted through the coach for a way out, but the entire vehicle was covered in Gus's icky feeling magic. If I used another spell, it would slam back and wound me.

Instead, I hunted for weapons, clues, anything to get me out of this and back to Zandra. There were candy wrappers, newspapers, abandoned purses, but nothing to use when fighting a demon. And I had no doubt that was what Gus was.

I forced open the toilet door and froze. Dumped on the floor was a pile of scaly skin.

Chapter 17

A serpent among us

The skin stank like cheesy feet. I delicately dabbed at a large piece and it stuck to my paw. The feel of it on my toe beans made me queasy as the dark magic nestled in the folds flickered to life.

I steeled myself to the unpleasant task and sorted through the pile of skin. After a few minutes of stomach-churning investigation, I found an almost complete skin suit. It was like an adult had shed a thick layer of skin or yanked it off their body and tossed it to one side. I could even see wrinkles on the forehead.

And the skin suit was a perfect fit for Gus. It couldn't be anyone else. I was dealing with a body-snatching demon.

Body snatchers took innocent individuals, killed them, then used their physical form to walk around unnoticed. Most body-snatching demons were globs of floating energy, so they needed a stable form to move around without drawing attention from Angel Force.

The dangerous magical practice of stealing another person's body was outlawed, but there were still some demons willing to do it so they could frolic and destroy without getting caught.

Gus had fooled us all with his affable helper act. He'd covered himself in the most innocuous form, pretending to be an overworked and underpaid savior to lonely old ladies who needed entertaining. He'd even helped us get everyone into the town hall. And then there was the show he'd put on of saving Old Mother Splinter, when he must have been trying to drown her after she'd seen the dark-hearted killer he truly was.

It was no surprise he'd ended her life. He'd probably have drowned her at sea, but the risk of being caught in the act had been too great. So, he'd waited until she was alone in the hospital and gotten to her at her most vulnerable.

My booping snooter wrinkled as the foul stench from the discarded skin intensified. I backed out of the toilet and shoved the door shut.

I was curious why the demon had maintained Gus's form for such a long time. Body-snatching demons needed a new body at least once a week, because the fragile physical form broke down, even when magic held everything together.

But this demon had been showing up, pretending to be Gus Bainbridge for weeks. Why? What was so special about Gus's form that meant the demon had to keep it? Why maintain the same disguise? So he could lure us into his trust, and we'd be easier to defeat?

Whatever his devious motives, I'd found him out, and it was time to stop this demon.

But first, I needed to figure out how to get out of this coach.

I edged open the toilet door again and peered inside. The waste pipe had to go somewhere. Could I squeeze through it? I shook my head. The prospect of such a mission was too foul, and I'd most likely end up locked in a container of waste. It would get me nowhere but a ruined fur coat and a mouthful of something unmentionably nasty.

"No swimming in sewage for me," I muttered as I shut the toilet door again and did a slow circuit of the coach.

I prodded the magic trapping me in, but it was strong and held firm.

Demon Gus must be worried about being defeated by me, since he was so determined to keep me trapped. And so he should. When I got my paws on it, that would be the end of this body-snatching demon.

I didn't need to worry about hurting the original Gus when the final fight began. He'd have died the second the demon set its sights on him.

I did two more circuits of the coach before my gaze landed on the air-conditioning vent. That must lead outside. Since I couldn't use magic to break out of this metal prison, I'd do things the old-fashioned way.

After jumping onto the seat closest to the vent, I coiled and leaped. I dug my paws into the vent slots and pulled back. The vent cover buckled but remained in place.

It took some negotiation, but I used my claws to wriggle free two of the screws. That did it, and the vent sprung free.

I dropped back onto the seat and stared at the ominous dark hole, not welcoming me inside. "That's my way out. That's my way to stop Gus."

Fortified by my pep talk, I jumped again and landed inside the vent. It was a tight fit. Maybe I'd put on a pound or two in the last few months. Vorana's food was excellent, and I often had seconds. And Sorcha always gave me extra-large portions at her café. Perhaps I should take up jogging to get back to my slender form.

I grimaced. So long as I didn't get stuck in here, I was perfect just as I was. And Sammy always said he liked something to squeeze.

Sammy. My poor fluffy friend was in league with a demon. How had that happened?

I wriggled and clawed, kicked and shimmied as I made my way along the length of the coach. Pale light filtered through another vent.

I hadn't thought through how I'd exit and had entered the vent headfirst, but my back legs were better for kicking, and I needed to use them to break through the vent.

When my booping snooter hit the grill, I peered through it. There was no sign of Gus or any non-magicals. The other coaches had gone, and the place was eerily quiet. It was so unlike the Crimson Cove I knew and loved.

After head-butting the vent grill several times and achieving nothing other than a sore head, despite the fluffy padding, I stopped to reassess. I leaned my weight against it, but it did nothing.

I was just figuring out if I had enough room to turn when my bond with Zandra pinged.

There she was! At the end of the street. What was my wonderful witch doing outside the protection of Angel Force? Gus could capture her. He knew we were poking around in his business, and he wouldn't hesitate to destroy her.

I tugged on our bond, and she stopped, her head snapping up.

"Juno!"

I tugged again, and she changed direction and headed toward the coach.

"Hey! Up here. I'm inside the air vent."

Zandra looked around, confusion in her eyes, until she discovered where the vent was. "What are you doing in there?"

"What are you doing out of Angel Force? You can barely stand."

Zandra leaned against the coach then grimaced and stepped back. "I had no choice. Finn fell asleep, then so did Elijah. Then something weird happened. Tinkerbell showed up. She went around the office checking all the angels to make sure they were asleep."

"Did she do anything to them?"

"No. Other than grumbling to herself as she looked around, that was it. What was she up to?"

"Did she touch you?"

"I faked being asleep. It was an effort to get my eyes open again when she left, but I knew I needed to move."

"I'm glad you did. Tinkerbell is in on this, too. She's connected to the demon who's doing this. And that demon is Gus Bainbridge."

Zandra pursed her lips, looking even more confused. "The coach tour guy?"

"He tricked us. He's a body-snatching demon. Get me out of here, and I'll tell you everything." I thumped the vent.

Zandra pressed a hand against the side of the coach. "What magic is surrounding this? It feels gross."

"It's a spell from Gus to keep me trapped in here. Any spell I use to break my way out repels and injures me. That's why I crawled through the air vent. I figured I could get out this way, but the screws are on the outside."

Zandra peered up at the vent. "Yeah, I see them. Give me a minute. I'll get you out."

As worried as I was for my witch's safety, I was thrilled we were back together.

Five minutes later, the air vent popped. Zandra must have grabbed something to stand on because she reached into the vent with ease and lifted me out.

Neither of us moved for several seconds as we hugged each other. I had my paws on her shoulders, and my forehead was jammed against hers. It felt amazing to breathe in my witch's familiar scent.

"So, Gus is the demon we've been hunting?" Zandra lifted her head, her eyes half-closed. "How'd that happen?"

I scraped my raspy tongue across her cheek several times, and she grimaced. "Stay awake and I'll tell you all about it."

"I'm awake. Kinda. Go on. I'm listening."

"When Gus didn't freak out about Sammy having a conversation with him, I knew something was wrong."

"Sammy is working with a demon?"

"It appears so. So is Tinkerbell. They're helping Gus. That's why Tinkerbell came to Angel Force. Gus needs the angels out of action."

"Why are they helping him? It makes no sense." My booping snooter wrinkled. "I haven't figured that out."

"Sammy is one of the good ones. They must have been forced into helping. Maybe the demon threatened to hurt you if Sammy didn't join him?"

The brief flicker of hope I felt died. Sammy knew I was powerful, and he wouldn't risk himself to keep me safe. "Whatever the reason, he's involved."

Zandra sensed my sadness because she gave me several gentle head kisses and hugged me tightly for a second. "You'll sort things out with Sammy. How did you figure out a body-snatching demon took over Gus's form, though? When they're concealed, they're impossible to detect."

"The pile of gross skins discarded in the coach toilet gave it away," I said. "Whoever this demon is, it used Gus's form to visit Crimson Cove so it could get its unpleasant plan into place."

Zandra climbed down, keeping me in her arms. "What does the demon want?"

"Something to do with power. It wants what Crimson Cove has, but I couldn't get any more than that out of it."

"It's weakening the magic users who live here, so it can take our power?"

"It must need the power for something. It won't be anything good." I inspected my witch's tired expression. "Do you need a break? I can find somewhere safe for you to hide."

"Not in this town. Not if a demon is about to unleash its gross plan on us."

I didn't want Zandra at risk, but I couldn't leave her alone. There had to be somewhere I could hide her where she wouldn't be in any danger.

"Stop thinking so hard. It makes you look constipated." Zandra kissed my head again.

"Maybe you should go to the bookstore. Sage can guard you."

"Uh-uh. We stick together. We always do. Demon Gus is deadly, but we can stop it together." Zandra stifled a yawn. "And I'll fight this magic, but I'm not sure how much longer I can keep going."

"Then hide!"

"Nope. I'm with you."

I loved my witch, but she was infuriating. "Then take my bangle."

She eyed the multi-colored band around my neck. "What's so special about this thing?"

I hesitated. "It has power."

"And?"

"That's the only important thing you need to know right now. It helped Vorana. It can help you. Take it."

She eased it off my neck and tugged it onto her wrist.

I stared into her face. "How do you feel?"

"The same. No, maybe better. Less sleepy. What you got in this bangle, Juno?"

"It's old. If it helps you, keep it."

"This'll keep me awake?"

"It'll slow things down. Oh! And Randal says pain keeps you focused."

Her eyes widened. "He's still awake?"

"He was the last time I saw him. Randal helped create the foul potion that encouraged the non-magicals to leave Crimson Cove. But he was working flat out to keep the magic wards stable."

She tugged on the ends of her hair. "You think the demon is behind the ward's instability, too?"

"It could be. It wants Crimson Cove vulnerable. Take down our wards to distract us, then we won't notice some sneaky demon creeping its malevolence through town."

Zandra's gaze drifted along the street toward animal control. "But Randal is fixing things?"

"He's good, but the sleep spell has gotten him. He could be asleep by now."

"Barney? Glenda? Anyone else awake at animal control?"

"No. Randal took them all to the hospital."

"If we were at full strength, I'd consider tackling this demon on our own—"

"But we aren't. Far from it. The angels are out. And Elijah told me Sorcha's asleep."

"We can't risk Vorana. That's if she's even still going," Zandra said. "But let's start at the bookstore and see how they're doing."

She stagger-walked along with me in her arms. I dug my claws into her shoulder.

"Hey! I know I'm dopey, but I won't drop you. You don't need to hold on so tight."

"Pain will focus your attention. I'm doing this for your own good." I also didn't want to get dumped in the dirt if Zandra fell asleep while standing.

She grunted her disapproval but stopped complaining.

We reached the bookstore to find the front door open. Vorana was slumped in a seat, her eyes shut and her mouth hanging open. Sage lay across her lap, also asleep.

I jumped out of Zandra's arms and dashed to my furry friend. "Sage!"

She didn't stir.

"I think the sleep spell is affecting familiars, too," Zandra said. "Elijah went down fast."

"We've been immune until now. Demon Gus even bragged about the brilliant plan to affect only magic users, so their familiars would be too panicked to notice what it was up to." I nudged Sage several times, but she wouldn't stir. This was no normal slumber. The magic had weaved its cruelty around her.

"Let's try the hospital," Zandra said. "Now we know the source of the spell, it could help the doctors figure out how to reverse things."

"I'll take us there." I touched her calf with a paw, cast translocation magic, and we arrived outside the hospital.

When we got inside, the place looked like a whirlwind had blasted through it. Chairs and beds were scattered around, takeout mugs of coffee discarded, and doors stood open.

"That's the doctor we spoke to." Zandra pointed to a tousled haired, middle-aged guy slumped over a gurney, fast asleep.

My heart sank as I padded along the corridor beside Zandra. Each room revealed beds occupied by sleeping people. Some had their familiars with them; others were alone. All the familiars were asleep.

"I hear something," Zandra said. "This way."

We hurried along the corridor and into a small room at the far end. Amenia was still awake! Her wings drooped, as did her antenna, but she was moving.

Her head lifted when she heard us. "Juno! My babies, they couldn't wake them."

"The sleeping spell is getting everyone," I said. "Your children, they're not..."

"Alive, they are. But still sleeping. Stable they seem, but I'm not sure for how much longer. I haven't seen a nurse or doctor for hours."

"How are you still awake?" Zandra said.

"Force of will. I'd never abandon my babies. And you?"

"I'd never abandon Juno."

I leaned against my witch. "Amenia, we need your help, but it means leaving your children for a short time. There's a body-snatching demon in town. It's enthralling the non-magicals and sending everyone else to sleep. If we don't bring it down, Crimson Cove and everyone in it will be finished."

Amenia stared at the bed where her children lay. "If the demon wins, my children will never grow up."

"Does that mean you'll help?"

Her wings lifted. "With you, I am. What do we need to do to destroy this monster?"

Chapter 18

Weapons at the ready

The clock hands slid past midnight as we entered the basement at Vorana's house.

"Stay standing and do jumping jacks," I said to Zandra as she staggered to the bottom of the stairs and headed for her bed.

"Coffee. I need coffee," she whispered.

"More than that, you need," Amenia said. "I kept zapping myself with a strange paddle-shaped device in the hospital. I pressed a button, made it hum, and then stuck it against my abdomen. Violently unpleasant, it was, but stayed awake, I did."

"You mean a defibrillator?" Zandra slowly blinked. "That could have killed you."

"More than a little electricity it will take to destroy this magnificent form," Amenia said. "Have one here, do you? Use it to stay awake, we could."

"No zapping my witch with killer jolts of electricity," I said. "Keep jumping, Zandra."

Zandra sluggishly moved her arms and legs as if swatting slow-moving flies. "The chest is unlocked, although I don't know what I've got in there that we can use to defeat Demon Gus."

"When Adrienne gifted you this magic-filled chest, she knew what she was doing." I hurried to the chest and shoved up the lid. "She gave you the tools to ensure you could achieve great things."

"Or maybe she got lucky when hunting in thrift stores."

"Your mother is far from faultless, but she got this right."

"Do that for my children, I'd like to. Give them the tools to be fearless and powerful. Sounds incredible, your mother does," Amenia said.

"Yeah, she's something else. She's also a ghoul."

"How intriguing." Amenia fluttered to the chest full of spell books, potions, magically enchanted items, and more.

Ever since we'd discovered the chest stored in Adrienne's attic, Zandra had been exploring the contents and seeing what the objects could do.

I set aside a phoenix wand, an ember cat's eye stone, and a vial of marauder potion. "There has to be something in here we can use to defeat this demon."

"Know the demon's name, do you?" Amenia said. "Many I've met over the years. If we had its name, we'd have power over it."

"No names. It uses Gus. That's the name of the guy whose skin it's wearing."

"Have you seen its natural form?"

I burrowed through the box, lifting out more items and placing them on the floor. "No. And that's bothering me. A body-snatching demon takes physical form to hide in plain sight, but it must renew its vessel regularly."

"At least once a week, before everything breaks down and they smell funky," Zandra said.

"Which makes me think whatever is hiding inside Gus's physical form is immensely powerful. They've kept the same form for a long time."

"Demon Gus has been visiting Crimson Cove for weeks. It first showed up at the animal sanctuary, didn't it?" Zandra sloppily jumped about.

"For all we know, it could have been visiting for longer than that. Perhaps it settled on Gus's form because it would give the demon an easy in. None of us questioned the friendly coach tour guide. This whole time, it was using Gus as cover to set its plans in motion."

"Another option, there is," Amenia said. "The demon could be stuck."

"It can shed its skin," I said. "That must help Demon Gus keep its disguise intact."

"Painful, that must be," Amenia said. "This demon sounds like a remarkable creature. Hateful and I want it dead but still remarkable."

"Remarkable and deadly," Zandra said. "And we need to get it out of here."

"And destroy it," Amenia said. "My children are my life. That creature put them at risk, so pay, it must."

"The demon will pay when we destroy it. What about this?" I pointed to an enchanted arachnid net. "If we cover it in the net, we can slow the demon."

"We need to slow it then reveal its true form," Amenia said. "I've destroyed demons."

"One this powerful?"

She sniffed. "Maybe not."

"Once we know its name, we'll have the power to control it. Then we can find out what it really wants with Crimson Cove," I said.

"Maybe it wants all of you," Amenia said. "Whenever I visit, overwhelmed by the immense power radiating from this town, I am."

I turned to face her. "On this visit, you said there was something strange about the energy. That must have been the demon tainting our magic."

"Yes, unpleasant, it was. My children felt it, too. This demon has been in the area for some time, weaving its malevolent desire through your foundations like a toxic weed. It intends to make this place crumble and bend to its will."

"Not now we know what it's up to."

Zandra shuffled over and inspected the items I'd laid out. "None of these will destroy such a powerful creature."

Amenia nodded. "Agree, I do. Conned you all, has this demon. No one noticed anything was wrong until it was too late. You can't defeat such a beast with basic spells and charms."

"These aren't basic." I hissed at her. "We know what we're doing."

"It might not be enough," Zandra said.

I hesitated, my gaze on the items. "If it wasn't for Old Mother Splinter seeing through the demon's disguise and it killing her, alerting us something weird was going on, it would have swept through the town, taking whatever it desired. We need something more powerful." I stared into the chest, but nothing inspiring revealed itself.

"What about your power?" Amenia fluttered around my head.

"Juno is strong," Zandra said. "Have you got something up your fluffy sleeve?"

"Old is your magic," Amenia said. "You must have seen a few demons like this over the decades."

"Juno's not that old." Zandra grinned as she swung her arms. "Although there could be a few grey furs among that white fluff."

I slid a pointed look at Amenia. She needed to stop talking.

She didn't take my hint. "Holding back, you are. Draw out something deadly and defeat this demon."

"Um... what are you expecting Juno to draw out that's so deadly?" Zandra slowed.

"Keep marching," I said. "You sit, and you'll sleep."

She huffed out a breath but stepped up the pace.

Amenia fluttered to Zandra. "Bangle magic can restrain and trap."

Zandra inspected the bangle on her wrist. "This thing! I still don't know what's so special about it."

"It contains ancient magic, but that magic can be unreliable." I glared at Amenia, willing her into silence. "It doesn't always work when I need it to."

"Convince it to work, you will," Amenia said. "My children's lives are at risk. Worthy cause to fight for, that is."

"What we've got here could be enough." I examined the items again.

We needed a boost of something special, but it had been a long time since I had all my power, and I was doubting myself. My magic was prone to mis-function and now wasn't the time for it to fail.

"Juno, powerful you are," Amenia said. "Defeat anything you set your mind to, you can."

"Whatever you're packing in this bangle, I'm willing to back you," Zandra said. "The way I'm feeling, my power isn't up to much if we have to go toe-to-toe with the demon."

"Give me a moment. I'll see what I can do with it." I gently tugged the bangle off Zandra's wrist, walked into a corner, and turned my back on Amenia and Zandra. I closed my eyes and centered myself, focusing on the magic.

You must be unsettled by what's going on. I never meant to abandon you. You were taken by force and thrust into this object without your consent. It must have been a shock.

The bangle warmed and shivered against my toe beans.

But I need you to trust me. That's a lot to ask, given what happened to us, but we must remain loyal to each other. This place is in terrible danger. If we let this demon take over, it'll warp the power in Crimson Cove into something toxic. It could be a threat to thousands of magic users.

The bangle trembled again.

"Anything we can help with, Juno?" Zandra said.

"I'm good. Just thinking things through."

"The time for thinking is over," Amenia said. "Act now, we must, if we're to defeat this demon."

"One more minute." I kept my eyes closed and focused on the bangle.

My intentions are pure, but I need you in this battle. If you don't wish to stay with me after that, you can leave. I'll miss you, but I understand if you wish to merge with another magic user. This fight matters. It's not about amassing a fortune or gaining territory. This is about keeping people safe.

"Clock ticking, it is," Amenia said.

The magic in the bangle flared to life, starting at the tip of my booping snooter and moving to the end of my tail. I shuddered as old power flooded over me, seeping through my fur and into my skin.

"Juno! You're glowing," Zandra said.

"Released her old power, she did," Amenia said. "Proud of her, I am. Fight there still is in this old creature."

"She's really not that old," Zandra said. "I was teasing about the grey fur."

"Know your familiar as well as you think, do you?"

"Not now, Amenia." I shook out my fur, my skin tingling. I whispered a silent thank you to my magic. Maybe it wouldn't stay with me long, but with this energy flooding through me, I was convinced we could beat the demon.

I inspected the bangle. It still held something back, and magic lingered inside it. I flipped it over my head. When I turned, Zandra had her hands on her hips. She arched an eyebrow, waiting for an explanation.

I didn't meet her gaze. "Let's find Gus and ask him some questions."

Zandra's expression was full of caution. "You sure you've got a handle on that power? Your eyes have changed color, and you have a shimmer of white all around you. I can tell that magic is not to be messed with."

I blinked several times. "It's temporary. You know what magic is like. All kinds of interesting side effects. I'll do a location spell to find Demon Gus."

Zandra still looked at me with caution in her eyes as we assembled, and I cast the spell.

Amenia zoomed around the shimmering map of Crimson Cove that had appeared. "Oh! Everywhere, he is."

Zandra's forehead furrowed. "Did you do that spell right? It looks like there are dozens of demons in Crimson Cove."

"We're not just seeing Demon Gus. We're seeing its energy." I studied the three dozen tiny dots that revealed demon power had seeped into every corner of town.

Zandra inspected the dots. "All this time, it was only one demon doing so much damage?" She blew out a breath. "We need reinforcements."

"What we need is to destroy this demon once and for all," I said. "Let's see if I can find Tinkerbell or Sammy. They're most likely with the demon."

"And then obliterate it, we will," Amenia said.

"Absolutely." An enormous yawn overtook me.

Zandra rested a hand on my head. "Juno, you feeling tired?"

Despite just having been gifted with a flood of power, my eyelids felt heavy. "It's nothing."

"It's something," Zandra said. "Hurry! Let's find Sammy and Tinkerbell before the sleep spell gets as all."

I cast another location spell and got a hit on the fluffies. "They're at the old apothecary shop."

"That's been closed since we moved here," Zandra said. "Who owns it?"

"No clue. But it's the perfect base for a demon to cast its final devious plans without anyone noticing," I said.

"Then let's go ask Demon Gus what it's playing at and stamp all over those ambitions." Zandra staggered to the stairs and heaved herself up.

I raced ahead of her, Amenia fluttering behind. I dodged onto the porch and ran into Bertoli. I bounced off his legs and crashed into Zandra, who'd emerged behind me.

"Bertoli! Greetings! And welcome home. You're finally back from your spa retreat."

"Looks like." He peered along the silent street. "What's going on? I saw your light, but you're the first people I've seen awake since I got back."

"There's a situation we're dealing with," I said. "How do you feel?"

"Good." Bertoli tugged on his shirt sleeves. "I'm glad I've seen you, Juno. We need to talk."

"Later. Much later. There are bigger issues to fix." This wasn't the time to work through Bertoli's enchantment, his unexpected spa session, or the fact I had anything to do with it. "Now, you have two choices. You can help us save Crimson Cove, or you can get out of the way."

He remained in our path, his wings fluttering. "What are you talking about?"

"There's a body-snatching demon in town," Zandra said. "And it's taken over the form of a non-magical. We believe the demon has been messing with the magic wards and bringing non-magicals into town to disrupt things. Its latest trick was to cast a powerful sleep spell."

Bertoli's tidy eyebrows rose. "That explains the old boy I found asleep in the street. I thought he was sick or drunk, but I couldn't wake him. I took him to the hospital, and the place was in chaos."

"That's all thanks to the demon," I said. "Do you want to help us take it down? It would make Cythera happy."

He nodded. "Tell me what to do."

I jerked back. "You're not going to argue or tell me I'm being reckless?"

Bertoli let out a gentle sigh. "My thermal spa treatment was thorough. I got talking therapy and signed up for mindset work while I was there. That's why I've been gone so long. It helped me to see I didn't always behave as rationally as I could."

Zandra and I stared at him with open mouths. Was Bertoli a reformed character? There was no time to ponder if this angel was an ally or if this change was temporary.

"Follow us. I'll give you the short version of what's been going on," I said.

Bertoli fell into step beside me as we dashed toward the old apothecary store.

"As you know, we've been dealing with issues with the magic wards and the unwanted attention of non-magicals," I said. "Then Old Mother Splinter was pulled from the sea by Gus Bainbridge after she went for a swim. We thought she was okay, but she died in the hospital. She died from a sleep spell."

"That this demon cast upon the town?"

"You got it. To begin with, I wondered if it was the scarabs. They're known for their mischief." I nodded at Amenia.

"Not us," Amenia said. "My children are sick, too."

"We also investigated Old Mother Splinter's estranged husband and her toy boy as suspects. They checked out."

"All this time, we overlooked Gus," Zandra said. "It wasn't until Juno found Gus talking to Sammy that she realized something was different about him."

"And I found an enormous pile of skin the demon had shed," I said. "That's when I knew what manner of devious creature we were dealing with."

"Why is it doing this?" Bertoli jogged beside us.

"Reason unknown." I stumbled ungracefully over my paws and almost landed on my booping snooter.

"You're suffering because of the sleep spell, too?" Bertoli said.

"We all are," Zandra said. "You will be, too, soon. The most powerful magic users can fight it, and the doctors slowed the spell's progression, but they're all asleep."

"What happens when the sleep spell takes hold of you?" Bertoli asked.

"Old Mother Splinter slipped into a coma and died," I said. "Everyone will go the same way if we don't find out what magic the demon cast."

"Which is why we plan on obliterating it," Amenia said.

"Not recommended," Bertoli said. "Angels arrest criminals. We don't kill them."

"Leave, you can, if you won't help." She fluttered around his head.

"It's a demon! Intent on destroying Crimson Cove and killing everyone who lives here," I said. "That warrants lethal force."

"Nothing warrants lethal force," Bertoli said.

"No good in it, there is," Amenia said. "Why keep alive something so rotten?"

"So it pays for its crimes."

"The demon can pay by dying," I said. "Best thing for it."

Zandra hummed under her breath. "My family has worked with many demons over the centuries. Sometimes, they're not all bad."

I jerked back my head and stared up at her in astonishment. "You're forgetting the demon Tempest dealt with most of her life."

"I've not forgotten. I still carry a tiny piece of Frank with me."

Bertoli stared at Zandra. "You're part demon?"

"No. And that's a long story for another time," I said. "Frank the demon made Tempest miserable."

"And he occasionally saved her life," Zandra said.

"When he wasn't trying to kill Aurora," I said. "Demons pretend to be good, but they never will be. And they always want something in exchange for that façade of goodness."

"Tempest came across a few who were helpful. Maybe Bertoli should arrest this demon. Besides, we can't kill it before we know everything. Maybe this demon has more planned for Crimson Cove."

"I'm on your side," Bertoli said. "We restrain and question. No killing."

I wasn't happy my witch had agreed with the angel and not me. I'd only ever heard awful stories about the demons the Crypt witches imprisoned. Still, now wasn't the time to argue with my wonderful witch.

We reached the empty apothecary store and stood on the other side of the road, watching for signs of life.

A light flicked on in a back room.

I cast another location spell, which confirmed Tinkerbell and Sammy were still inside. There was also a dot suggesting Demon Gus was there, too, but because its malevolent energy was so prevalent across Crimson Cove, it was hard to get a fix.

"We'll sneak around the back, break in, and grab Gus," I whispered.

"I can take him," Bertoli said.

I snorted. "You have no idea what kind of demon you're dealing with. This beast is in a league of its own."

"I'm also in a league of my own. During my spa sessions, I had hypnotherapy and focused on improving my confidence and self-worth."

I hid a smirk. "Which is wonderful, but now's not the time to pretend you're a superhero."

Bertoli pulled back his shoulders. "I can be anything I want to be. All I have to do is believe. And you putting up barriers to my success is unhelpful." He marched to the front of the apothecary store.

Zandra dashed after him, and after an exasperated sigh, I followed with Amenia beside me.

"Idiot, is this angel?" Amenia whispered.

"More like misguided and slow on the uptake. Be ready if Gus tries to tear off his head."

Bertoli knocked on the door.

"Stop! You can't let them know we're here," I said. "You're ruining everything."

"I'm showing this demon I'm not afraid. I'm sure the creature will be reasonable when it sees it's outnumbered and you have an angel in charge."

"I'm sure the demon will blast Bertoli into a million pieces," Zandra muttered to me. "We should get out of here while we can. Figure out another way to bring down Gus."

We were inching away when footsteps approached the door, and Gus pulled it open.

Bertoli squared his shoulders and his wings flared. "Gus... The demon? You're under arrest."

Chapter 19

Best laid plans

Gus's black gaze moved from Bertoli to us. He laughed, the tone mocking. "Shall I hold out my hands, so you can shackle me?"

"I'd appreciate that." Bertoli missed the sarcasm. "You've done wrong, and it's time to pay for your crime."

"What crimes would they be?" Gus held out his hand. "I don't think we've met."

Bertoli went to shake it, but I jumped and scratched him. "This demon can't be trusted."

"He's being reasonable. He knows he's in the wrong." Bertoli yanked his hand away and inspected the scratch marks made by my claws.

"I'm a terrible creature and need to be reformed." Gus's gaze shifted over Bertoli's shoulder.

I turned and discovered a small army of non-magicals lurking close by. They swayed and groaned like they were more walking dead than living non-magicals. "Release them from your power."

"Make me. They're the perfect tools. Why would I want to get rid of something so biddable?"

"Because you're killing them!"

Demon Gus shrugged. "At least I give them a purpose. Restrain the angel and his companions. Keep them out of my way until I'm finished."

The non-magicals lurched toward us.

Bertoli yelped and batted away their hands as they grabbed him. "Stop that! Behave! There's no need to do that. Ouch! My wings are sensitive. How are you even seeing my wings?" He looked at me with a bewildered expression on his face.

The non-magicals focused on Bertoli as he squeaked and shoved, but he used no magic. He was a well-trained angel and knew how dangerous it was to inflict even the lightest of angel magic on someone with no power.

"Revenge, we will have." Amenia shrieked and shot toward Gus, magic blazing from her antenna.

The magic slammed into Demon Gus, and he stepped back. His hand shot out, and he grabbed her. "You have power. Although it's been weakened by my slumber spell. Perhaps we should work together."

She fizzed and shrieked, squirming in his grip. "Dark heart, you have. Never work with that."

Demon Gus tilted his head from side to side. "What if I bring your children out of their eternal slumber? I'm sure you can turn some of that sly power toward my ambitions and still have time to enjoy life."

"Don't do it," I cautioned Amenia. "Demon Gus can't be trusted. It's been lying to us ever since it arrived in Crimson Cove."

"My word is my bond." Demon Gus pressed its free hand to its heart. "What about you, Juno? With power so old, you must have come across a hint of darkness over the years. It tastes incredible, doesn't it? Makes you want to get down and party while crushing a few skulls."

"Juno is going nowhere with you," Zandra said. "Neither is Amenia, right?"

Amenia had stopped squirming, her antenna quivering. "My babies will be safe?"

"It's manipulating you," I said. "Demon Gus knows it can't win if we stick together."

"But my children—"

"Won't be safe if they're under a demon's command. You don't want your children to grow up with dark hearts and menacing minds. You want them to be free to play and enjoy life."

"I enjoy life," Demon Gus said. "Or I will once I finish what I started. Join me, all of you, and we'll be magnificent. You can even bring your witch, so long as she promises not to take me to her family's prison."

Bertoli yelped as he was buried under a pile of non-magical bodies and they hit the ground.

"Old Mother Splinter saw straight through you," I said to Demon Gus. "She recognized the falsehoods you told. That was why you killed her."

"Is that so? Maybe she was just too irritating and self-satisfied to remain alive. Some people deserve to die."

"You admit you did it?"

Demon Gus smirked. "You're forgetting, I was the hero and pulled her from the water after that foolish old crone went night swimming. I almost drowned. She weighed a ton."

"She was under your influence. Had you already cast a sleep spell on her before she went swimming?"

"Does it matter? She's gone."

"Because of what you did to her."

"Old Mother Splinter was weak and past her prime. It was simply her time to go."

"She'd have lived many more years if it hadn't been for your interference. You murdered her so you could keep your devious plan going."

"Will somebody help me?" Bertoli was just visible beneath the non-magicals. They weren't hurting him, just keeping him pinned to the ground.

"Bring him here." Demon Gus clicked its fingers, and the non-magicals dragged Bertoli over. "Kneel. I have no use for an angel, but those wings will fetch a pretty price. Minus the body, of course."

"Leave Bertoli alone," I growled.

Demon Gus slid a large hunting knife out of the back of its pants. "You don't even like him. I thought you'd be pleased I wanted him dead."

"My feelings about Bertoli are unimportant. He's one of the good guys."

"You don't consider him good when he's hassling you. I see you, Juno. I've watched you while I've been here. You have your own way of doing things, and if someone doesn't approve, you're unhappy."

Demon Gus turned the knife slowly and inspected the tip.

Zandra zapped out a spell, but in her weakened state, it barely touched Demon Gus.

It waggled a finger in the air. "There's no need for unkindness. I've been a benevolent demon whilst here."

"There's nothing good about messing with our wards, bringing in non-magicals, and sending everyone to sleep." I stood in front of Zandra to keep her safe.

Red flickered in Demon Gus's eyes. "Perhaps I'll burn this place to the ground. It has been more trying than I thought it would."

"Because we don't want demons ruining our town."

"Bored now." Demon Gus squeezed Amenia in his fist and tossed her to one side. She landed on the ground and didn't move. "Your attempts at resistance are over. I have everything I need." It pressed the knife against Bertoli's wing.

"I don't believe you! There's something you need before you can get what you want." My gaze flicked over Gus. The demon looked tired, its edges frayed. "We know you're a body snatching demon, yet you stayed in the same body all this time. That must be painful."

Anger lit an unnatural gleam in Demon Gus's gaze. "Things will change when the time is right."

"Not here. We plan to keep Crimson Cove exactly as it is."

"Even your friends?" Demon Gus stepped back and made a come here gesture with its hand.

Sammy and Tinkerbell staggered out of the apothecary store, their eyes bleary and movements sluggish.

"What have you done to them?" I took a step toward Sammy, but he hissed at me.

"Showed you things must change. You thought you had it so good with Sammy, your obedient little pet, but look at him." Demon Gus tapped the knife on top of Bertoli's head.

"He was much more than that to me. Sammy, what's wrong?"

"You're here. That's what's wrong." Sammy blinked and yawned.

I flinched. "You cast the sleep spell over them, too. Why?"

Demon Gus nudged Sammy with its foot. "These two have served their purpose."

"Monster! Sammy, fight the sleep spell. You're strong, so I know you can do it. Don't let the demon beat you."

Sammy yawned again. "You can't tell me what to do anymore."

"You want to live, don't you?"

"He doesn't want to live if it means putting up with you," Tinkerbell said. "You've been a nuisance since you moved to Crimson Cove. No one wants you here."

"I love this place almost as much as I love my witch, and I'll fight to stop any darkness from taking over."

"You fight as long as you like, but you've already lost," Demon Gus said. "I have an army of obedient non-magicals who I know you won't dare hurt. I have powerful familiars doing my bidding, despite what I do to them, and everyone else is weak or asleep. Even you, Juno. I see it in your sluggish movements. My magic is too powerful to resist."

"Let's get rid of her," Tinkerbell said. "Take out the trash and move on."

My paws grew leaden, and I stamped my feet to keep the circulation going, hissing at Tinkerbell to let her know if she made a move, I'd crush her. "You almost got away with it. Your good guy act had us fooled."

Demon Gus smirked. "I did get away with it. I own Crimson Cove, and soon I'll absorb all its power."

"People won't give you their power."

"If any are still awake to refuse me, they'll die. Their deaths won't be painful. They'll slip into an eternal slumber." Demon Gus spread its hands, pointing the knife at the sky. "I'll look after what's left of Crimson Cove, if that makes you feel better."

"I'll feel better when you're obliterated."

"Language! You'll upset a demon by talking about something so disagreeable."

"She's like that," Tinkerbell said. "Juno talks about kindness and doing the right thing but only when it suits her."

I glanced over my shoulder, and my heart froze. Zandra had sunk to her knees, and her head was down.

I raced to my witch and thumped my paws on her knees. "Stay with me. You can't go to sleep. We're close to defeating this demon."

"Are you? Really? Your scarab sidekick is unconscious, your angel is about to lose his wings, and your witch is unresponsive. What else have you got? Not Sammy," Demon Gus said.

My focus was on Zandra as Gus taunted me, my head throbbing and my heart aching. "I can't lose you. We've got so much to do together. There's so much I want to show you."

"Juno, look past your panic and see what you're missing. This witch bond you have was only temporary. You have bigger plans than spending your life in this boring little town, doing boring little things, with boring little people."

I hissed at Demon Gus. "You can't think it's that boring, since you want to take everything in Crimson Cove."

"I want the power, not to set up home and pass the time gossiping about local trivia over a mug of sugary coffee."

I was done with this demon. I sent a silent, powerful intention to the bangle around my neck, and the magic flared to life, just as I hoped it would. This was all I had. If this didn't get Zandra on her feet, nothing would. And if I lost my witch, I may as well lay down and submit to this demon.

The bangle didn't resist as I removed it from around my neck and placed it on Zandra's wrist. I dropped my paws over it.

"Take your time to say a final farewell, but then you must choose," Demon Gus said. "An incredible life with me or death."

"We don't want her," Tinkerbell said. "She's a troublemaker."

"We can find something useful for her to do. What will it be, Juno?"

I ignored Demon Gus and Tinkerbell and focused on Zandra. The bond between us pulsed erratically. She was fighting, but it felt like she was losing the battle.

My magic had to work. I breathed in and out, keeping the bond active. A wave of power shifted from the bangle and across Zandra's torso. I knew it had been holding something back.

Zandra's eyes flicked open, and she blinked. "What's going on?"

"Stay awake! And keep out of the way of Demon Gus," I whispered.

Zandra blinked and smacked her lips together. "Why do I feel so strange?"

"Go with it. It'll keep you alert."

She shook her head. Her eyes glowed as her gaze flicked to Gus. "Got it. We focus on bringing down this demon."

"Ah! Interesting. What power is this you're wearing? Not Crypt witch magic. It's something else." Demon Gus licked a finger and raised it in the air. "This'll be fun."

Zandra staggered to her feet. "Not for you."

"Reveal your true form." I leaned against Zandra's leg. "There's no need to hide anything from us. We know your secret."

Demon Gus clenched the knife in one fist. "I will, soon enough."

"It must be exhausting, maintaining the same body. What's so special about the original Gus's form that you kept him for so long?" My gaze roved over the demon.

"Maybe I find this form appealing. I'll change when I'm ready."

I shook my head. "Amenia was right. You can't change. You're stuck as Gus. That's why you're here. You need Crimson Cove's power to get free from that skin suit you've gotten wedged inside."

Zandra's eyebrows rose, and she hooted a laugh. "The demon messed up its own spell and got trapped as a non-magical?"

Demon Gus bared its teeth. "What if I did? I'll be free soon enough."

"It doesn't look like you're going anywhere," I said. "You picked Gus because of his job. It's the perfect disguise, allowing you to travel in and out of Crimson Cove to set things up. But what happened? He wore out and when you looked for a new vessel, you couldn't get free? How did he trap you if you're such a powerful demon?"

"Show some respect," Tinkerbell hissed.

Demon Gus stabbed the knife into the wooden door frame, and smoke drifted from its nostrils. "This dumb body had a hint of magic in it. I didn't know when I took it, since it was dormant. But then... something happened."

"Oh! Gus's ancestors must have had magic," I said. "You made a mistake by picking him."

The demon shrugged. "It's of no consequence."

"It kind of is since you're trapped and slowly dying in a suit of skin you stole," Zandra said.

"Enough! Sammy, Tinkerbell, destroy Juno and her witch. I won't look at them for another second." Demon Gus sounded petulant, disappointed we knew the truth about its humiliating situation.

Sammy and Tinkerbell crouched, moving apart in a semi-circle, their eyes black and hisses issuing from their mouths.

I stepped in front of Zandra again, but she nudged me aside and stood beside me. "I can't expect you to take down your former furry snuggle buddy. I'll deal with Sammy."

"I can do it. He's not the Sammy I once knew."

"You still care for him, though."

"I won't let that get in the way of stopping him." I stretched my murder mittens. Zandra came first. My heart may bruise if I injured Sammy, but I wouldn't let her be harmed.

Zandra also crouched, her gaze on Sammy and Tinkerbell, who skulked ever closer, taking their time. Her hand rested on my head, and although no words passed between us, I understood the meaning behind the touch. We were a team. We helped each other. I wasn't just her protector. She was also mine.

I drew strength from that pure, steadfast love. "Do you plan on prancing for much longer? We have a demon to take down."

Tinkerbell growled. "The smug witch is mine. You deal with Juno."

Sammy nodded. The cold-steeled gaze he settled on me made my gut clench. But he didn't pounce. I'd expected him to blast magic at me, but he just stared at me. It was more unsettling. What was going through his mind? Did he still care for me? Was he having doubts about the side he was on?

"We've got this," Zandra whispered to me. "Remember, together, we can achieve anything."

My heart thudded with a mixture of fear and adrenaline as Tinkerbell lunged at Zandra. I hit Tinkerbell in mid-air, and we slammed to the dirt in a bundle of claws and teeth, hissing and snarling.

A spell exploded close to my ear, sending a ringing blast down my spine. I rolled over, taking Tinkerbell with me, my claws latched onto her belly.

She howled and blasted a scatter of repulsive-smelling magic. It stank of disease and death.

"Zandra! Look out!" I yelled.

She was already ducking, avoiding the worst of the spell.

I pinned Tinkerbell for a second. "What happened to you? Your magic is rotten."

Tinkerbell snapped her teeth at me as she fought to get free. "This is true power."

"Demon-infused power. You were always cold but never evil."

Her murder mitten slammed into my gut, raking claws into the skin. "I'm powerful. I don't care how I got it."

Sammy shot a spell at Zandra, but she cut it off with a hand slice and fired back. The blast sent Sammy and Demon Gus flying.

A spell of frigid cold poured over me, rattling my bones. I reacted with fire, protecting myself in a bubble to destroy the foul magic flooding out of Tinkerbell.

Her tail caught alight, and she rolled to put out the flames. With murder in her eyes, Tinkerbell fired at me repeatedly. The magic was twisted and malfunctioning. Demon Gus had ruined her power.

It had taken what it wanted and no longer cared about her.

Where was the demon? It should help its followers, not cower in some corner while my witch hunted it.

I thrust the most powerful knockback spell I could summon, sending Tinkerbell bowling through the air, curses flying from her mouth, and raced to join Zandra in the fight against Sammy and the demon.

Magic shimmered between Zandra's outstretched hands, and she whacked the full weight of her spell into the demon just as it stood.

It back-peddled, its arms waving as if to ward off the spell, but the magic hit it in the chest, and it dropped to the ground, its body twitching.

"You deserve to be obliterated." I raised a spell to finish the job, but Zandra stopped me.

"That demon is going nowhere. Where's Tinkerbell?"

"Out cold in the dirt. Sammy? He's not..."

"No, but he's injured. Not by me. He got in the way just as Demon Gus cast something nasty, and the magic hit him. He dragged himself away." She pointed to a shadowy corner. "He didn't look good. Go help him. I'll make sure Bertoli and the non-magicals are okay."

Panting, I ran in the direction Zandra had indicated. Sammy didn't deserve to die. He'd gotten in deep with some dangerous magic, but he could turn things around.

I discovered him disheveled with smoking fur. He lifted his head when I drew near and growled. "I'll still fight you."

"No, you won't." I inched closer, my heart a tumble of grief. Was Sammy dying?

"Think you can finish me, then? I'm not so easy to kill." His chest heaved in and out, a rattle of pain echoing from his open mouth.

"I don't want you dead. I want you back. The Sammy I cared for deeply has been missing for too long. I miss him."

He fizzed a spell my way, but it was weak and easy to disperse with a simple paw wave.

"You need help. Gus has done something to you—"

"He opened my eyes. Made me realize I could be so much more without you."

"This is what you want?" My words were sharper than I'd intended them to be. "To be downed by the demon who was faking being your ally? This is to be your end?" My heart slammed against my ribs. There had to be a way to reach Sammy and bring him back to me.

"I want... I want..."

"Yes? What is it?"

"For you to die!"

White hot pain punctured my back as fangs sank into me. I howled and rolled. Tinkerbell was on me.

Sammy dragged himself over, a dark pulse of toxic magic oozing from his paws. He pressed a cold paw against my side.

I bucked Tinkerbell away and staggered back, stung by his power. His magic felt awful. Not just laced with the darkness of a demon, but there was something else underneath it. Something toxic and sticky that made my skin crawl. The thought of him touching me again made me gag.

I shook the spell off, but Tinkerbell launched at me again and sunk her teeth into the back of my neck, drawing more blood.

Zandra yelped, and her magic flared in a wild arc as she was blasted backward.

Demon Gus was on its feet, striding over, magic blazing between its palms. "You made your choice, Juno. Now watch your witch die."

I squirmed in Tinkerbell's grip, desperate to get to Zandra and keep her safe, but Tinkerbell wasn't letting go.

"You'll soon be reunited." Demon Gus lifted its palms.

This couldn't be the end. My gaze flicked to Bertoli. He was rolling around on the ground, no use to anyone. Where was Zandra? I couldn't see her, but I could feel her. Our bond was alive, which meant so was she.

"Relax. I'll make this quick. Not that you deserve it." Demon Gus smirked. "Maybe I should let my familiars finish you. They're having fun playing with you. Such a pity all that blood has stained your beautiful fur."

Sammy went to touch me again, and I shied away from him, repulsed by the thought of that gross magic polluting me.

My power was weak, and I couldn't fight them on my own. The pain in my back intensified, and blobs of darkness floated through my vision.

Zandra! I couldn't give up. She was alive, and she needed me. I dug into the old, broken magic inside me. It was there, wary and unsure what to do. It wasn't enough. I was failing.

"Zandra! The bangle! Rip it apart to release the rest of the magic. Set it free and use it." I hoped she could hear me, and I hoped the magic wouldn't destroy us all.

Demon Gus shook its head. "She can't help you. She's taking her final few breaths. Just as you're about to."

The demon was wrong. I'd only accessed part of the power in that bangle, and now was the time to open the magic gate and let it pour out.

Zandra slid into view. One side of her face was blotchy and her eyes unfocused. She was yanking at the bangle, but it wouldn't pull apart. She grabbed a stone, tossed the bangle to the ground, and slammed the stone on top of it.

"Close your eyes!" A wave of power hit me like a freight train. Tinkerbell's fangs vanished from my back as I flew, warm air lifting me and turning me over again and again.

"Juno!" Zandra screamed.

"It won't hurt me." I hoped. And I'd pray to any goddess that demanded it that this would work and my witch remained safe.

I circled higher, the air growing cool. Tinkerbell and Sammy were gone. Demon Gus was flat on its front, but it was already moving, and Zandra stared up at me, waving her arms.

"The demon," I whispered. "It must be stopped. Hold it. Take whatever you need, but don't let that monster go."

My magic didn't obey. Instead, it slowly lowered me toward Demon Gus.

"No! That's an order. The demon must be obliterated."

Demon Gus was on its feet. Fire licked from its mouth, charring the skin. It was headed for Zandra, but she was watching me.

"Look out!" I was too high for her to hear. I flailed my paws, but she stood below me, her hands up to catch me.

Demon Gus lumbered toward her, getting closer by the second, those dark flickering flames growing bigger.

My heart fought to escape my chest. The demon would kill her. Panic tore at my throat, but I forced it back. My eyes closed, and I leaned into my ancient magic. "The witch. Zandra Crypt must live. I gift you to her. Be with her for the rest of her days. Keep her safe. I release you from my hold."

I dipped lower, the magic I'd been seeking fading as it rained down on Zandra, twisting around her in a sparkling white circle. Then it punched into Demon Gus with the fury of a dozen tornados.

With no magic to support me, I plummeted. I twisted, seeking a soft place to land, but my injuries and the sleep spell undid me, and I tumbled, paws over whiskers and tail over booping snooter.

Warm, strong hands caught me, and Zandra's delicious, familiar smell filled my booping snooter. "I got you."

I nuzzled her cheek and pressed my head against her chest. She'd gotten a lot more than she realized. I'd never gifted my magic to anyone. But now that power was hers, and I'd never get it back.

"I'm not sure what you just did, but you saved my life." She kissed my head.

"I'd do it again. In a heartbeat." I may have lost a piece of my magic, but I'd kept my witch.

Zandra lifted me and peered into my face. "Same here. But this feels... different."

The non-magicals stopped pinning Bertoli. They looked around, confused, then ambled away, not seeming to realize they'd been unwitting participants in a fight between good and evil.

Bertoli groaned as he dragged himself toward the barely conscious Demon Gus, flipped it over, shackled it with a binding spell, and hauled the demon to its feet. "You're under arrest."

Chapter 20

No place like it

"I need to sleep." Zandra leaned against the wall, her breathing shallow and her forehead sweaty.

"Not yet. If you fall asleep while the spell has you in its grip, you won't wake." I stuck claws into her calf.

She staggered away. "Then we need to deal with that demon scum. It has to tell us what magic it used to put everyone into an eternal slumber."

I nudged Zandra along. "Then keep up with Bertoli. We need to be involved in the interrogation."

"It won't be an interrogation. I'll be using my advanced interview techniques to get the information we need to fix things," Bertoli shot over his shoulder.

"Just in case those awesome skills don't work, I have an idea. Something that demon won't be able to resist."

"I'm not sure your threats of obliteration will be enough to get it talking." Zandra lurched along to catch up with Bertoli, weaving as if she'd had one too many witch's brews.

"Not obliterate, although that's what the beast deserves. But Demon Gus desperately needs something, and you can provide it."

"Hurry!" Bertoli said. "I need to get this creature behind bars before it gathers strength and fights back."

"It won't misbehave." I trotted along, nudging Zandra with my booping snooter every time she faltered. "Not when it hears our proposal. It'll be life changing."

"Let's keep it moving just the same." Bertoli strode along, tugging a reluctant Demon Gus beside him.

"What do you have that you think I need?" Demon Gus growled out.

"Freedom. At least, a version of it. You've been trapped inside the same skin suit for a long time. That's got to hurt," I said.

"What if it does?"

"I hate to see a person suffer. Well, a demon. Much."

"This thing deserves no less," Bertoli muttered. "Not after what it did to the town."

"Even so, it's suffering because of its failed quest to take over Crimson Cove and absorb all our magic users' power so it could break free from its self-imposed prison. Did you really think you'd win?" I was goading the demon a touch.

"I nearly did. If it wasn't for you and your interfering witch getting in my way, I'd have everything I desire by now."

"Thank you. We always appreciate compliments when our quest for justice is appreciated. Now, be better mannered, or you won't hear our proposal."

Demon Gus grunted. "I'll hear it. You like the sound of your voice too much to stay silent. Suppose you're gonna brag."

I glanced at Zandra. My wonderful witch was suffering, but she was up to this challenge. She had her power and some of mine pulsing through her now. It would give us what we needed to make this work.

"Go on, cat. I'm giddy with excitement." Demon Gus lumbered into Bertoli and almost fell. This demon was in a world of hurt. Bertoli didn't look too good either.

"Don't go making any deals." Bertoli continued toward Angel Force. "Cythera won't be happy if you haven't cleared things with her first."

"She'll be happy to rid this place of a demon. However, she's asleep, so if we don't make this deal, she'll never wake, along with most of the residents of Crimson Cove. That won't look rosy come appraisal time."

Bertoli muttered under his breath as he reached the doors of Angel Force and pulled one open.

"Glad you're in support of solving this situation," I said. "Let's get Demon Gus in a secure place, and then we'll talk some more."

We kept a watchful eye on Bertoli as he processed Demon Gus. I wanted nothing to go wrong at the last minute and for this demon to escape.

"What have you got in mind, Juno?" Zandra marched on the spot, although her slowness suggested her boots were made of concrete and not leather.

"You know demons better than anyone else. Better than some Crypt witches."

"Debatable. My dad hung out with shady demons over the years. We both know Tempest rounds them up and eats them for breakfast. I expect Granny Dottie used to mess with them, too, when she was younger."

"No doubt, she still does. And you've learned from them all." I lifted my chin. "You have the power to release that demon from the skin suit it's trapped in."

Her eyebrows slowly rose, and she glanced at the entrance to the holding cells. "Why would I do that?"

"We're making a deal with a demon. Demon Gus gets free from the skin suit in exchange for telling us what it used in the sleep spell. Once we know the exact magic, we can reverse it. Everyone will wake, and Crimson Cove will go back to normal."

"I can barely keep my eyes open. I can't do that. It's too big of a spell."

I leaped onto my witch's shoulder and pressed my head against hers. "You're a hundred times more capable than you think you are. And I'll be by your side. We can't fail if we do this together."

She held out her hands. "I don't know what you did to me, but I feel different. Stronger."

"I shared a little of my power with you."

"This is yours? But it feels so... musty."

I nipped her ear. "It's because you're not used to it. With our magic combined, plus your skills with demons, we'll get what we need from Demon Gus. It'll never go free, but it won't be trapped in a degrading skin suit. Being trapped like that must be driving the creature insane. It'll snap up this chance to get out of that skin prison."

She lifted her shoulders. "It's worth a go if you think I'm up to it. What do we need to do?"

After I'd made Zandra down two strong coffees, we went to the cells. Demon Gus was secured in the far end cell, and Bertoli stood on the other side of the door.

"The demon isn't talking. It won't say what it did to the town."

I stood close to the door. "Demon Gus, here's our proposal. If you tell us what magic you used in the sleep spell, my witch will rid you of your skin prison."

Its dark gaze lifted from a spot on the floor. "She can do that?"

"Um... Sure. I mean, I've never done it before, since you don't meet many body-snatching demons. I've been around plenty, though. I'll make it work." Zandra cracked her knuckles.

Demon Gus tapped its chin with a finger, its gaze flickering over Zandra. "Will I be free to leave?"

Bertoli snorted and shook his head. "A truth seer died, and there are dozens of critically ill people because of you. You'll pay for your crimes."

Demon Gus was silent for a moment, its gaze not leaving Zandra. "Do I get a choice of prison?"

Bertoli puffed out his chest. "That'll be for the judge to decide."

"Serving a sentence will be more pleasant in your demon form than trapped in a decaying skin suit. The pain will become unbearable," I said. "And as for the smell..."

"I know an amazing demon prison." Zandra smirked. "I could put in a good word for you. The family who looks after it isn't unreasonable, so long as the demons behave."

"I'm not going to the Willow Tree Falls prison." Demon Gus paced the cell several times.

"This is a limited-time offer." I tracked his movement. The demon squirmed to be free, the skin flaky and pale.

It spun on its heel to face us. "I agree. I must get out of this body. I want to scratch myself raw."

"The sleep magic details first," I said.

Demon Gus's eyes widened, the flicker of a smile on its cracked lips. "You don't trust me? I'm hurt."

"You'll get over it. Give us the details. We'll make sure we can reverse your magic, and then we'll release you."

"What if you fail? I'll get nothing from this deal."

"The options aren't great for you, but at least you have some." I flicked my tail. "So, what will it be?"

"Give me a pen and paper."

Ten minutes later, I stood around a table with Zandra and Bertoli.

"This is the last ingredient." Zandra dropped a sprig of thyme into the small cauldron on the desk. The liquid glowed red then flashed a brilliant white before settling into an attractive shade of pink.

"That's it?" Bertoli peered into the cauldron.

I rested a murder mitten on his arm, claws out. "It took skill to formulate that potion. And ingredients don't enchant themselves."

His cheeks flushed. "I helped. I donated a feather."

"We all helped," Zandra said. "And it looks good. The potion is stable."

"So long as that demon didn't lie to us about what it used," Bertoli muttered.

"Demon Gus knows the price of lying." I dug my claws into his hand.

Bertoli swiftly moved his hand away. "How will we get it to people in time?"

"Feel up to a flight around town?" I said. "You fly, and I'll scatter the potion so it gets in the air and people can breathe it in. It's not as potent as drinking it, but it'll get things moving and buy people time so they can get a full dose of the potion."

"You want to come with me?"

"Not particularly. Flying with angels makes me queasy, but I'll use a scatter spell while you fly. It'll be the quickest way. Once more people are awake, they can find others who need help and bring them to the hospital."

"What about me?" Zandra said. "I want to help, too."

"You made the potion. And you're having a dose now. Get it down you," I said.

"I should help to distribute the reversal spell. We need every pair of hands."

"You'll be much more use watching the demon who caused this trouble and getting the rest of

Angel Force awake. I'll go with Bertoli." I nudged the cauldron with my hip, and after a second of hesitation, Zandra took a small amount and swallowed it.

Her skin turned a startling pink, and her hair stood on end as if she'd been given a jolt of electricity. She shuddered and then stretched. "Whoa! It feels so good not to be exhausted. I feel like a new witch."

"We can celebrate later." I hopped to the floor.

"Just a minute. You're next," Zandra said.

"I can keep going for a few more hours."

She fixed me with a glare a Gorgon would be proud of. "Juno, lap up some potion. You too, Bertoli."

"I... I don't lap."

She tutted, scooped a dose of the potion into an empty mug, and thrust it at him. "We need to be on top form to wake everyone. And if you crash while flying with Juno, I'll make you sorrier than a dragon who let out a keto fart at a family wake."

Tiredness had seeped into my bones, so I drank some potion, admiring my fur as it turned briefly pink. The soul-wearying ache vanished from my limbs. and a shiver of energy fluttered from my stomach. My power switched on, and my brain no longer felt like it was swimming in treacle.

Bertoli also turned pink, and while most of him returned to his normal color, his wings remained a beautiful pastel pink shade.

He inspected them, a scowl on his face. "How long will I be stuck looking like this?"

I chuckled. "It suits you. Follow me. We have a demon to deal with."

Bertoli continued to protest about his new wing color while I strode to the cells with Zandra. It felt so good to stride rather than lurch or shuffle like an old lady with a dodgy hip wearing slippers that were too big for her.

Demon Gus was slumped on the floor of the cell. "You came back."

"Unlike you, our word is our bond. Let's get this over with," I said.

The demon stood and pulled back its shoulders. "What do I need to do to get out of this skin?"

"Don't fight us when the magic hits. And don't break out of that cell," Zandra said. "If you do, my familiar will obliterate you."

"A deal is a deal. Get this itchy thing off me. That's all I care about."

I jumped on Zandra's shoulder and ensured our bond was strong. She grinned at me and pressed a hand against my side. Our magic connected and swirled around us in a vibrant shield of gold. It had been a long time since I'd felt this good or this powerful.

Zandra pressed her free hand against her chest. "Release, reveal, remove, rewind." Wind lifted her hair, and a bolt of magic slammed into Demon Gus's chest.

The demon slammed against the wall, struggling for a second as our power consumed it, then black smoke shot from its mouth. What was left of Gus, not the demon version, slumped to the floor in a soggy, flaky mess.

The black smoke swirled around the cell before settling into an amorphous blob near the door, pulsing and wavering. Two red eyes appeared in the smoke. They blinked once.

I nodded. "You're welcome. Now, we have work to do."

❧ ❧

"Do we have to get up?" I was stretched lengthways along Zandra's warm back.

"Yes." She didn't move.

After releasing the demon, I'd spent hours flying around Crimson Cove with Bertoli, dispensing sleep reversal magic. Once the potion was in the air, we'd stopped at the hospital, woken the doctors and nurses, given them the spell reversal information, and let them get to work. By the end of it, we were all exhausted, and I'd insisted we go straight to bed. Although Bertoli hadn't been invited to join us.

"Let's stay here for another few hours," I muttered.

"I want to see everyone," Zandra said. "And Vorana's expecting us at the bookshop in a few minutes."

"We saved Crimson Cove. Everyone will understand if we have a lie-in."

Zandra pulled herself out of bed, and I lost my warm snuggle buddy. "It's almost five in the evening. We've had enough sleep. Besides, I want to find out how everyone is doing. So do you. And Sorcha will be there, so there'll be amazing food."

Reluctantly, I pulled myself out of bed, had a quick grooming session, then we headed up the stairs and over to the bookstore.

The door was open, and the smell of fresh coffee lingered in the air as we entered. I was delighted to see a plate of smoked salmon and cream cheese alongside the cookies.

Finn and Sorcha were already seated. Finn had three cookies balanced on his knee and a broad smile on his face. All traces of tiredness were gone.

Vorana came out from behind the counter, a huge grin on her face, Sage strapped to her chest in a comfy papoose. "The guests of honor are here. Welcome. You're right on time."

"We're nothing special." Zandra waved away Vorana's words.

"We are. Thank you. These last few days have been an adventure I don't want to repeat." As I looked around, I was relieved to see everyone looked a hundred times better than the last time I saw them. The sleep reversal potion had worked.

Once everyone was settled in seats with coffee and refreshments, Zandra leaned forward.

"So, what's the latest on Demon Gus?" she asked Finn.

"Sullen but cooperative. It knows it's been beaten."

"Thanks to Juno and Zandra," Sorcha said. "It's all people have been talking about."

"It was nothing," Zandra said. "We were just the last ones standing, so we had to help."

"It was something," I said. "We risked a lot to go up against that demon. And with the other suspects hiding things and keeping secrets, it made our challenge much harder."

"Juno, you're amazing," Finn said. "I don't know how Angel Force managed until you came to town."

I ignored the hint of sarcasm in his voice. "You're welcome. Have you dealt with all former suspects?"

Finn mock saluted me. "Yes, ma'am. Other than the scarabs, who remain elusive. Robin didn't hide his relief that this was over and he now had no option but to move on. And Harlan admitted he wanted out of the relationship. He was with Old Mother Splinter when she went swimming, and he didn't help her."

"That's shady behavior," Vorana said.

"I don't disagree. The guy felt trapped, and he made an idiot move. He'll get a reprimand but nothing more."

"Has everyone received a full dose of the sleep reversal potion?" I asked.

Finn nodded. "As far as I know. We've been doing house to house checks and getting neighbors involved. We don't want to miss anyone."

"How are the people at the hospital?" Zandra said.

"They all made it. The only fatality was Old Mother Splinter."

Vorana set down her mug. "I'm sorry about what happened to her. And I'm really sorry I hid my struggles with the business. Maybe everyone really thinks books are boring, just like you, Zandra."

"Anything but, they are." Amenia zoomed through the door with her children. "Leaving, we are. Came to say goodbye and thank you."

"It was our pleasure to host you," I said.

Her antenna quivered. "Even though murder suspects, you thought we were?"

I ate some salmon. "Anyone can make a mistake."

Amenia hovered close to Vorana's face. "Boring, books are not. Teach us about creatures like Demon Gus, they do."

Vorana's bottom lip jutted out. "I think this place is amazing, but maybe I'm out of touch with reality. Everyone's so busy these days. Too busy to read."

"You're not thinking of closing, are you?" Zandra said. "Is the rent still going up?"

"It's too early to say for certain, but Old Mother Splinter would have had things in place to make sure her business continued. I'm sure the rent will double just as she intended."

"A problem, this is?" Amenia said.

"I'm not sure I can afford to pay so much rent," Vorana said. "I may have to look for another job. Maybe I could get a night shift job. Something out of town."

"A moment you will give me. Children, follow me." Amenia flew around the store several times, pausing to inspect various books and nooks and crannies.

"What's she up to?" Zandra whispered.

I shook my head. I was as bemused by the scarabs' behavior as everyone else.

Amenia re-joined us. "Invaluable, knowledge is. And Crimson Cove, I have to thank for keeping my family safe."

"Technically, she has us to thank," I muttered to Zandra.

She grinned and bit into a cookie.

"Gift, I will give you," Amenia said. "A lifetime sponsorship deal for the bookstore. Rent will be covered. The rest, you must do."

Vorana stood from her seat, her eyes wide. "I... I don't know what to say."

"For how long?" I said.

"Lifetime sponsorship. Live to be at least a thousand, I will. Not enough?"

"That's a generous offer. What do you want in return?" Scarab deals were never to be entered lightly without knowing what they desired from you. The price could be steep.

"A tiny thing. A scarab logo on the sign. That is all. My gift to the town."

Tears filled Vorana's eyes. "This'll change everything. With financial backing, I can keep the store open and start my expansion plans. I... I'm lost for words. What should I say?" She looked around the group.

"Say yes then goodbye. Go, we must. Be in touch, I will." Amenia and her children shot around the store one more time and then left.

Vorana sank into her seat, her hand over her mouth. "Did that just happen, or am I still under the demon's sleep spell?"

"You're not dreaming," Finn said. "You've got yourself a guardian scarab."

"I don't know whether to cry or laugh. It's good, right?"

"It's excellent. I can see an adorable scarab nestled next to the store's name. If you'll excuse me for a moment." I hopped off Zandra's lap and headed outside. Bertoli lurked close to the door, looking like he wanted something. "Greetings. Will you join us?"

He scuffed a foot on the ground. "Sure. And I owe you an apology. Probably more than one. I've been a jerk to you since you moved to Crimson Cove."

"There's truth in that. I understand you being cautious around new people, though."

"It wasn't caution. I was jealous. You and Zandra made friends easily, and you got on with Finn straightaway. I'm not good with people. I say things that make them think I'm weird."

"Also partially true."

Bertoli pursed his lips. "I want to change. Be a better angel."

I walked over and pressed a paw against his foot. "You will. You already are. Change can be good. Come and join us. We have cookies."

"I don't eat sugar after noon."

"Then you're missing out. Sorcha made them."

His gaze went to the cookies. "Maybe one. I don't want to get in the way, though."

"You're welcome. And you can give us an update on the case. We were just talking about it with Finn."

Bertoli's shoulders stiffened. "It's an ongoing investigation. I can't share confidential information with outsiders."

I looked up at him and tilted my head. "If you don't trust me and Zandra by now, you never will. We really are here to help, not cause you problems."

He opened his mouth then snapped it shut and nodded. "Sure. I'm figuring that out. Change is hard."

"But easier if you don't do it alone." I turned and headed back into the bookstore, and after a second of hesitation, Bertoli joined us. He accepted a coffee and a cookie from Vorana and chose a seat.

"Any sign of the non-magicals returning?" Finn said to Bertoli.

"They've gone. Once Demon Gus was out of action and Randal fixed the wards, they no longer wanted to stay. They were eager to leave."

"Which means our magic is stable again. The wards are repelling non-magicals," I said. "What a relief."

"It'll feel good not to hide our powers anymore," Vorana said. "I was always checking over my shoulder before casting spells. That got stressful."

We all nodded in agreement.

"Any news about what happened to Sammy and Tinkerbell?" Finn said.

The joy in my heart sank. That was one issue we had unresolved.

"No sign of them," Bertoli said. "We're looking for them, but it's likely they've left town. They know they'll be arrested if they stick around."

"In Sammy's defense, there's something wrong with his magic," I said. "When we fought, it felt nothing like his usual power. Demon Gus must have done something to him."

"And Tinkerbell." Sorcha had been unusually quiet since we'd arrived. She still looked pale, as if she needed a good night's rest. "I failed that cat. She'd been behaving strangely for a long time. I should have done more to help her. I should have seen she was struggling."

"It's not your fault," I said. "Ever since I met Tinkerbell, she's been unpleasant."

"Because she was forcibly bonded with a demon. And Demon Gus's arrival must have triggered terrible memories. I've been so busy, but I should have done more. I let that cat down."

"You did what you could," Zandra said. "Tinkerbell isn't the easiest of cat familiars to get along with."

"We all have our moments of being less than amazing, but that doesn't mean people should give up on us." Sorcha slumped in her seat. "I'm taking a break and shutting the café."

"For how long?" Zandra exchanged a worried look with Vorana.

"A few weeks. Maybe longer. I need a change of scene and to think things through. My priorities feel wrong. Tinkerbell would be happier and healthier and may never have gotten involved with Demon Gus if I'd been more attentive to her needs."

I wanted to argue the opposite had been true, but Sorcha was deep in a self-guilt trip, and anything I said would only make her feel worse.

"Take all the time you need," Vorana said gently. "Zandra and I will look after any waifs and strays that need feeding until you're ready to come back."

"Sure. And when you come back, because you will come home, you'll feel like a new almost vampire," Zandra said.

Sorcha's smile looked strained. "Thanks. I don't want to leave, but the break will do me good."

While everyone talked through the logistics of Sorcha's amazing café shutting, I settled in with a snack and closed my eyes. Crimson Cove was safe once again. The demon was gone, the non-magicals purged, my witch was safe, and my magic strong.

I pressed a paw against Zandra's thigh. Some of my magic was gone forever, though. I'd sacrificed a piece of it to ensure my witch was strong enough to defeat a demon and save the town. I wasn't certain what that sacrifice had cost me yet, but I'd had to do it. Zandra Crypt was my bonded witch, and I'd do anything to keep her safe. Even give up on a long-held dream.

I'd figure out a solution. I always did. Although at that moment, I was out of brilliant ideas to ensure everyone got their happily ever after.

Although I had the Sammy issue to deal with, Tinkerbell was missing, and the delicious treats from Bites and Delights would be out of reach for a few weeks while Sorcha healed her emotional wounds, life was still good.

I snuggled against Zandra's soft belly, made biscuits with my murder mittens, and relaxed into a slumber I knew I'd wake from.

About Author

K.E. O'Connor (Karen) is a mystery author living in the beautiful British countryside. She loves all things mystery, animals, and cake.

If you want to practice spells, solve a few murders, and spend time with amazing witches and their talking familiars, join her weekly newsletter.

Sign up today.

Newsletter:
https://BookHip.com/GXDVFRA

Website:
www.keoconnor.com/writing

Facebook:
www.facebook.com/keoconnorauthor

Also By